BY N.JOY

N.Joy   Jill

This novel is a bio-fictional work. The background, appearance and circumstances surrounding the actual events and characters are the work of the author's imagination. Any resemblance to actual events relating to any persons is entirely coincidental.

Copyright © N.Joy 2017

Printed and bound by Amazon

Find out more about the author and her work @ www.nljdesigns.co.uk

ISBN 978-1-9997358-0-7

My first novel has been an experience and some due respect and thanks go out to Zeb Poole for his educational knowledge, to Nathan Fussell for his expert knowledge on Victorian surgery & tools (and smells!!), to Rob Long of Hiron's and Sons butchers for his help in the slicing and dicing department and to the staff at Kenwood House for being very helpful and lovely.

Local authors Mike Cumiskey and Veronica Henry have been more help than they would ever know with their words of advice and to the vast array of published authors that line the shelves of my bookcases – thank you, I hope to one day join you.

To Carl Hawkins, thank you for your advice, invaluable.

Thank you to my inspirational English Lit teacher Lin Redhead for being a great teacher and fostering my love of literature.

The staff at the Writers year book – Thank you.

A massive thank you to my beautiful baby sister Gem who proof read Jill for me, sorry about the spelling mistakes!!

To Mum and Dad, thank you for creating me!!

To my amazing children Charlie and Paige, thank you for putting up with me. Sorry I couldn't get an agent. One day I will have a book deal that turns into a movie franchise!

And finally, to my husband who was very lucky not to become a victim, sorry you're not getting rid of me on a world-wide tour and thank you for all the technical stuff!!

N.Joy   Jill

N.Joy   Jill

For my family & friends

Your belief in me means everything

1

I woke in the early hours of the morning, the night still hung in the sky, an orange glow from the industrial chimneys that surround us billowing into the air and leaving a blanket over the sky, hiding the twinkling stars and half full moon that I knew decorated the ceiling of our world. I clung to the memory of the amazing dot-to-dot of silver against black, witnessed on yesterday's rare family outing to Stratford in the summer of 1876. I could still remember the scent of honeysuckle that hung in the air as we waited for the sun to set, heralding in the darkness and signalling an end to the day's pleasantries.

The carriage ride back should have probably scared me as the two large brown nags charged seemingly through the pitch of the night, along the uneven tracks and pathways that lead back to old London town, the noise and smell of the city increasing with every stride that brought us nearer our destination signalling the end of the care free day. The image of the great steam engine would stay with me for years, whips of steam exited into the sky as the machine sat stationary. It was chomping at the bit, shaking with raw power but held still, it's great wheels prevented from turning. People marvelled at the gleaming paint work and shining metal, the operator stood proudly at its side, oil smeared across his clothing and face.

It was inevitability beyond my control that tomorrow I would have to return to the seemingly endless torture that would be thrown at me as I sit uninspired and rigid at my predesignated desk in the freezing dull classroom at Well Street Chapel Free School, a choice of convenience on behalf of my parents.

A typical day would consist of Miss Clarke, a woman of small stature with her white ringlet hair worn in a short cut and a face with delicate yet pinched features all nestling for space in the centre of her weathered and stern face, droning on about the benefits of arithmetic's and the requirement to learn reading and writing which they referenced to as the three Rs as well as the teachings of the Church of England, the importance of religion and the discipline that should be displayed in the service of her majesty Queen Victoria.

Once I was old enough I did enjoy the practice of handwriting for I had a keen eye for detail and relished the chance to write elegantly and fashionably. These were not lessons designed for girls, although there were some twenty more than their male equivalents. We had been taught from the outset that we were the inferior sex, that our place was in the house, raising children, keeping home and being at the beck and call of whichever man had decided to lay his claim upon you, a misfortune that we were powerless to alter.

The government had eventually decreed that, although we were due little else, a female should be educated alongside her more superior male counterparts providing that they remained a docile as church mice, and as quiet too, however the physical punishment given without a thought on behalf of the teaching staff on a daily basis was enough to keep the majority in our places. In some fairness to the system girls were taught skills such as sewing so they could become a seamstress and fractional working that would assist them in their daily home chores as well as measuring fabric in addition to good etiquette so that we could gain employment in service.

My own mother received little education at all, her family too poor to afford a governess but she was made literate through attending Sunday School due to the fact that in 1831 it was decided that children should receive basic lessons in reading and writing that were to be delivered through the church in the attempt to provide them with more opportunities, a luxury that was not in existence in my grandparent's time which lead them to the physical occupations that they held and the beliefs that they instilled into my parents. My father and uncles were afforded the luxury of extended schooling as they were male, which they latter squandered in labouring and in the towns taverns, as their fathers did before them.

Only recently had we all received a state funded education which was introduced in the year 1870, when I was just four years old, meaning that in less than a year I would spend every week day in education placing the plans my parents had been dreaming of using my income for on hold. Some saving grace for my father, who was particularly angry about my delay into the workforce, was that for the most part I only had to attend in the mornings so I could still be put to good use in the afternoons to earn a few extra farthings, none of which I benefited from in the way of new clothes, a toy or a little additional food on my dinner plate but it did seem to keep father at the local tavern for a little longer most evenings.

My favourite hobby, which I could pass off as attempting to earn a crust was to walk along the banks of Regents Canal, down in Camden, looking for lost treasures which had fallen from a boat passing through the waterways or been dropped by a passer-by that could be salvaged, cleaned up and sold on but the pickings were slight and often I came home empty handed.

The best venue for this was down on the Thames, due to its size and frequency of ships of all shapes and sizes with various forms of cargo and passengers, however it was a journey of over four miles and everyday saw all manner of Londoners as well as foreigners scurrying around, hoping to find that one golden nugget that would see them through and change their fortunes, as Father would often say "where's there's muck there's brass". I preferred the stretch under Waterloo Bridge, there is no real reason for this, it isn't any more attractive than the remaining miles, but I had been lucky on a few occasions, once finding a whole penny which I kept concealed within the folds of the only bow that I owned and several small trinkets and items of jewellery that I took home and mother sold at Camden market. I had trialled and failed at several apprenticeships, but no-one really wanted my unskilled efforts and school for me was more of an exercise in mass brain washing than teaching, but it gave me a change of scenery from the mundane scrubbing   that mother always insisted I do or against the boredom and hardship that was my childhood.

Personally, I found the education system a nightmare, consisting of uneventful and tedious lessons, unwelcome punishment which was delivered through the birch wood canes that seemed to be an irremovable extension of many of the teachers' hands and a series of degrading remarks that spiralled my general feelings of low self-worth and compounded my feelings towards those that hold a position of authority or power over me. I had only received the cane on a couple of occasions, once across the palm of my right hand and the second on the back of both my legs but I stood firm both times, never shedding a tear although the pain ran through my body like a hot knife through butter and every time I wrote for several days after my hand felt like it had been held above a flame.

Miss Clarke, being particularly harsh to deliver the punishment to my writing hand, was secretly expecting me to abandon any resolve allowing her to continue in her punishment unabated on my left hand. I had witnessed the punishment inflicted upon those who were unfortunate enough to be dominantly lead by their left hand, so I persevered through the pain to be the victor of that battle.

For some the purpose of school appeared to be a daily challenge to see who could receive the most amount of punishment, for which the honour usually befell John Ward who I had witnessed being caned on the backside more times than I had had hot dinners, which was not a major achievement as many of the teachers seemed to care more for the reprimands than the lessons they taught and their purpose of school seemed to be who could produce the most impressive welt on a child.

Another way that the teachers could humiliate you was to make you stand in the corner of the room up against the wall facing away from your class mates wearing the shameful dunce hat. I wasn't the brightest child in the class by far, but I could grasp concepts quickly enough and assimilate new information to compliment what I had already learnt or use it as a building block for new knowledge as well as being able to rapidly assess a teachers' manner and temper, so I managed to escape this penalty which was ordinarily awarded to Emily

Brown who had been singled out as the most balmy in class.

I found no subject especially troublesome, but I did struggle against the lack of creativity displayed in the teachers and deficiency of opportunity to be able to express myself for I craved the freedom to be able to use the emotions that I had to keep hidden from my parents to grow as an individual and develop a sense of my own self. Many of the teachers took to hurling the chalk board erasers across the room at any child that seemed distracted, effectively using us as target practice which would result in a white dust cloud erupting around the area of impact and a trail of white particles descending from the flying implement onto the children that it passed on its way to the intended victim. After coming home on one occasion with white marks on my clothes mother went ballistic, I went without supper and she threatened to have my guts for garters if it happened again, so I learnt to remove the chalk with water before getting home.

Sometimes the punishments were a welcome distraction from the crammed conditions of the classroom, I shared my desk with a girl called Annie Sheppard, we were best friends of a sort, given that we sat in such close proximity of one another, in fact we actually touched, and we were on par in our abilities although I moved from slate and chalk to paper and ink three whole weeks before she did.

Like me Annie lived in Mile End in the old East End part of London and she had parents whose lives mirrored those of my own parents but that is as far as our friendship went, we did not see each other outside of the school's walls. Being in such crammed conditions on a daily basis was unavoidable as the entire school consisted of just two rooms which was more tolerable when I first started but as we all grew I became more uncomfortable and the smells emanating from my peers which mixed to produce a heady scent of body odour and the herbs used in an attempt to conceal them would cling to the tiny hairs of my nostrils and be carried around with me as a constant reminder.

We had two schools to serve our densely populated suburb which was a small mercy compared to those bigger inner-city schools who had as many children per class room as we had in the entire school. Although many of my peers would attend school with a cold or coughing all over their desks and each other I was spared from this infectious behaviour, or I possessed a wonderful immune system, however it did not stop the contraction of head lice which was one area that my mother was particularly fussy over resulting in a weekly inspection which would leave my scalp reddened and often bloody with few patches containing less hair than it should due to my mother's examination technique of sharp finger nails and a keen eye. She would then cover my head in cotton lavender which she had prepared herself by boiling it on the stove, and thus making the escape from the potent smell impossible as it seeped into every room of the house, roughly massaging it into my hair then smearing handfuls on top of my sibling in the fear that I may infect them.

For the most part the journey to and from school was the most appealing part of my day. My usual route would be to enter Victoria Park at the south end, off of Globe town then I would walk all the way up through to the North gate exit onto Lauriston road and past the St John of Jerusalem church which is located on the right. Whilst it looked warm and inviting on a cold winters day after a long and laborious day I felt no inclination to seek refuges in the sanctity of God.

The school was not far, it's external appearance was far less appealing than the stained-glass imagery of the church containing highly intricate carvings, sleek wooden benches of the churches pews that retained a faint smell of incense used during services in contrast to the bear stone walls of the classroom that complimented the depressing atmosphere and the high windows that prevented any form of imagination from infiltrating the walls of the education prison.

Sometimes, particularly if rainfall had been heavy I would trudge along the pavement adjacent to the residential squalor of Grove Road, passing under the bridge that carried the loud dirty trains, past St Barnabas church and into Victoria park and onto school via my customary direction. I had seen Queen Victoria in April 1873, when I was six, when she visited the gardens, I had never seen so many people in the park before, there was such a wealth of finery about the place, such fine hats and fashion on display for all of London to behold. The Queen herself, adorned in her crown veil and magnificent dress that ballooned all around her, was strategically surround by a sea of red and black but I got a glimpse of her as she surveyed the grounds, her expression sober yet amused, that had been named in her honour.

Each route would last around twenty-five minutes, the latter route offering more in the way of smog, fumes and filthy streets but not as scenic as the stroll that took us through the majority of the park. For the first few years I walked alone, being the eldest of my siblings I was the only one old enough to attend and having only been shown the route once by my mother, I soon learnt the short cuts and developed the ability to fade into the city's surroundings, passing largely unnoticed.

For a short while I was accompanied by my younger sister Amelia, who I called Mills, but following the accident with the carriage which took her life I returned to walking to school on my own for a few years before having to drag my little sister Lottie, who was easily distracted by every little whim that took her fancy but a few stern words and a threat of the back of my hand kept her on track.

The day of Mills accident started out the same as every other morning although it had been uncharacteristically harsh the previous evening for so early in the season which resulted in the world waking to a crisp frost that had settled over the cobbles and roofs producing a glacier look and feel to the streets of London. The first rays of sun had yet to penetrate through the smog and melt the ice paths that had laid themselves the previous night.

After taking the first precarious steps with due care and without so much as a minor slip or slide I decided that we could accomplish a quicker pace to avoid the wrath that is guaranteed for any pupil that should dare to be tardy and to reduce the numbness that was starting to infiltrate the thin layer of fabric that clung to my feet which were encased in holey boots that father had procured on his way home from work several months ago.

To avoid the inevitable moaning that would emit from Amelia's mouth with the quickened pace I increased the speed gradually and she kept up, marching beside me with no cause for concern. As we trudged up Grove Road one of the adjoining side streets had caused the wind to whip around us like a chilly blanket, stinging my ears and forcing me to squint into the distance as we began the approach to Victoria Park.

I did register the sound of a horse and cart, but the whispering wind distorted the noise and I failed to realise how close the carriage actually was to us. The streets path narrowed due to the merchants having piled discarded crates against the sides of the buildings forcing us to walk on the edge of the pavement. By this point my face was stinging from the chill and dust particles that the weather was hurling at us that I blindly moved around a pile of crates that had tipped over spreading further across the pavement knocking into Mills who had inadvertently come up on my right, her footsteps silent behind me on the ground in her soft shoes.

At the same time that Mills foot slipped on the polished kerb a wide eyed powerful black horse pulling a high topped and ladened carriage hurtled past in a thunderous roar that almost drowned out the screams of Mills as her flailing arm was sucked into the momentum of the air swirling around the carriage and she disappeared from the path and into the road. Before I had time to register what had happened it was all over, the carriage, driver and occupants had vanished beyond the gathering throngs of people that had begun to congregate around the small still bloodied figure that lay motionless on the cobbled road.

The wheel that had left its mark across the chest of my little sister was large enough to encompass her completely and she barley caused the carriage to become unbalanced as the wheel climbed from one side of her body to the other accompanied by a sound which equalled that of twigs breaking under the foot of a heavily boot. The silence that fell in the aftermath was unsettling and eerie as if the whole world had stopped to mourn this tragic individual but all too soon it was broken by the hurried voices of adults as they rushed to intervene. I stood there transfixed by the striking image of her scarlet red blood as it seeped from the pool that had formed under Mills head, dividing into the ruts between the stones as if in race with the other droplets to an undisclosed destination, mixing with the crystallised ice to create intricate and beautiful patterns over the ice that still cling frozen to the ground.

It took the physical intervention of a stranger shaking my body to bring me back to reality where I was surrounded by men and women, one woman with owl like eyes and a shrill voice was positioned next to my face yelling "You, where are your parents? Girl, where do you live?" Before I could answer a burly man, sporting the standard waistcoat and trouser ensemble with a mismatched jacket and a flat cap balanced upon his balding head, shouted in a thick Cockney accent, between the pipe hanging from his mouth, that we belonged to the Wheelers of Maroon Street and that he knew father and would fetch him at once.

There was nothing to be done, Mills had been covered by a dirty piece of linen that some woman had recovered from on top of the pile of unwanted crates, but I could still see, for the image was imprinted upon my memory, her emotionless glossed eyes staring accusing at me from underneath the makeshift coffin.

The funeral was held three days later. My mother and the growing bump of the unborn child that would fill the gap in her heart that Mills passing had ripped waddled arm in arm with my father as they trudged together to say a lonely farewell to their second born daughter as she was laid to rest in an unmarked grave in the pauper's section of the local cemetery. For a time, I would visit the spot where she was buried, leaving a fresh flower harvested from an unsuspecting flowerbed but after several months I stopped going as it emitted such a lethargic atmosphere it felt like the fingers of death hung ever present over the site, flexing its limbs whilst it waited for its next victim, I eventually forgot the exact location of her body, just the general direction in which she was interned. For the time after the accident that I walked alone I didn't change my route and not one of those strangers who had surrounded me that fateful day ever looked in my direction or acknowledged my existence.

I cared little for those that passed us, squirreling away, conducting their affairs in any manner they saw fit however, just every now and then, I would notice a young filthy child and think 'what happened to you?' and I would imagine what chain of events had occurred that lead them to that moment in time. Mostly my only thoughts were about what would happen to me and to my life, what would I become and what had the world in store for me?

I was born in Igtham in Kent, but father relocated us to London when I was just two years old. I have no memory that I can recall of that time, only the dirty paths and walls of London, the skyline littered with plumes of filthy smoke, of the noises that filled the streets; the horse's hooves against the flagstones, machines in factories and the hustle and bustle of daily life for the inhabitants of this cramped city.

For a few years we resided at a small dwelling of just two rooms at two William Street, but mother became pregnant again, so we moved to sixteen Maroon Street which was larger, but we shared the house with the local Buckley family. I found the place to be more oppressive and although I had the Buckley children as company I missed my friend Tom Shaddick.

Tom lived next door, he was a stick of a creature with crazy curls for hair and a face that possessed so many freckles he was like a human dot-to-dot, but he was kind to me. We would help each other with whatever tasks our mothers had set us too and when we'd finished we would disappear together exploring the area, playing in the park and causing a slight nuisance to the local traders at the various markets that were held around the town. After we moved I saw less of Tom and I think he eventually forgot about me because he stopped coming down my street and I haven't seen him since.

Our house on Maroon Street was sandwiched into a long brick row of bland identical facades, a door and window on the ground floor with two windows, facing a mirror image, on the second floor capped with the regimental slate roof. The gap between the two rows of facing homes was large and allowed for easy passage of carriages whilst games were played by the streets children without a fear for an accident occurring which was good as the back yards that accompanied these properties were little more than claustrophobic pits housing the water closet and the scraps of fuel squirrelled away for the winter months with was no space for a child to entertain themselves.

It wasn't an uncommon site to see people wandering looking lost and confused as the area was being developed and streets were being renamed in a seemingly insane manner, ours only recently bearing the name Catherine Street which had now ceased to exist in name but not memory.

The house was nicely divided to give each family their own downstairs room, ours being to the rear of the property with upstairs comprising of three bedrooms of which we had the use of the two smaller rooms at the front while the Buckley's slept together in the back bedroom. For the most part I interacted very little with them, meeting on the stairs and queuing in the mornings in the minuscule yard. I found John and his brother rather dull and lacking in the trappings of youth and Harriet was working as a maidservant at the local school so was rarely around, but Mrs Buckley seemed nice and it appeared mother had made a friend in her.

The main room in William Street had been of similar

dimensions to that of the bedroom that I shared now in Maroon Street where here our main room was larger which allowed each piece of our furniture to be placed so that it no longer had to touch another and for the first-time mother had a real stove to cook upon. In the centre of the room opposite the door a brick frame had been built against the wall standing five-foot-high by at least two-foot-wide which housed two small metal kiln like stoves with an open grill in the middle, it was compact yet versatile. There was even enough room for mother to store her limited pots and pans and she now had the capacity to warm an iron, if only she had the money to buy one.

It was rather grand but how father had managed to procure a room with such a luxury was beyond my comprehension for he was only a labourer now following his resignation from his employment as a delivery foreman. We had a round table with six chairs of varying different origins, but all fit for purpose and a dresser that was worn and marked but solid in its testimony to the craftsmanship which was adorned with the trinkets and treasures that mother and father had massed over the years and hid our chipped crockery and megger food supplies. A narrow bench that had been constructed by my father from crates that he had scavenged from the docks lined the wall under the window, mismatched pieces of fabric thrown over it in attempt to offer a little comfort. The decor was dismal, a dispiriting landscape of multiple shades of grey or brown, the exposed floorboards worn smooth with the endless passage of feet but ingrained with years of use.

In the corner, furthest to the back of the room was a small tin bath that mother used for washing everything from dishes to children, clothes and linen were constantly suspended from ropes hung horizontal from wall to wall. The room smelt of a strange mixture of herbs and spices, which mother used to compliment her cooking. It also worked well to disguise the odour of humanity which was only tolerable owing to the powerful scent of the herbs, hence we didn't open the window often as if was close to the water closet.

The rocking chair sat prominently by the hearth, a beautiful example with delicately crafted spindles, indented seat and sleek feet that deliver a smooth and reassuring rock. I always liked the calming feel of the chair, swaying in the warmth of the stove, dreaming of a life yet to happen.

Mother and father's bedroom had bare floorboards and the pale walls were smudged with reminders of the previous occupants. It was just big enough to contain a double bed, which was pushed firmly against the wall and a wardrobe that had been crammed into the space between the bed and the adjacent wall. A small wooden chair that would have been fitting in museum, nestled behind the door. It was the throne to my mother's prized possession, a tatty but loveable bear that her grandmother had given to her on her fifth birthday.

The only decoration in the room was a small mirror framed in wood and a truly awful portrait painting that looked like it had been done by a drunk donkey. On top of the wardrobe, pushed as far back as it would go was a box, I often wondered what was in that box and what secrets it held.

The bedroom that I shared with my brothers and sisters had two crudely made wooden crate beds divided by a battered chest of drawers that had as many drawers as there were children, so we got a draw each, mine was at the top. For a while it was me and Mills in one bed with Lottie and Charlie in the other, as Johnnie was still in with mother and father, but after losing Mills I had the freedom of the bed to myself until Johnnie was old enough to be tossed in with us and I had to share my bed again.

The room was sparsely furnished for it contained little else except a child sized rickety chair, a pot stood in the corner by the window for emergency calls of nature and a sprinkling of cherished toys. The ritual naked floor was matched in sadness by the faded and peeling paper that covered the walls, a jumbled collage of flowers in an ever-repeating pattern. We were expected to keep the room clean and orderly and if we didn't the candle and food rations would be decreased but there was little to keep tidy, so this particular punishment was rarely used as justification.

I lay upon my straw mattress, the chill of the early morning seeping through the cracks in the brick work around the lattice window, whispering between the holes of my moth eaten ancient blanket. The gentle warmth the seeped into the floorboards from the Buckley's stove below was long absorbed into the night so was no match for the icy fingers of a frosty morning. I began to imagine what this day would bring, what events would unfold around me and which would be attributed to my actions and how far the wave of consequences that resulted as a course of my decisions would go.

By the time I left Well Street Chapel free school I was just shy of my twelfth birthday. I was the oldest pupil there, ninety percent of my peers, including dear Annie, had left by the time there tenth birthdays arrived, yanked out by their parents and thrust upon the nearest employer that would take them, or succumbing to one of the many diseases that plagued the streets.

The remaining handful dwindled rapidly so only I remained. As I had already learned every lesson taught I found myself being used in every way imaginable from scrubbing the floors to aiding in the teaching of these retched creatures, a daily torture of infantile scribblings and rancid dribbling orifices. The sole reason that I remained trapped within the education system for so long was due to the personal request of my mother to ensure the safe arrival of my remaining siblings for little did my mother suspect that I was the one responsible for the untimely death of Amelia and it was certainly not for the benefit of furthering my knowledge so that

I could engage in a respectable occupation.

I had wrongfully expected some form of acknowledgement on my final day, Monday May twenty-fourth, 1878, a deserving nod from Ms Clarke, a well done or good luck but as usual they all seemed oblivious to the lives of the young people in their care. As I walked through the large nondescript double doors, that had been wedged open with a viscous looking stake of wood, I felt a small twinge of sorrow at what I would lose. I knew that I would never have to return and face the rigmarole of the day but the realisation that I would now have limited time, and even fewer resources, to produce the elegant writing that I had perfected. My imagination that had been permitted to fly but would now be caged as I would be expected to join the masses as a cog in the great London workforce, earning a crust for the family.

The joyful feeling of freedom was short lived as tomorrow would see me arriving at Ms Killners door for a six o'clock in the morning start. I had been apprenticed to Mrs Killner since the tender age of eight, working four afternoons during the week from two o'clock until five o'clock. Ms Isabelle Killner was a plump kindly lady with a face so full of lines she looked every bit of her fifty years. Isabelle was unmarried and childless and worked from the front parlour room of her tiny cottage that still stood tucked away, harbouring from the on onslaught of dwellings threatening to swallow it, at the end of

Green Street, which I accessed through Globe Road.

It was always warm and welcoming despite the often depressing and dismal atmosphere that hung around like an unwanted guest. Much of Mile End Old Town had already morphed to the sardine housing that was taking over London, foot after yard being gobbled up and built upon. As an apprentice, I earned two farthings a week which was a pittance but to be fair Ms Killner could have managed adequately without my presence, so I was grateful for her goodness.

The arrangement with Ms Killner had suited all parties involved; the halfpenny that I would bring home was hidden away and saved for the pleasure of a whole family outing, Ms Killner received a willing apprentice who was eager to learn and who provided welcome company, mother was safe in the knowledge that I was not creating some mischief that would come back to haunt me and I had some spare time to pursue my hobbies.

Even now I still enjoy drudging through the banks of the Thames, squelching mud sucking me into the cold earth, looking for my fortune but mine was for pure pleasure unlike the impoverished Mud-Larks. As I idly poked holes in the ground with a stick hoping to detect a clang of metal I watch the Mud-Larks wading through the mud from Vauxhall-Bridge to Woolwich, that remained on the shore after the tide had receded in clothes that camouflaged against the mud, drying hard in the summer to form clothes resembling board, stiff and unforgiving.

The majority of them were mute in their search, resisting the urge to tamper with docked boats or fleece an empty coal-barge for scraps but some were bold which often ended in a brief, but welcomed, imprisonment in a house of correction. What I found of use I took to the rag-shop Simmons, opposite Tower Bridge, he'd pay a farthing for a pound of wet rope although the best was dry rope which he would offer at three farthings a pound and the best place to source that was from the hanging man after the user had finished their obligatory two-day swing.

One of my common duties was to sit upon a pile of books to flatten the fabric underneath so that it could be arranged in an orderly and neat fashion for Ms Killner to access. Ms Killner hired her Singer sewing machine and paid two shillings and six pence per week for its hire. The clientele that used the services provided by Ms Killner, who was renowned for her sewing skills, she specialised in patching up old garments and creating new ones from miscellaneous material, salvaged rags or from one of the second-hand clothes markets as well as individually styling partly made bodices to match the accompanying skirts and occasionally fashioning short notice mourning attire for a desperate grieving woman.

Unfortunately, many locals were beginning to buy clothes that were being mass produced by the factories at a reduced cost or opting for repairing their own clothes which resulted in nightmare Frankenstein creations wandering the city and a severe reduction in the volume of work that arrived with us, some days we would be lucky to earn one shilling. It also meant that because I had left school and become a full-time apprentice Ms Killner increased my pay to a thrup-pence a week, but this proved to be unsustainable and she was forced to end my apprenticeship, as my father would not permit me to bring him home any less than the three pence.

I was regrettably retired before I had any experience on the actual machine for I had previously not possessed either the technical understanding or achieved the height or strength required the make it possible for me to operate the pedals, wheel and the cloth without becoming unbalanced.

This lack of ability was to have a detrimental impact on securing any form of adequate employment as my impressive stitching was lost in the sea of a hundred faces all desperate for the chance to pace a better existence for themselves. My sewing skills were beyond average, and I could repair a hem or stitch a cuff as well as Ms Killner but alas, it wasn't to be. As that chapter of my life ended another began.

N.Joy   Jill

2

To say that I missed my time with Ms Killner is an understatement but there was nothing that I could do to alter my circumstances other than continue to seek employment and escape the trappings of the life to which I have been bound. The longer that I spent with mother the more our personalities clashed for we seemed to share no notion or thought the same although we were eerily similar in appearance, especially now that I had entered womanhood and was developing a body that any whore would be honoured to display. I think that she still found fault with the way that I tore my way into existence, rendering her near death and I could tell from the look in her eyes when we walked together that she resented me for the admiring glances that I would receive as these were once hers to relish in.

One saving grace for me was that I was too large to fit inside the breast of a chimney which rendered me unless in the employment of being a chimney sweep and the market of being a crossing sweeper was a smelly one which was generally reserved for the younger of my generation which I was thankful for as the smell of horse offering was bad enough to scurry past without being required to sweep it off the streets and away from the path of those who lived a lifestyle that was lavish and plush and a stark contrast to that of my own.

As a result of my inability to slip directly into a new job, a fault that father laid squarely at my door, I was required to make the weekly Monday morning trip to Taylors pawn shop, or rather the crowded front room of a residence down on Globe Road, to pawn our Sunday best. Not that it was in any way the best of anything, but it was superior to the rags that formed our usual attire. We always found a way to source the money required to buy them back on the Saturday so that we would be presentable when we attended service, but the cycle would start again on Monday.

My salvation came in the small pox death of a local resident and friend of mothers, old Mrs Jones who lived on the opposite side of the road to us. Mother would look in on Mrs Jones several times a week as her husband had been dead and buried the fifteen last years and her only surviving child, who was rather dense and childless themselves, had succumbed to tuberculosis last winter.

As mother was the only person to show kindness without recognition she was the first to discover the body which was unfortunate for her as Mrs Jones lost her fight with the pox shortly after Mothers last visit, so the body had laid undisturbed for several days.

Owing to my lack of employment I was required to assist mother in every aspect of daily life and had been conscripted to accompany her lately when visiting Mrs Jones which I didn't mind as it broke up the day and offered us both solace from one another whilst simultaneously providing an abundance of attention for the old girl.

I called her old Mrs Jones, but she was only a handful of years older than mother, but life had not treated her kindly which left her resembling an image ripped straight from the pages of ancient text to describe the withered old hag of a witch. She smelt permanently of lavender, which was only offensive if you didn't like the suffocating scent whilst her face reflected every second of her years, her features all scrunched up in the centre of her face with only a whisper of her greying hair escaping from the bonnet that she always wore strapped tight over her skull.

The only aspect that gave away any clue to her true age was the distinctive twinkle that shone in her eyes which seemed to sparkle even brighter when in the company of anybody of a young age or when she recalled anecdotes and tales from her past. She had kept many of the warning symptoms of the pox hidden from us, not acknowledging any headaches, explaining a persistent back pain on slipping the previous day and blamed her increasing confusion on her age.

I was the first to notice the rash but neither adult seemed concerned, so I thought no more of it. Mrs Jones was not a large woman, but she was certainly not skin and bones either, so I did see the change in her appearance each time we visited for she looked gaunter on every visit but attributed this to her decrease in appetite and the faint smell of vomit that greeted us on entry was ignored by all parties.

The last time that I saw Mrs Jones alive her visible skin had begun to show the signs of the classic pus filled blisters, evident in small clusters around her mouth and nose which she was unable to conceal from us unlike her attempt to disguise her hands with the arrival of never before seen black oversized gloves, that I assumed to be a relic of her late husbands, that she wore on the pretence of being cold and needing to keep her fingers warm and circulated so that she could construct the matchboxes as well as the fact that her shawl was permanently nestled around her neck.

Mother blindly swallowed the old gals' charms and never once questioned her responses, perhaps she suspected or maybe she was ignorant to the evidence that greeted us on every visit, either way she took no steps to see that Mrs Jones received any form of treatment or attention from an educated source.

When we called on that gloomy day the smell was the first

thing to assault our senses as Mother let herself in, it was an overpowering concoction of decaying flesh, human excrement, festering vomit and the sickly-sweet smell of the herbal perfume used to fragrance the property which did nothing to disguise the scent of death. As she stood rooted to the spot, unable or unwilling to move further into the house I shoved my way between Mothers ample frame and that of the flaking wall of the entrance hall and made my way to the open door of the front parlour room where I had spent many an hour in the recent weeks.

I was confronted with a barrier of ice cold air as the room had had no heat move around it for days and the smell that had filtered into the hall. The mixture of this and the anticipation that was building up inside my stomach over what would await us forced me to urge as the bile in my stomach made a desperate attempt to escape my body and join the revolting odour that crept out like a sea mist.

The site that met me was grotesque yet fascinating at the same time. A combination of the pox spots at varying stages of contamination, from small weeping sacks to large white pods, from circular blemishes with black centres to crusted scabs as well as gaping lacerations in the skin exposing the rotten and diseased flesh. She made for an artist's palette of red, orange and yellow with a brownish staining of dried blood covering every visible inch of Mrs Jones that I could see, and I suspected that her clothes hid an identical image. She was such a sorry sight, slumped in the chair that I had last seen her sat in, her eyes only half closed above a mouth that was open as if she was in the process of an unwanted yawn exposing teeth that looked as rotten as the flesh that supported them and housing a tongue that was swollen and black.

Although it meant the end of a life it was also fortunate for mother as being the first on the scene meant that she was the first to discover what had been left behind. The linen was all stained from the bodily fluids that had leaked from Mrs Jones as she had passed on the only piece of comfortable furniture in the property but there were a few pieces of chipped crockery that joined our own dilapidated collection.

Mother was privy to the hiding place of Mrs Jones possessions and was quick to instruct me to retrieve the small wooden box that she knew was carefully concealed beneath a pile of old papers under the chair in which the deceased Mrs Jones still occupied. I was thankful for the papers as they absorbed the fluids that had steadily leaked from the expired Mrs Jones and I managed to avoid them touching my skin and infecting me by a swift flick that sent them slithering to the floor.

The box contained a little shiny tanner and a two-bob bit which was the first time in my life I had actually seen a florin, two whole shillings, an old photograph of Martha, Mrs Jones' insensible daughter, and a beautiful maroon coloured shawl. By far the greatest treasure was a table top brimming with unfinished matchboxes that mother swept into the shawl and removed at a speed that I was unaware she was capable of achieving.

This was to be the start of a new venture for we gained the revenue for completing and distributing Mrs Jones boxes which allowed us to gain the commission to continue to make and supply them with Lottie being utilised to sell them on a weekend as well as assisting us in producing them on an afternoon when school had ended as their small fingers were ideal for scale of the matchboxes, but the boys were not trusted to sell them. The image of little Charlotte when she was trussed up ready to earn her keep was a comical site owing to her looking more like a pile of moving rags than a girl but the essentials were on show, her podgy miniature fingers protruded from the ends of fingerless gloves that were more hole than material and her eyes, nose and mouth peeped out through a canopy of cloth like a street urchin spying through the circle made in the frost covered glass at the lavish lifestyle of those more fortunate, her gentle voice escaping with the white vapour of winter as she enticed buyers for our wares.

For the most part the time I was required to spend putting together and filling matchboxes was an exercise in constraint as I was unable to express my true opinions for fear that I would beguile mother and make the whole day intolerable. After each monotonous morning, I found that my shapely hands were a curse in the box production industry as the carboard was stiff to work with and the process was fiddly. I was used to delicate work through the intricate stitching that I learnt whilst with Ms Killner and she permitted me frequent breaks to flex my limbs which mother perceived as unnecessary to instate in her workhouse regime. It mattered little in the long run as I was to embark on a new venture just ten days after witnessing the festering corpse of Mrs Jones.

She had hardly had the time to lay cold before the landlord had seized her remaining property and installed new tenants within the dwelling, the Thomas family. Their arrival was swift but they all appeared to display a welcoming disposition which ingratiated them to the street along with the fact that they were a local family and were known to many, including mother and father. As they were an older couple only one child remained with them, a lad by the name of Joseph who at fifteen was a few years my senior who already held a position as one of the tea boys at Kenwood House, an apprentice footman who would soon earn that title. Mothers nature afforded them the courtesy of the daylight hours to become accustomed to their new surroundings before launching herself upon them as the self-appointed street advocate, dragging us with her like a hoard of minions.

My initial feelings of embarrassment subsided the moment I meet the gaze of Joseph, who looked as uncomfortable with the intrusion as his parents, turning instead to one of giddy excitement at the prospect of seeing him in the full light of day. I found sleep that night an elusive creature as my mind whirled with the heated imaginations of a young girl as the first dawning of love began to settle over her.

The sound of a door closing snugly into its lock aroused my semi-conscious mind and I pulled back the rags covering the window to steal a look at the young Master Thomas as he embarked on the journey to work, his pitch-black trousers and coat blowing in the early morning breeze, the first rays of sun just visible enough to reveal his charcoal coloured hair swept neatly over his head in a side parting that was a stark contrast to the ruffed mess that adorned his head the previous evening.

I had the good fortune to be returning from a trip to Victoria park with my siblings when I happened to encounter Joseph returning from work. I wasn't sure that our visit had been appreciated so was delighted when the smile that I offered was returned and he kept pace as we walked back to Maroon Street.

In the short walk I learnt that he had three older brothers, all of whom had left London to fight in the Boer War that had broken out in the continent and the loss of their income had forced his parents to seek smaller accommodation. Joseph had no interest in serving Queen and country, determined to raise through the ranks at Kenwood House to ultimately become the butler for he was an educated but not an intellectual individual.

By the time we had reached our respective doors he had

promised to enquire about any vacancies within the great house that I could fill and report back to me the following day. The day seemed to be endless, every second taking a minute, every hour seeming to drag on longer than the last and when I finally saw the lone figure in black walk past the window my heart leapt at the news I so desired he carried. My heart sank seconds later into a pit of despair as he didn't knock as I had expected but instead continued to his own door, disappearing inside.

I watched in horror as all my dreams of the last two days began to unravel inside my mind and the glittering future as Mrs Thomas, the wedded servants of Kenwood, dissolved into an image of Ms Killner, a spinster, alone in life and love. I barely registered the tapping on the door and it was only the shrill shriek of my name coming from mothers' sour mouth that brought me out of my self-imposed exile to my bed. As I slunk down the stairs I was astonished to see the silhouette of Joseph in the doorway, his smile widening as I approached, me hoping that my face had not betrayed the pleasure that I felt at his visit. I could see from the shadow that escaped from under the door that mother was lingering behind it, her attempt to discreetly listen disguised to her knowledge but blatantly obvious to mine.

Just to vex her I persuaded Joseph to remove himself from the doorway and state the reason for his visit out in the street, hoping that I would not be disappointed with what I was too hear. Joseph delivered the news I was desperate to hear, he had secured me an interview the very next morning with Ms Francis the housekeeper as well as Mr Grimsby the House Steward, which would mean that if I was successful then I would be joining the staff up at Kenwood House and would be in service to an earl and not the great Wheeler of Maroon street. Mother was not impressed at the thought of losing an able hand to construct matchboxes although she did unwillingly accept that I could provide a substantial income to the household and granted permission for me to attend the interview.

I experienced another restless night, this time due to the nerves that had settled within my stomach which threatened to render me un-presentable to my potential new employer and rob me of the opportunity to expand my experience and earn independence. I was stirred from my slumber by the sound of small stones hitting the thin glass that formed the window of our bedroom. I looked down into the street to locate the perpetrator to find Joseph already dressed beckoning for me to join him.

Reluctantly I dressed as quickly as I could in my Sunday best, which was a hastily bought purchase from one of London's many market stalls at Petticoat lane that consisted of an ivory coloured long puffed sleeve blouse, a skirt made of the itchiest material known to man that rested suffocating around my chest accentuating my bosom in a shade that was once black and which had belonged to countless previous owners.

For the occasion I took mothers good boots and frock coat determined to make a good impression although my entire appearance looked like I had simply stolen the clothes off a person who was several years my senior. Joseph suppressed a giggle as I made my way silently from the house into the street, making no comment on my attire but instead gesturing for us to proceed.

The distance we would need to walk was seven miles, the first was completed in silence, the following two were uncomfortably balanced on board a cart trying to keep my appearance respectable, for Joseph knew the trader and would regularly hitch a ride for part of the journey, with the remaining 4 miles being filled with Joseph telling me about his role and the dynamics of the staffing arrangements as well as the etiquette that I would be expected to display.

The first signs of the estate were visible a mile before we would reach the house itself, as the view of the city gave way to the trees that surrounded Kenwood House we approached the first gatehouse which we slipped through with barely an acknowledgement from the gatekeeper who was more concerned with chastising a young stable hand than detecting any intruder that may enter the grounds.

By now the sun was settling into the sky and the houses servants had sprung into a hive of activity as they prepared this huge dwelling for another day of splendour. This was the first time that I had been on the grounds and was marvelling at the sight when Joseph pulled me from our current course to take a well-trodden path that lead around the left side of the house to the service wing.

Maids and grooms buzzed in and out, criss-crossing to complete their duties on time and to the satisfaction of their superior, the occasional glance thrown in our direction or a nod of the head. Joseph shoved me through the first break in service traffic he found and into the small hallway that lead to the downstairs of the great house which was the domain of the servants. He hurried me along the corridor until he stopped outside a door that was open a crack allowing the warmth to seep into the cold neglected corridor in which I waited, a welcome blanket of heat wrapped around my stockinged legs. Joe rapped lightly on the door and stood back to await the reply which followed almost immediately with the summons to enter.

I took a deep breath, fixed a smile upon my face and confidently pushed open the door, careful not to reveal how anxious I was as I stole one quick glance backwards to witness Joe winking at me before disappearing at speed to another part of the house. Both Mr Grimsby and Ms Francis could have competed with any of my former tutors at school for they possessed the same demonic quality of sternness and discipline that was fostered at Well Street with their uniforms pressed to a regimental standard and faces painted into place by a disgruntled artist I could detect no inclination of how well, or how badly, I was performing until the horrendous ordeal had come to a conclusion and they delivered their verdict.

After what seemed like an eternity, which later transpired to be about forty minutes, I was requested to wait outside the building whilst they deliberated my responses and would send for me in due course. As a waited outside the door that Joe had brought me through I observed the work that was being carried out and the expressions of those that scurried past me in the line of their duties. Most were consumed by their allocated tasks that they paid me little to no attention with the occasional individual showing genuine delight in their work and there were some that acknowledged me with a distrustful look in their eyes, perhaps wondering how and where I would fit into the workforce or if I would fit into the position that they held.

The agonising wait to see which direction my future would take was drawn out in excesses of two hours or more. Whether they had forgotten about me or if it was a test of character I never found out but I did as they had asked and duly waited until I was called for again, ushered into the same room by a harassed young house maid dressed in a white pinafore with black arms protruding out the sides, one wrapped around a valuable looking vase decorated with ornate blue flowers, the other carrying a cloth that was intended to clean the mentioned vase.

I found myself stood before the two imposing characters, again with no idea what they had decided as not a flicker could be established from their expressions. To my relief I was offered a position as scullery maid with an annual income of eleven pounds a year although I would have to complete a provisional period of one week to ensure that I was suitable, at a pay of five shillings providing that I was not tardy and completed all the tasks presented to me to a sufficient standard in an adequate time scale.

I was to report at seven am sharp to Mrs Newcombe, the cook, as my main task was to wash the dishes created by the earl and his guests as well as by the staff that resided at the Kenwood house and I would be required to make a soapy start on the breakfast dishes as my first task. Mother was thrilled to say that one of her offspring was in service to the fourth Earl of Mansfield, William Murray, and I'm sure the whole of the street was aware of this before I had even commenced upon my first day. Again, Joe accompanied me on the trek to Kenwood House, spelt Caenwood by most locals, leaving me in the warm fragranced kitchen to collect my uniform and start the employment that could change my life.

I was to discover later that day that the position I now held was vacated only the day previous due to the clumsy nature of the previous young whippet, so my arrival was set in bad feelings as she was much liked by the under cook and kitchen maids who were pained at her loss for which they seemed to lay the blame at my feet and the cook treated us all as if we were her personal slaves although she would offer a sly smile or gentle wink in my direction when she wasn't being observed by her peers.

Being a scullery maid required nothing in the way of intellect and lacked any form of challenge with the exception of the extra attention I needed to prevent any form of damage to the array of china that passed through my hands although the large metal pots and pans that Mrs Newcombe used daily to prepare the various different meals required little care due to their sturdy construction but did require, on occasions, for me to almost get in the sink with them depending on what cook had prepared and how long it had stood in the pot for and what attempt it had made to melt into the fabric of the vessel.

I completed my probationary period without incident to become an official member of the Kenwood House staff just shy of my twelve birthday, an event that was ignored by all with the exception of Mrs Newcombe, who I had named Cookie in my own head, had left a small piece of fruit cake wrapped in a plain piece of cotton on my stool. It was gone in one mouthful, but I savoured the taste and memory for months to come. At first the privilege of using hot soapy water on a regular basis was a novelty and I enjoyed the scent that soaked into my skin but this feeling waned and my fingers would be left feeling enlarged with a dulled sensitivity, I could feel the beat of my pulse vibrating through my skin, my hands and fingers tingling with the retained moisture, they felt as if I was wearing invisible gloves or that they belonged to another and I was struggling to adapt to the sensation.

As a scullery maid I worked in what they referred to as the wet kitchen, a room off the kitchen, that was twice as large as our main room at home, painted white with a stone floor that was cold to the touch day or night, rain or shine. There was no decoration to distract me, just a wall of mismatched shelving below rows of rods suspended from the ceiling to hold the laundered sheets and clothes. The basins used by the laundry maids were shallower than mine and ran adjacent to me, their mangles stood in the centre of the room allowing for them to manoeuvre the sheets and the floor standing clothes dryers were positioned in the corner around the entrance, often being moved to make the best use of the heat that filtered in through the windows.

I soon found myself no longer requiring the assistance of the crudely made stool that Mr Burton, one of the grounds keeper, had constructed to allow me to easier access the deep white fire-clay sink, large enough to comfortably bath an infant, that stood, supported by bricks, underneath one of the windows, maximising the use of the natural light to reduce the resources that we used.

Having been upgraded in 1845 to accommodate a new cast-iron open range, so that Cookie could spit roast the kitchen, was awash in a sea of stunning white and vibrant blue as Cookie had managed to amass a collection of matching sets, from a London pottery company that had opened in 1869. All were inscribed with the name of the supposed contents, not that this held much relevance for the vast majority of the maids were illiterate and could not read the labels so relied on their customary position on the shelves and the appearance of the vessel. This it didn't stop Cookie from having to be vigilant, as on more than one occasion a footman was heard cursing as his tea contained salt instead of sugar or an afternoon tea had been seasoned with sugar instead of salt. I'm sure that Kenwood must have been their best customer, whether Ms Francis was aware of it or not as some of the items I speculated had been purchased for their originality value as opposed to their functionality, but that was only the internalised opinion of a lowly maid, of which I had many but kept them securely in my own mind, desperate to avoid any unwanted attention that could make my position untenable.

My first year passed without much interest or merit, the Mansfield family preferred their Scottish Estate Scone Place with William only in residence at Kenwood for approximately three months every year, which brought with it an increase to everybody's work load which resulted in frayed tempers and short abrupt communications when just days previously there would have been jovial conversations or hushed gossip escaping our mouths as well as secret smiles exchanged between forbidden lovers, all placed on hold as the service staff effectively held their breath until the family vacated and we could relax again, only the iron fist of Ms Francis to avoid.

My second year passed much the same way as the first with nothing note-worthy to report, although not valued I was now excepted for my role as I was courteous and had yet to break or even chip an item that had passed through my hands. I had become more adventurous and would occasionally sneak unseen into the house to marvel at its splendour or spend time in the gardens, seeking out a groom or stable boy that were idle in their responsibilities.

Joe still accompanied me to and from work and had transitioned into a strapping young man who looked more physically fitting for the stable than the house, but he had progressed up the ladder and was now a recognised footman whilst I remained a scullery maid, an achievement owing to my delicate handling of the crockery. My plain features allowed me to blend into the background, mostly ignored by the occupants of the great house and their guests I found that I could pass virtually unnoticed if it appeared I was engaged in some errand or another and I was often carrying a pitcher to aid my deception. Despite the fact that I got teased hanging around the stables, with the calling of "neigh" and such like, I cared little for what the trivial boys had to say for they influenced no-one of importance and would receive a clip round the ear or a harsh word if their disrespect fell upon the ears of the senior staff for they likened me often to the magnificent creatures in their care owing to the rather unfortunate formation of my teeth which protruded at such an angle that they did remind, even myself, of a horses teeth.

On one of the rare days that I was not employed in scullery duties I found myself pacing the flagstones of Westminster. I should have spent the day with the family, completing any chores that mother saw fit, but I had taken the day in my own hands and ventured to a part of London that, although I had visited before with mother as a young girl, was unaccustomed to me. Many of the sights and sounds could have been found on my own doorstep but it held a prosperity that was lacking in the slums of the East End, this was the heart of the city, where decisions were made for Queen and country, where the lords held court, where the prestigious youth were schooled, and their mothers paraded their siblings in perambulators, all polish and lace.

As with every inch of my home it was littered with an array of society, a stone throw from the glory and beauty were the institutions that held the criminal and the insane, many a Londoner had been sent to Bedlam for losing their mind or held for a myriad of crimes whose penalty would range from incarceration or transportation to death.

The view from Westminster Bridge was breath-taking with various wharfs invading the banks of the Thames, a busy hive of hustle and bustle and building that stood so tall they could pierce a cloud. The opposing bank allowed the infirm held within the walls of St. Thomas's hospital a scenic view, the adjacent magnificent palace gardens a credit to the ochre brick castle that was Lambeth palace, the fit and ample home of the Archbishop of Canterbury although the towns place of worship was not to be outshone and stood tall above the highest turret of the palace.

By far the splendour of Westminster was the Houses of Parliament, the vast golden building was no less great then I remembered it to be, the clock tower that stood regal at its side boomed i's chime for all to hear, the sound of Big Ben, as it became known, stirred in me the memories of standing as a small child and looking up the length on the tower, convinced that it would lead me straight to heaven should I climb it. Even now I was dwarfed in its presence, I felt small and insignificant. I have often wondered over the years what path the city would have taken if Guy Fawkes had succeeded in his gunpowder plot to blow up the houses of parliament although I am sure that the powers that be would have gained control and it would have been chalked up to a misfortune in history.

I took in some of the scenery at Saint James Park, ate a pie whilst watching the ducks on the pond before heading towards Buckingham Palace to envy the residence of the monarchy. I stood with my bosom and face pressed up against the cold metal of the railings that prevented the public from gaining access to our great sovereign and imagined what life would be like as the Queen. Did she eat cake all day and decide whose head should be chopped off or were there more pressing matters that required her attention, or did she simply spend every day as she chose, being entertained by court jesters and served by a bevy of servants, I could only imagine.

The day would turn out to be more eventful that I would have ever thought that it could, I had witnessed the best and worst of the cites architecture, humanity in its glory, it's hardships and I was about to witness how brave those in service could be. The day was drawing to a close which meant that I had to make my way back to Mile End before it became too dark as not every street had the new gas lighting and unsavoury characters came out of the woodwork when the sun disappeared from the sky.

I inhaled the obnoxious smell of burning before I happened upon the source of the fire, the dimming light had masked the smoke that bellowed from the upstairs window of a terraced house, the occupants and neighbours watching in horror as the orange destroyer danced within and licked the brickwork. The clatter of the horses' hooves on the cobble was the first indication that help was on its way, followed closely by a white charger pulling the fire engine and men to where they were needed.

The firies jumped straight into action pulling a large flat length of material from the back of the engine and facing it toward the small inferno that was emitting a sheet of heat. There was little room to move as the force of the fire yielded anyone unable to stand within the vicinity of the building, but a crowd had gathered to watch the fate of the stone and mortar and offer sympathy to the family that had been rendered homeless.

The moustached firie who were efficient if not sympathetic looked sterling in their black uniforms, if not a little silly with trousers that spilt out over long black boots, the glow of the flame reflected from their polished buttons and axes hung from their belts like the pistol of a wild west gun slinger. Similar to the helmets worn by the beat bobbies those of the firies were a shimmering gold and capped with a ridge, a shining surface for the events of the moment to be played out should one not want to look directly into the heart of the destruction.

I did not stay for the duration, only witnessing the initial flood of water as it shot from the hose and damped the flames, knowing that as it was man's work there would never be a place upon the force for a woman, besides I was more enamoured by the beauty of the colours of the flame than putting them out.

My third year was shaping up to be much the same as the first two albeit with a growing list of responsibilities and a growth in my internal confidence. As most meals were eaten in the confines of the kitchen little food escaped onto the estate which suited Mr Grimsby and Mr Burton as it kept the outside image of the estate looking respectable and the vermin could not be unduly attracted by the scraps and crumbs discarded by the young lads although many a pocket left the kitchen with the addition of a crust of bread to later be munched under the guise of concentrating on retying a knot or re-buckling a horses' harness.

Henrik was an easy target, he wasn't from these parts, came from some cold country across the sea I'd never heard of and his grasp on the English language was challenging. He had made very little progress since arriving at Kenwood and was surround by boys and men with thick cockney accents and even if he had been able to explain his feelings or opinions he would have likely been disregarded or branded a trouble maker if he had made a fuss. Henrik was in no way an instigator of my torment, he was simply following suit and copying the behaviour of the other boys, but he didn't defend me either which made him just as guilty in my eyes and fair game on any punishment that may be metered out. He was as feeble in strength as he was in character, a stick of a boy, unnaturally tall for his age, all long bony legs clad in breaches that fit him loosely around the waist but fell short of his ankles exposing his pasty limbs and twig arms under the cover of a roomy stained shirt. His hair was a golden blonde, an envy of the young ladies, that fell like a mop upon his head.

It was the work of a moment, an irresistible opportunity that presented itself in that instant, a spilt second decision that I had made before I'd even considered any possible repercussion. My walk around the estate, permitted when I had finished all allocated tasks, had become customary for there were always items to be collected or returned and I was as good as any to carry out these errands, better that a maid is put to any use than is left standing idle.

Owing to the several years of outstanding service that I had under my belt and an innate ability to recognise and carry out duties without consultation my presence was not unexpected in any area of the estate which allowed my movements to pass largely unnoticed and a flattering smile or flirtatious word would prevent the senior grooms and gardeners from reporting back to Ms. Francis that I was trespassing on their allocated areas or causing a distraction to the young stable hands.

Henrik had been given the unenviable task of clearing the summer debris in the form of autumn leaves and moss from the ground level gutters and roofs of the stable and around the service wing as several established trees stood regally in the vicinity and the fallen leaves lodged themselves in the gutter preventing the water from forming easily in the buckets and producing sporadic waterfalls when the rain is heavy.

Henrik had been at the task for two days already, this being his third, for he was a slow worker and was left unattended for large periods of the day, his presence within the stables not missed by colleague or master. His technique was to climb to the top of the ladder and extended himself as far as he could before sweeping the leaves towards himself, a cascade of brown, yellow, red and green falling to the floor like discoloured snow or sodden lumps clumped together that he had gathered in handfuls from the open pipe that he dropped onto the stonework with no care for who or what was below him, not that he could see for his arm would come to the side, he would make his release and repeat, all whilst facing up the slopped roofs.

The moss was the most problematic part of the clean as it secured itself under the tiles, clinging like a barnacle to the side of a ship and Henrik would slither further, his torso flattened on the roof, his legs suspended in the air so that he could manually pull the moss from the tiles.

As I discretely watched on my approach from the scullery I observed Henrik do this several times, his feet leaving the safety of the ladder so that he could gain additional length then rocking back until they impacted with the top rung of the ladder again. He did this as I approached, oblivious to my silent step which was aided by the soft leather of my boots but also the skill that I had perfected in walking with a light step that left my passage as quiet as that of a church mouse.

With a quick glance I checked that we were alone, that the stable boys were occupied elsewhere on the estate and no other maid was skulking around. I tiptoed innocently past, my focus locked on the great knolled oak tree that stood at the edge of the path, as I drew parallel to the ladder I turned slightly, extending my own arms to grip firmly onto the sides of the ladder and lifted it a foot to the left before releasing it silently against the wall as if had never moved at all and continued on my journey, never looking back to see if I had been observed or breaking pace until I had disappeared around the corner of the house.

I slipped into the little used entrance, for it was low and was often the cause of a footman curse so staff had discontinued using it, and made my way back towards the kitchen, the smell of Mrs Newcombe's freshly baked bread wafting towards me as if were a beckoning a Sheppard lost at night towards his warm bed. As soon as I was safely back inside the confines of the scullery my mind starting racing, questioning itself as to why I had just done what I did, guiltily hoping that no significant harm would befall the boy for he was only guilty of not befriending me, or even really acknowledging me at all, of trying to better his own life in a country that was not his own and for carrying out his duties with the same effectiveness that I prided myself in.

I heard the commotion around maybe ten minutes after I had returned, a shout through the wall that got louder as John, one of the stable boys came hurtling into the kitchen as if the hounds of hell snapped at his heels, breathlessly informing Cookie of the tragic accident before skidding into the scullery to retrieve a pail of clean warm water and whip a clean piece of linen from one of the dryers. I knew this was to bathe the wounds that Henrik had suffered in his fall from the roof as the buckets used around the stables with collected rain water were used to clean the stables and water the horses but not considered adequate for human consumption, and in this case for sterilising the injury.

I hadn't been able to hear every word that John had uttered and in his hurried state he could only manage the words "Henrik...fall...roof" so my mind concocted a myriad of injury's that could have been caused; bones protruding at odd angles and severed limbs on blood-soaked stones.

One thing was certain, Henrik was not dead. It was early evening before I managed to leave the four walls of my scullery to investigate the exact extent of Henrik's wounds for the day had been longer than usual owing to the kerfuffle caused as a result of many staff tending to Henrik or trying to ascertain what had happened and Joe had waited for me even though he had been dismissed from his duties hours previously. I was disappointed by Joe's lack of knowledge, and interest, in the plight of Henrik and he knew no more of the boys' fate than I did and even less of the circumstances surrounding his mysterious fall which meant that I hadn't been discovered as the perpetrator. As we hurried along the darkened streets our thoughts were turned inwards, me pondering Henrik and Joe's on whatever a young man thought of.

I had hoped that mother would have been concerned for my well fair as I had returned home hours after my expected arrival, but she did little more than scoff with a twitch of her head in the direction of the stove to indicate that I had a plate of uneaten food waiting for me.

It took several days listening to various accounts and viewpoints to piece together the nature of the injury's Henrik sustained in the fall. It transpired that he had broken both legs, although the drop was little more than 8 foot he must have landed in an awkward position on the hard surface below or had weak bones for the damage to be so dire, surely, he must have made some attempt to prevent the fall or cushion his landing. His leg had fractured above his right ankle, all inside his body so the only evidence could only be gleamed from the unnatural angle and swelling of the skin, but his left calf had snapped in half, the white shards of the splintered bone slicing through the skin like a chick bursting from its egg. He had also suffered a knock to the back of his head which had rendered him quite senseless. Mr Burton had bundled Henrik into one of the carriages that very night and spirited him away to one of the voluntary infirmaries so that his wounds could be properly addressed by a doctor. He was never seen at the estate again, so I have no clue as to whether he survived his injuries, was left paralysed or made a recovery and I made no effort to find out beyond my unsuspecting wondering.

Little did I deserve it but the day of our family outing to the zoo had arrived. Excitement had been building in the house for the best part of a week, the younger ones positively fit to burst. All I had heard was talk of the elephant that carried children on its back and the lions that could eat a man should they be let loose. I was proud of the knowledge that my wage had contributed to the visit and we had been able to take the train, arriving in relative comfort, delivered at Chalk Farm Station with only a short walk to memories that may last a life time. Despite the zoological gardens having been open for the last fifty years and more it was a constant draw to visitors and locals alike. A steady stream of people flowed in and out of the entrance, families reminiscent of the caged apes, their feet itching to explore the enclosures, couples hand in hand seeking a quiet corner for an embrace and artisans with easels and paints in hand ready to capture these exotic creatures forever on canvas.

The first dilemma to solve once we had passed through the arch and handed our ticket to the capped attendant was to decide which exhibit to visit first, the boys rather eager to get to the sandy coloured magnificent felines whereas Lottie was persistent in her attempts to see the giant grey mammal. I was happy either way as I understood that we would be entitled to visit every exhibition and animal on display and we had ample time for it wasn't even yet noon.

Father took the deciding hand and directed the family, as a collective, past many enclosures and directly to the Fish House. It was a large building that looked rather like a majestic greenhouse and was home to an array of fish that varied in size and colour, an apple in the zoos eye I found the aquarium to be a tranquil environment, the inhabitants safe from the hook and line, unaware of their appeal as they idly float around.

Lottie was thoroughly impressed with Jumbo the elephant and he meet every expectation that she held dear although she was unable to touch or ride him she was satisfied to be in his presence. He was indeed impressive on a grand scale, yet my affections lay with a creature whose species name was as ridiculous as the name they had given him, Obaysch the hippopotamus. He was a creature of a moody disposition with sagging wrinkled skin and a face that had seen better days. The cats did not live up to the boy's imagination as they were feeble looking animals that spent most of the time laying down and lacked the blood and dismembered bodies that I am sure the boys had expected to litter the cages. As a surprise to all mother favoured the reptile house and father was taken by the giraffes, their ungainly necks supporting a minuscule head and a tongue that caused even the most serious to part with a discrete snigger. The day ended with a supper of fish and everyone went to bed dreaming of the animals that they had seen, some for the first and only time.

Life returned to normal at the estate, Henrik's mishap
becoming a distant memory, the Murrays still only visiting for
a few months a year. Within that year of 1880 I celebrated my
fourteenth birthday for which Cookie made me a little cake,
small enough to fit in the palm of my hand, which I got to
savour all to myself.

I went through two new dresses too as I had grown in height
and stature with the dress making a desperate attempt to
disown my boots and my breasts swelled out of the second
much to the exasperation of Jessie Issacs, a local seamstress
employed to repair linen and uniforms and who considered
maids to require nothing more than mere rags to cloth them as
they should remain in the background, neither seen nor heard
though thankfully Ms Francis required us to be presentable as
you never knew who may come calling at the house.

With the increase in the size of my breasts came an increase
in my interest in the opposite sex and the stable boys that I
once found futile and irritating had morphed into muscular
physiques and handsome faces that I often imagined pressed
closely against mine, day dreaming in the scullery of flings in
the hay and stolen kisses behind the hedges.

As much as I was noticing the male of the species I was
beginning to observe that they were also noticing me but
finding mutual attractions was not as easy as it would appear

for I seemed to like those that had no desire to know me and those whose glances I had detected fall upon me I had no inclination to know further. It had never occurred to me that Joe would find any attractiveness in myself for we had been friends for many years and he was courting one of the parlour maids but occasionally I would see him looking at me as if I were a succulent pig hanging in the butcher's window which aided in my determination to find a suitable partner in which to enter adulthood.

My first kiss was not the passionate and beautiful affair that I had dreamt that it would be but a snatched moment of reality that I had not expected. I was still a regular around the stables and had been developing a closeness with one of the grooms, a dark feather haired boy of equal height to myself and a build that was slight yet portrayed strength and an accent that screamed I'm meant for better things.

On this particular occasion he was in the process of mucking out one of the estates fine mares and had spotted me enter before I had located his position. As I walked past the stalls admiring the magnificent beasts held within Harry appeared like a jack-in-the-box, startling me enough that a surprised cry escaped me making him laugh and my cheeks redden. I was about to chastise him for such a petty act when he leaned forward and embraced me, his soft moist lips pressing against mine resulting in a fluttering inside my chest that was new to me, unexpected but not unpleasant.

It felt to me to last for minutes as my head filled with euphoric thoughts but would in fact have been seconds as we were interpreted by the stable master making his entrance that Harry's ear had become accustomed to over the years and he was already working by the time old Thomas had made his appearance, oblivious to the corrupting scene that had been on display just moments before.

With a sharp "get girl, back to your kitchen" I was dispatched, the memory of the kiss lingering, the excitement dissipating as I floated back to the scullery however my mind was suspended in time, replaying his touch unable to focus on my tasks which had little bearing for I was accomplished in my dish washing abilities and I did not require the full use of my mind for it. Over the following weeks we shared many brief kisses, some planned others spontaneous but all respectful and short.

I envisioned that no kiss could be delivered sweeter, but I was disparaged by the lack of experiment that Harry was willingly to try, and I was becoming disillusioned by the notion of romance. One or two of the older boys thought that they would attempt the same tactic as Harry and tried to kiss me, but their advances were rebuffed.

I stayed away from the stables for a while, fearing that I had a reputation starting to form around me. James McCall was one of the footman, arriving from Ireland in the late months of 1880 and became the focus of my attention, his polished shoes and pristine uniform adding an air of grandeur to his position, his oily mud coloured hair a betrayal of his heritage. At first, we exchanged small smiles and glances that were unnecessary, the excuses to be in each other's company becoming more frequent and blatant.

We had yet to touch lips, but our hands had meet many times, a stroke as we brushed past each other in the narrow hallways that left me giddy from anticipation of sharing our first embrace which I imagined would surpass the first but this one was delivered in a different manner.

It started the same, a brush of my soft skin against his but he was more forceful moving his jaw to part my lips. As I settled into the rhythmic motion a stirring began to happen in my loins and I started to feel a desire to have him press firmer against me, my breathing increased and my hands that were grasping his jacket began to involuntarily tighten.

What came next both ended any chance of a relationship between us and brought me to the stark realisation that I was still only a child at age fourteen and not yet the woman I desired to be.

His kiss was experienced but I was far from ready from the intrusion of his tongue as he projected it into my mouth, a slippery snake of wet flesh that whipped around my teeth, jousting with my own tongue. The feeling was unexpected and alien, I pushed James away and ran back to the scullery, unsure why he would have done such a thing, not yet aware of the pleasure that can be gleamed from a passionate embrace for my experience had been limited to childish pecks on the cheek or lip-locking that progressed little further than both lips leaning stationary against one another.

It was several weeks before I left the comfort of the scullery. The duties I performed within the main house were carried out quickly whilst my confidence to be in the presence of the opposite sex was restored.

First returning to the familiar surroundings of the stables, the distinctive scent of horse infiltrating my nostrils and clothes bringing a slice of the country to the smog of the city. It wasn't long before my confidence returned, and I was of the mind to appreciate the fine features of the male staff although I was content to look and not touch, or be touched, for the time being.

The next object of my affection arrived in the form of a young male relative of the Earl himself, a son of a cousin through marriage but nonetheless a wealthy adolescent with eyes that shone like the sapphires that adorned his mother's ears. They had arrived to spend the Christmas festivities in residence and to experience the delights of the great capital.

As was usual when the family was home we were expected to be on our up-most behaviour and the work load increased tenfold offering me little in the way of escape from the scullery, but it kept my attention focused on the task at hand until Alastair Ramsey came investigating the deeps of the mansion.

I was first alerted to the strange presence by the unusually polite voice which was emanating from Cookie, although a kind-hearted woman she was characteristically short in tone with others and was accustomed to barking orders at lesser staff to ensure the smooth and efficient running of the kitchen, but her tone was humble and accommodating.

I poked my head around the door to see who was eliciting such a response from old Cookie to be meet by the curious young Scot who was not only testing Cookie's knowledge of the house and the surrounding area of Hampstead but also testing her patience. Although her exterior exuded calm and professionalism I could tell from her eyes that she would rather wring his neck than be questioned like a criminal, but she never betrayed herself.

I had glimpsed Alastair many times since their arrival in mid-December but had yet to meet his acquaintance. This would happen shortly before Christmas day, I was scurrying down the servant staircase that lead behind the library, arms laden with dishes to be washed when Alastair rounded the corner directly into my path.

It was a pure miracle that I saved the crockery from harm, avoiding a disciplined dressing down from Cookie.

Alastair's guilt over his part in the narrowly avoided accident lead him to take a share to the scullery, opening the pathways of conversation that lead me into the next chapter of my life.

3

Alastair and I meet as often as we could, on a basis of friendship, two kindred spirits yearning for excitement and adventure but tied to the circumstances of our upbringing and conformities of society.

The family were attending a church service followed by dinner with the Duke of Devonshire at their Kensington residence on Christmas day, so I wasn't required to report to work until late morning allowing me to return home on Christmas Eve.

I had arranged to meet with Al in Victoria Park to celebrate the festivities along with the masses who congregated to watch the performers and part-take in roasted chestnuts, sing and dance.

The whole family was in attendance which made it difficult for Al to slip away but he managed to make his escape to mingle with the common folk of London. We were quickly swallowed by the crowds, the Yule tidings drifting through the air, mixed with temporary happiness and whispered promises that never materialise.

As we weaved among the human maze Al slipped his hand into mine mid swing, a motion that he didn't acknowledge with his face with the exception of a slight smile that would have passed unnoticed to anybody that he wasn't acquainted with. The feeling of his hand in mine felt different to when I held Lottie's hand or from the memory of holding mothers hand when I was small girl, his soft skin, a contrast to the rough surface of a labours hands, made my heart flutter and my breath quicken but I acted as if I was overcome by the throngs of people as opposed to being overcome by his touch. The night ended quickly but sweetly with a swift kiss and sweet dreams.

I had stayed over at Kenwood on many occasions, especially when the family was in residence for they had a liking for entertaining the countries aristocratic and artistic society or if the house was the host of a function that required me to start earlier and finish later making the journey to and from home an inconvenience for all involved, so I would bunk down in one of the rooms allocated for staff accommodation. The heralding of a new year was one such occurrence.

The house was at its capacity, every room a hive of activity swarming with stunning gowns of every colour imaginable spliced with sparkling jewels reflecting the glow of the candles burning around the house like little stars twinkling. A colony of servants strategically worked the gathering ensuring that the evening ran smoothly, my part was, as always to ensure a constant supply of clean glasses.

The persistent drone of the orchestra and thudding of dancing feet penetrated the floorboards, the shrill interruptions of rapturous laughter mixed with the elegant conversation floated down the stairs, I felt a little envy of their fortunes, wished for once that I was dancing and drinking, making merry with the nobility of England.

My thoughts were broken by James bringing a fresh batch of plates and glasses to be dealt with, we exchanged a brief greeting before he retreated with the clean replacements. It had been a little strained between us since our fleeting dalliance, but I no longer had eyes for him, my affections lay elsewhere. As my hands automatically began the process they had been doing for the last three years, the warmth of the water a caressing comfort as I toiled alone daydreaming of a future filled with parties and extravagance.

I was so absorbed in my fantasy that I had not heard the footsteps on the stone floor and the sudden realisation, when a hand touched my shoulder, that I was not alone made me jump, the glass that I was holding flew from my soapy hands smashing into the wall before falling to the ground in a waterfall of shattered crystal.

Despite the noise from above the distinctive sound of the break echoed down the corridor bringing Ms Francis into the room.

With a flustered expression and arms fluttering beside her like the wings of a demented bird she took one beady look in my direction, to the broken glass, back to me and my guest before saying "apologises young Alastair, forgive me for the intrusion, I do hope that everything is in order. Mary, the cost of the glass will be deducted from your wages, carry on. Alastair, may I escort you back to the party?"

This wasn't posed so much as a question but an instruction so reluctantly Al allowed himself to be led from the floor under the disapproving gaze of the miserable old blower.

The celebrations had run their course and Cookie with her maids had long since gone to their rooms. I was ready to retire, exhausted from the days' labour, drying my hands on my apron I moved around the room extinguishing each candle with a tired sigh. The only remaining candle lightening the darkened room was waiting for me by the door, ready to light my way to bed.

As I approached the flame began to dance wildly and a shadow fell across the doorway.

The silhouette of a man came into focus, with baited breath I slowly reached out to take hold of one of the rods that the maids used to prod around the linen. As the apparition drew near I gripped the smooth wooden rod in my palm ready to defend myself if the situation required it. My heart beat ferociously in my chest, filling my ears with a steady beat, my eyes unable to blink fixated on the point of entry, the rod scrapping on the floor as it vibrated through my shaking grasp.

The figure stepped into the doorway revealing not a man, well not yet, but Alastair, still clad in his expensive glad rags, his pearly whites shining in the light of the flame beneath a cheeky smile, his eyes lustrous like precious jewels. He advanced in a heartbeat to stand in front of me, just inches between us, I had to tilt my head to continue to gaze into his eyes for he was taller than me. Without breaking eye contact his hands found mine, he moved purposefully against me so as to cause me to take a step backwards continuing in this fashion until my heal impacted with the palate holding the pressed linen for use the next day.

Before I had registered what had happened I was laying on top of the pile of pure white cotton, Al's body suspended above mine. His slow measured breath met my more rapid version as time seemed to slow down my mind raced at a thousand miles an hour, crazy adult thoughts colliding and exploding revelations in parts of my body that were unfamiliar and new.

An alien thought entered my mind and refused to leave, getting stronger and more forceful with every seductive second that passed. A primeval need to have Alastair consume me, join with me, an involuntary response in my hips forcing them skywards, inviting the union of two bodies, a warm yearning spreading over my laycock.

No words were exchanged only consensual murmurings and unspoken desires given through the mutual communication of our eyes. Al worked with the expert skill of a horseman, one arm supporting his frame retaining a gap between our possessed bodies, the other starting the journey of descent down my torso before disappearing into the folds of my uniform, invited by my legs that I found were no longer straight but bent enabling my hips to gain the upward momentum that my body craved.

At some point Al had released himself for I felt the warm sensation of flesh gently pressed upon my skin where before only myself or linen had touched. I arched my back, straining my neck so that I could take his soft lips in mine, the sweet taste of champagne mixed with the salty tang of sweat was evidence of his restraint, any conscious thoughts lost to the moment. Momentarily breaking the eye contact that had tethered me to the last strings of innocence I plunged my tongue into his mouth, feeling my way across his teeth, caressing his lips with mine, my hands that previously lay at my side found a passion of their own, bracing against him, tracing the patterns in his expensive shirt, trying to find any entrance to his skin.

In one purposeful movement I secured my hands over his buttocks and thrust myself upwards, taking him into me in one swift move that was both the source of the most severe pain that I had yet to experience in my short life but also one of satisfaction, my body reacting equally in waves of pain and pleasure, Al matching my movements in a rhythmic action until a rapid surge of energy that resulted in him entering me to the fullest before burying his face in the moist skin of my neck and becoming alarming still.

I lay trapped beneath his weight, the throbbing of his manhood bracing inside me, my arms still locked around his body, his breath tickling my neck sending shivers down my spine. Although it felt like an age, my mind whirling with the possibilities of the repercussions with the thought of actually being caught never entertained, in reality the whole episode probably only lasted a fraction of the time I envisioned.

Alastair's limp body gained a surge of life, he looked me in the eyes, a satisfied smile spread across his face whilst slowly slipping from me. He planted a delicate kiss on the tip of my nose before standing straight and making his retreat from the room, adjusting his attire so that no suspicion would befall him should he encounter another living soul before reaching the safety of his bedchamber leaving me alone in the near dark scullery, a chill beginning to settle on my exposed legs as no body now lay between them providing human insulation.

I pulled my piny back down to cover the shame that began to swirl around me, as I shuffled off the pile of linen I was meet with a sensation of aching limbs, not dissimilar to the feeling that I observed after I had been on my first horse trek around the estate and an openness in my nether region that was irritable and damp. I blew out the remaining candle and made a slow amble to the first of the servant's rooms, slipping in discreetly without waking the occupants and falling into a fitful slumber on the floor.

Thankfully I was first into the scullery that morning which prevented a lengthy explanation of the discovery of blood that had stained the sheets the night before. I would have been alarmed for not the discovery of trickles of blood on the inside of my thighs and on the lining of my underwear which lead to the realisation that the blood was a result of the previous evenings intercourse. The maids were known to be idle in their duties so had left the cloth that adorned the tables to soak overnight, not wanting to tire themselves unduly which provided me with the opportunity to dispose of my secret under the pretence of assisting them in their tasks.

I failed to manage to concoct a meaningful reason to escape from the servants' wing so had to suffice with a glimpse of Alastair on a feigned errand to retrieve a missing pot, but I was rewarded with a smile for my efforts. Joe was waiting for me early that evening, excited with the news that he was to propose to his girl, so I could not wangle another chance encounter without raising suspicion.

As I returned the next day the estate was already a buzz of activity, the carriages were being readied and loaded with armfuls of trunks, matching in design but varying in size and contents, as the Murrays and Ramsey's' prepared to return to the highlands to recommence trade and education. I set sombrely about my duties, lost in a haze of self-pity and realisation that I was to be left behind, abandoned like an unwanted mongrel, used like a common whore with no monetary benefit.

Even though servants were discouraged from admiring the beauty of their surroundings I had always found solace in the music room and this is where Alastair found me, admiring the beautiful but disproportionate portrayal of Mrs Tollemache by Reynolds, under the pretence of dusting the harp. We all looked the same to the master and his family so nobody ever questioned my presence providing I was busy and blended into the back ground. We had barely embraced before we were interrupted by the arrival of the earl himself, mistaking the situation for a servant being accosted by an individual of superior breeding for it was Al's arms that held me tight and his face that loomed above mine, forcing me into the richly upholstered green canapé.

William Murray was a kind man and had lived a life not devoid of adventure, although he was no longer young at the expiring age of seventy-five he understood the trappings of youth, so I was released and sent about my duties, losing the chance to say a goodbye to my sweetheart but retaining my position, while Alastair was required to remain and embark on a lengthy conversation about morality and responsibility.

I started a great sickness mid-February, a persistent nauseous feeling on waking that I could not shake and which would dissipate towards midday regardless of the amount of food that I consumed or the tonic that I had secreted from the store hidden in the cupboard that stood sentential in the nook outside Old Francis office, although I felt well in my mind the sickness was accompanied by a niggling pain emanating from the bones supporting my midsection.

After several weeks the situation had not improved, and my mind had begun to self-diagnose what was wrong with me, had I contracted Cholera or was my stomach infested with a hideous parasite that would rip its way into existence. Despite the daily purge I had lost no weight, not even an ounce and developed no other aliments to accompany the sickness with the exception of a general air of tiredness that clung to me like the smell of the fish that hung around the merchants.

It was the lack of vigour and feeling of near exhaustion towards the end of a laborious day that was compacted with the endless stretch of repetitive mile that stood between my bed and the scullery that made me feel far beyond the tender years that I was, gone was the springiness of youth and clouded were the thoughts of a future yet to be written. I had started the feminine bleed years previously but wasn't yet able to make an accurate prediction as too when it would come so the lack of a regular bled wasn't an indication to me of my impending condition.

I wasn't innocent of the world but in my defence, mother had made no effort to inform her brood on the how's and whys they came into creation.

The notion that I may be with child only began to emerge through the accumulation of small identifying factors that individually could point to any number of medical conditions but combined with the gradual swelling of my tummy made me suspicious. I was never a girl of slight stature, but I had always admired that I had a relatively desirable figure and clothes fitted me well but of late my uniform was constricting and uncomfortable to wear, Cookie had even uttered a few remarks about my expanding waist line and increased appetite. It was only when the bubbling sensation in my stomach could be felt on a daily basis that I could no longer continue to ignore the situation in the hope that I was either mistaken or face the possibility that I had contracted a deathly illness that would incapacitate me.

What would father say? The shame that I would bring upon the Wheeler name would expel me from their company for a lifetime and even if it didn't I was looking at a stretch within one of the workhouses which, as with many, could prove to be my downfall for an eternity. I decided that I would have to inform Alastair as my first course of action as to the predicament that we found ourselves in. He was as responsible for the life growing within my womb as I was for taking him inside me on that cold but magical night that heralded the ending of one year and beckoned in another, but the Ramsey's were in Scotland.

The Earl and his associates returned shortly before April to conduct some business before the family arrived for the Easter celebrations, although the Ramsey's did not accompany him. My plight was becoming obvious to even the most unobservant of onlookers, although some would just assume that I was becoming greedy, and I failed to escape the notice of William who, behind eyes filled with disappointment, arranged for a me to be seen by an esteemed doctor to determine the term of the pregnancy so that arrangements for its future could be put into place. It was Ms Garner, the discreet lady's maid to the Earls good lady wife Louisa, that spirited me away with assurances that my replacement only held my position in my brief absence and that I would return to the estate forthwith with a solution that would benefit all parties affected by the unfortunate situation that was fluttering within me.

The impressive abode in Harleyquinn Street was a combination of an established and trusted private medical practice as well as the private residence of the physician and his family in addition to a few private rooms that accommodated his esteemed clientele for overnight stays should they be required to remain for the duration of their treatment. As I descended the marble steps that disappeared below the streets surface the world took on a surreal towering feeling as if it were conspiring to consume, belittle and humiliate me for the predicament that had led to my very presence in this affluent area of top hats and feathered bonnets.

The outside of the property reflected the status of the owner but did not betray the image with any signage to welcome patients or identify it against the row of similarly presented houses which made me wonder how a client was to find the desired address. The clinical brightness of the waiting room gave the appearance of being inside a giant sugar cube but without the sweet taste to dilute the sterile smell that hung around the same way a pub would inheritance resonate in the stench of spilled ale and tobacco. Ms Garner had no intention of being any more involved in this scandalous predicament than she need be so after a hushed conversation with Dr Lee she resumed her position on one of the cushioned chairs with as much care as if she had dropped of a garment to be mended.

I was beckoned into the doctor's office to be examined with an indication by a bony index finger curling like a worm that had been decapitated. The door was locked behind me, a bolt of metal sliding into place, trapping the condemned in a windowless box. Dr lee held no pretence over his disgust for the way in which I had conducted myself and a series of orders were barked out in a manner that was not becoming of a doctor of his reputation. These were intersected with ramblings on the depravity and ungodliness of youth which was no more effective than a priest preaching to the fallen or a groom closing the stable door after the horse had bolted.

The bed on which I was required to levy myself was harder than the linen pile on which this situation arose and offered little in the way of comfort to soften the shame that having a stranger's eyes exposed to my parts would bring to me. I was truly ignorant in matters of a medical nature so was unaware of what would occur during such a procedure and aghast at Dr Lee's insistence at the depth of his physical exam.

I positioned myself on the bed allowing Dr Lee to feel my stomach, pushing firmly at the top, bottom and from each side, his pale skeletal fingers disappearing into my skin, feeling about for the sack that contained another life like one of the little urchins feeling around in the mud for a jewel that will change their fortune. It wasn't painful as his nails were cut short and his hands manicured but it was uncomfortable. However, I sensed an increasing feeling of frustration and anger emanating from the doctor the longer his examination continued, his gentle touch becoming rougher, his care dissipating like the flow of water from a butt during the peak of the summer season.

I was uncertain were his next request would lead for the request was to remove my under garments for a further examination. I reluctantly wiggled free, retaining my modesty through the length of my uniform although this was short lived once I was re-confined to the bed I lay flat on my back with my legs bent at the knees forcing my uniform to gather in folded layers of black and white, my bare legs unprotected from the cool temperature of the surgery, my parts involuntary clenching at their exposure.

From my horizontal position in my agitated state I caught a glimpse of what I thought was Dr Lee making a move to release his trousers and take advantage of his position, a violation that I was not prepared to permit so I slammed my legs closed and started to sit up, anger and bile rising in equal measure, to observe that Dr Lee's attire was in fact as it had been previously. The motion had been him fastening a gown around his own body to protect his finely tailored suit, leaving me feeling both stupid and remorseful that I had even entertained such a notion but perhaps sealing an idea into Dr Lee's mind that antecedent was only a wish never to be acted upon.

A trolley was laid with terrifying metallic instruments of varying shapes, sizes and uses, all gleaming brightly, reflecting warped images of the room, pulled close to make it easily accessible.

The internal examination was a different story in terms of pain, the first initial touch was professional, careful and delicate but what came to follow would forever change my opinion towards the world and its inhabitants, it would alter my perception of what a human could be capable of and what limits they could be stretched to. Dr Lee gruffly explained the reason for this kind of examination was to determine the exact period of cessation and this was deemed to be the most effective method combined with the external measurements of any evidence of the pregnancy and that if I was to relax I was not to cause extreme discomfort to myself.

An experienced finger teased into my womanhood with a gentle yet firm poke, softly exploring my entrance, pushing and twisting, widening the gap until he inserted a second finger where they fought like soldiers before joining in unison to force a space wide enough to allow his thumb to form a tripod from which he could open me further. I held my breath, suspended in a dreamlike state, in an effort to distance myself from the stimulation that I was experiencing.

I was desperate to avoid Dr Lee misinterpreting it as an invitation, my vaginal muscles contracting and releasing in response to the controlled intrusion while my mind fought against the surreal images it was producing. Despite the knowledge that I was in the hands of an aged professional of impeachable character the arousal that I was experiencing was making my tract moist accommodating his touch to the extent that he it was becoming lost inside the cavern that had opened between my legs. By now my laycock was throbbing, aching in the memory of that New Year's Eve, my eyes closed as I imagined it was Alastair that was touching me. I opened my eyes, looking down the lengthen of my own body I noticed a change in Dr Lees demeanour, a cloud settling over his face changing it, extinguishing any emotion in his eyes, leaving lifeless pools of blue, devoid of humanity, legitimacy being replaced with revenge.

The next few minutes lasted an eternity as the pleasure that I was experiencing turned into an excruciating nightmare, the warmth of skin being replaced with the sharp coolness of a foreign object maintaining the hole that the doctor had titillated followed by scrapping and pinching as well as a violent stabbing, my legs thrashing at the doctor, body rolling on the bed in an attempt to extract myself from the torment.

The echo of my pitiful screams mixed with the pounding on the door, as Ms Garner tried in vain to gain entry to discover the source of the animalistic noises that escaped from the room. These were the last sounds that I heard before drifting away into blackness, consumed by the thought that my young life was being extinguished.

I was welcomed back into consciousness by the jarred motion of the carriage as it wound its way back towards the estate, Ms Garners face swimming into view as it hovered above mine, eyes full of concern, akin to a mother's gaze as she watches her sleeping infant as it recovers from a disabling illness. Her tender smile, tinged with guilt, conveyed the worry that she felt but did little to ease the sinking feeling that had settled within the pit of my stomach or erase the fragments of memories of the last day. She murmured hushed soothing's and lightly stroked my hair before I again lost the battle and was consumed by darkness, this time waking on a bed in one of the uniform servant's rooms, a wet flannel on my brow to ease the feverish symptoms that were evident through the clammy feel of my skin and uncontrollable shaking of my body.

It was three days before I was to process a rational thought and gain any resemblance of the person I was before my ill-fated delivery to the practice of Dr Lee. It later transpired through the grapevine that the doctor had that very evening previous learnt that his beloved wife was in the throngs of a passionate affair with an influential politician and that Dr Lee had condemned all woman with the view that they were adulterous wrenches.

To be presented with an unwed servant who had been clearly wanton in her actions was the proverbial straw that broke the camel's back accumulating in me bearing the brunt of Dr Lee's rage.

Although what was discussed between himself and Ms Garner

never materialised there remains the realistic possibility that I was taken to this legitimate doctor so that an illegal abortion could be performed under the order of William Murray under the pretence of an internal examination to negate any suspicion that may befall him or his client. Mr Murray however appeared truly sorry for the dramatic turn of events and the messages relayed to me assured that he had no intention of the outcome and that it was the result of the deranged manner in which Dr Lee had been affected by his personal circumstances.

It could not be denied that the consequences were an advantage to all involved, the family avoided that scandalous reputation that would hang around the estate like flies around the manure at the stables. Alastair could pursue his ambitions without the hindrance of an illegitimate off-spring and undesirable association with the struggling hub of the city and I would not bring shame upon my own family.

It did regrettably end any dreams that I may have held on the possibility of bearing a future family of my own as the botched actions of Dr Lee had rendered me unable to carry a foetus and irrevocably changed my view on the very nature of humanity and lead into the next chapter of my life.

N.Joy   Jill

4

I found myself back at home permanently, sixteen Maroon Street, with a negative outlook and a generous severance pay for the 'accident' that rendered me unemployable by the estate, a matter that meant mother and father would be suffice for the mean time provided my recovery was not for an extended period.

At the beginning it was the physical pain that was at the fore front of my mind, unavoidable as I was reminded with every breath I took and every movement I made. I never asked what lies my parents had swallowed and they never questioned me about the nature and circumstances of my 'injury' for none was evident in my appearance and I only displayed signs of discomfort when walking or sitting yet mother remained silent over any suspicions see must have had, being experienced in the ways of womanhood with the delivery of five children, one being an endowed daughter of an age where innocence was fleeting, if it remained at all.

I'd been incarcerated at home for three whole days before I found the strength to venture into the front parlour to seek the company of mother, in need of human contact to distract me from the loss that my body was experiencing. It still felt that I was with child, the nauseous feeling still plagued me from dawn till noon and I could feel any material that brushed against my breasts as they were as tender as a poppy in bloom, but they subsided giving way to the feelings that I'd buried deep inside, twisting their way to the surface in an eruption of emotions that were tinged with hormones, anger and pity. But I knew in my heart that I was alone on this earth as I could sense the flow of blood leaving my body, soaking the cloth that I had wedged inside my undergarments, wondering how I could sustain such a loss of blood without shuffling off my mortal coil.

When I was little I had suffered from a few minor convulsions that I had no real recollection of, just a distant memory of feeling unlike myself accompanied by a brief uncontrollable twitching that would often leave me bruised and mother exasperated with the chore of caring for me. It had been years since I had had an attack but as I left the room to use the outside facilities I felt discounted from my own body and blackness consumed me. I was powerless to stop it as it closed around my eyes, an echo of the past reverberating into the present, my last conscious image was the blurred floor rapidly raising to meet me.

I woke with a throbbing pain, a drumming beat though my head and an acute stabbing feeling in my left hand. The world crashed back to reality with a collision of colour and smell and mothers face etched with concern hovering above me like a solid apparition.

The cause of my childhood seizures had returned with a vengeance rendering me temporally senseless and wholly dependent on the care of mother. This dwindled rapidly for mother's sympathy was short lived with the realisation that I had caused myself little further injury, yet the bruises would remain evident, taking the best part of a week to fade resulting in me being confined to the tiny dwelling, unpresentable to prospective employers and a source of embarrassment to mother that would have the old tongue of Maroon Street wagging.

On the cold evening of the third April an official looking man dressed in a matching suit knocked on the door and questioned father about the tenant, enquiring about occupations and dates as well as places of birth and recording everything that father said onto a sheet of paper before making the same enquires of the Buckley family. I vaguely recall the same thing happening ten years previous at our old address for it wasn't often that such dapper looking gentleman called, and I was quite taken with his shiny shoes.

The look that I received when the ordeal was over reflected the embarrassment that father felt informing a stranger that his soon to be fifteen-year-old daughter was neither a scholar or in any paid employment and started me on a journey that would weave a distorted path throughout the remainder of my youth and into adulthood.

Fathers temper was impacted due to the increase in journalism visits, or curious gossip mongers that stemmed from a thirst to understand the behaviour of a distant relative by the name of Thomas Wheeler who had murdered a well-liked local farmer called Edward Anstee and had become somewhat of a local celebrity for his crime. Father was disgusted with the association to the Wheeler name but to me it opened up a fascination for death, one that had plagued me since childhood and would continue to be a reoccurring theme as I matured from adolescence in to adulthood.

Although Joe had been courteous and well-mannered on the rare occasions I had managed to orchestrate a chance meeting as he returned home he had made no effort to establish my well-being by calling at the house, a disappointing end to an admiral friendship.

I only realised that I had spiralled into a pit of depression when I realised that my thoughts were consumed with the notion of departing this life, to find solace in the knowledge that I may be greeted by peace, but another part of me refused to believe that I was worthy of the redemption of death and would forever flounder in the misery of my own actions.

The decent was gradual, the first whisperings starting when I woke from my ill-fated visit to Dr Lees address, but I was ignorant to such conditions of the mind that could take possession of a person's thoughts or feelings and could bend them so unforgivingly that that person can no longer evaluate the trappings of life without a veil of darkness extinguishing any joy that may be gleamed from such an inconsequential existence as my own. The recent events playing over in my head like a drama on loop at the Theatre Royal in Convent garden, and endless repetition of the same acts night after night. I was all but recovered from the physical ailments that had been a constant throughout the year to date, but the emotional wounds were still raw, septic and infected with the vileness of humanity, a scab that would not heal, picked at by my own thoughts and distorted by my unaligned feelings of self-loathing.

June was upon us, May was a blur of empty nothingness and the day of my fifteenth birthday arrived in a haze of worth-lessness and desperation.

Cookie had not forsaken me as I had imagined and had gotten a small package wrapped in a floral off-cut of material with a tiny hand-made card attached through the twine that held it together to me, probably coercing Joe into making the delivery for her, regrettably he had added no gesture of his own. Cookie's gift contained a small brass compact decorated with an intricate painting of three women and a dog with a mirror and powder concealed inside.

Mother and father presented me with a new snow-white ribbon fashioned into a bow that could be worn in my hair or as a brooch, perhaps an attempt to convince them-selves that their daughter was the virginal display of purity that they so desperately wished to believe, the ultimate contrast to their used and unwholesome offspring. Lottie and the boys had procured some wild flowers on their way home from school, a rainbow bouquet of buttercups, bluebells and pink champions gathered in a backdrop of balsam, a hint of floral summer impregnated into their petals.

My continued existence was a story with no end, a miserable tale that benefited none and had no ending that would make a heroine out of the damsel in distress. It had been a week since my birthday celebrations and the joy of that day had been fully consumed by the reality of life. As the day progressed my mood became more sombre with every passing minute, the gloom hovering like a mist, clouding my judgement, preventing me from seeing any future for myself. The mundane routines of life weighed upon me, compressing my feelings of loneliness and lack of self-worth, finally accumulating in a moment of lucidity, a solution that would provide the answer to the burden of life, a trip on the eternal one-way journey that would carry me from this world. My subconscious mind had made the decision for me, moving my body without consulting my conscious thoughts.

I found myself already half way to Tower Bridge without any knowledge of how I had got there, no recollection of passing through Limehouse or past the Docks but aware of the intention for my journey, yet I continued to proceed to my doom. I had walked almost three miles before my mind caught up with my physical actions, a wave of emotions flooding my brain, the indecision and dilemma fighting with the natural instinct of self- preservation, I couldn't tell what would prevail and which path I would take.

The cold chill from the dirty waters of the Thames snapped at my exposed face, the steel of Tower Bridge icy under my grip. I opened my eyes with a clarity that was a stark contrast to my earlier mood, a steely determination that I would show the world that I would not be defeated, that I would carve a way in this world that was of my making and that I would control my own destiny. As I looked out over the water I recalled a story that mother used to recite about a time that the Thames had indeed frozen over and people actually walked from one side to the other although I am sure that it was only a tall tale spun to fuel the imagination and encourage us to sleep.

Though the cloud of lethargy had settled over my demure as

the dark rain clouds settle in the winter sky the tiniest ray of sun began to shine a minuscule hole in my blanket of despair. A slither of hope that not all was forsaken but this slither came in the form of alcohol that dulled my sensitivity and reduced my need to depart this earth. Little did I know that it was not the object of salvation that I had prayed would enlighten me but was a worse demon in the guise of pleasure, one that would twist and turn its way through the degraded streets of London yet pose as a highway to redemption.

I had little treasured memories of my early childhood but one that had stayed with me was a visit to the fair. I recall not how old I was, but I can have been no more than eight or nine. I remember it as if I visited yesterday though had no inclination to relive any memory for fear that it would degrade those that I already had. The carousel was a spectacle to behold, beautifully painted horses chased one another in an endless race, captured in varying degrees of motion. The ride offered a measured rhyme that gentle rose up and down.

The big wheel was not as fun at it had appeared, the higher we rose the greater my fear threatened to tip the carriage and spill us onto the floor below. Mother had been quite cross with my behaviour and I received quite a tongue lashing for my fright. I would not climb the tower with the slide. Stripped stalls offered food and games of skill. My favourite attraction was the ghost house, a Gothic themed attraction of the macabre. Father disappeared inside the boxing saloon leaving mother to navigate the crowds.

I'd barely taken much notice of my appearance in recent months and cared little for how I was viewed by others. I passed mirrors with a glance for I had no interest in what would be reflected back at me. Where I would once stop to inspect the visual aspect of myself I now hurried past, diverting my eyes from any reflective surface for fear of catching a glimpse of the woman that I was becoming. This was a practice that I would soon have to forsake as mother had secured me an interview at a local factory, a shirt-makers trading from Mile End that had established their London factory over a decade, so I had to be reasonably turned out as my forte for sewing alone would not guarantee me a position in a warehouse that employed hundreds of women with the same skills that I possessed.

The small foyer that was the holding room for the interviewees was cramped, bland and full of females from varying ages but similar backgrounds which made for an unusual aroma that was neither pleasant nor vile, all hoping to secure a position and avoid whatever degradation that was taking hold of their existences. A tall pig nosed gentleman in a grey suit sullenly ushered me into an adjoining room and indicated that I take a nervous position on the rickety wooden chair in front of a panel of stern looking faces, a panel of judges who would decide my future.

I presented a brief abridged version of my accomplishments to date, lingering on the skills I had mastered as well as started to learn through my years with Ms Killner. Whatever I said or did in the interview secured me a position within the firm, my interview was followed by a rapid tour of the factory, an introduction to Mrs Kane who was in charge of the floor on which I was to be working, I had a beige coloured smock that had already had several previous owners shoved in my direction and instructions to return at 6am the following day to commence my employment with McIntyre & Hogg before finding myself back out on the street of Mile End facing my last day of freedom.

My first day saw me arrive with the sunrise, into a procession of beige shuffling mutely along Copperfield Road towards the monotonous labour awaiting, stitching shirts for the worthy, pristine white cotton cut and shaped to produce fine looking apparel for the hard-working middle class and privileged upper class of our great city. The patterned pyjamas and collars were produced on different floors, but all were fashioned to fit and woven to wear.

It took approximately ten minutes for the line of female workers to be swallowed by the thick wooden doors, consumed for twelve hours of sweltering finger tingling work before being spat out into the world, a weary trek to our abodes for a meal left waiting or yet to be prepared and a fitful sleep upon a mattress of straw before commencing the charade the following day.

The gloomy exterior of the factory was reflected in the equally retched appearance of the ragged school that was housed on the opposite side of the road, backing the canal, both multi-floored with bars securing the ground floor windows, constructed of dirty looking brick with regimentally placed windows and pulley systems allowing for heavy objects to be moved between floors without disturbing the occupants engaged with their given tasks. It was now that I wished I was two years younger as I would have been out within six hours although I was grateful that we were not required to work on Sunday.

No promises of holidays or the arrival of a weekend slumber to break up the mundane pattern that was to bridge the slender gap between the last verges of my childhood and the inevitable reaching of adulthood where sins could no longer be covered by innocent naivety or soothed away by mother's business-like embrace.

The day passed without incident, I was ushered into a position between Matilda and Louise, the proverbial boss of the floor, Mrs Kane, showed unregulated kindness in allowing me time to familiarise myself with the environment and make-up of the factory as well as become accustomed to the noise and workings of the lethal machines that could stitch a finger as effectively as a shirt. Although the machines had been fitted with safety guards many years ago in accordance with the 1844 Factory Act accidents still happened due to the negligence of those using them which further reduced the moral of the workforce, blood had to be removed without a trace and could result in costly claims for the business although McIntyre and Hogg had not experienced an episode for several years.

The kindness was not to last for my second day brought forth a full day from the moment we were seated at our allocated positions, the manufacturer starting with the industrial drumming as the machines were started on the ground floor for a day's production, echoing up and around the high-ceilinged stone walled floors that were stacked one on the other to maximise of space and staff. Being on the upper floor our hearing was relatively protected from the thunderous noise that erupted from some of the larger machinery.

There was little talking heard, it was not encouraged that we participate in idle chatter for it could reduce our capacity to carry out our duties or trigger an accident that would hinder production.

We were a fortunate floor for I saw little change in the workers, faces became recognisable in a matter of weeks, some became friends, but most remained just faces for the duration of my time with M&H. As I was employed alongside the adult workers I was granted the pay of seven full shillings a week, two more than I earned at Kenwood, yet the work was five times more demanding than even the busiest of days as a scullery maid. Mother and Father were ecstatic at the extra income that was brought into the house, allowing me to keep 6d every week, I wrapped the tiny silver coins in a floral piece of linen that I kept pushed inside my mattress so that my siblings would not find them, occasionally taking one out and tracing the minute wreath of laurel and oak and the miniature crown with the tip of my littlest finger.

To my right was Matilda Littleton, a forty-five-year-old widowed skeleton who was nothing but skin and bones, translucent skin with protruding veins and blood vessels, a green map showing through her wrinkled body. Her vivid blue eyes where sunken behind razor sharp cheekbones and had seen over forty years of life but had a haunted aspect that indicated that she had seen exceptional hardship and suffering. Although we became friends I learnt nothing of her personal circumstances except she had once had a husband and had born children she no longer had any dependants though I never found out the details of her loss. Her tone and general air of grace made me believe that once she had held a position of note in society but had lost it all with the loss of her family.

To my left was a plump girl, senior to me by a year with two months' greater experience, who was born with the name Jacqueline but used the abbreviated "Leeny" when referring to herself. This was a habitat that I soon began, I asked her once why she had chosen to name herself Leeny and she replied that

Jack was a boy's name and she had not considered shortening it to Jackie, although she admitted that she preferred that but had spent to long as Leeny to change now. She must have had a predisposition to carrying weight for her family was larger than mine and lived in Repton Street, an East End slum, which was renowned for the level of poverty that kept its tenants barely above the line of survival so the possibility of excess food was not even a consideration let alone a possibility so her ample frame must have been an inherited trait from her mother who was a round dumpling of a woman who waddled from side to side when she walked, both had as much charisma as they did flesh.

McIntyre and Hogg were fair employers for every day at noon the factory would grind to a halt and the workers were permitted a whole thirty minutes to consume whatever food we brought with us. Petitions could be made by the paupers to be feed by the factory, for a reduction in wage for those aged over thirteen years, usually consisting of a sloppy meal of watery porridge but it was at least substance of a sort.

My wages would earn me an apple and portion of bread every day that mother wrapped in cloth that I brought back daily for use the following day. Every now and then mother would substitute the bread for a round oatcake, a dry bland experience as mother seemed to skimp on the ingredients, adding no a sugar at all from the taste I'm sure.

On one occasion, some cheese had been secreted inside the bread, it was only a morsel but a feast for one of the many rats that had made the factory it's home, but none-the-less an appreciated and well-remembered addition. I never questioned why mother's generosity made a rare appearance, just hoped that it would happen again.

It was eight months and the passing of my sixteenth birthday that next saw my lunch anything more than near stale bread or cardboard oatcakes. This time I had in addition to my bread and fruit both a mouthful of creamy cheese as well as a cut of boiled bacon, a sweet sixteen gift to see me through until I returned home that evening.

McHogg had granted its workers a reprieve from slavery to celebrate Easter, I spent the Monday in South Kensington pulled along with the thousands that had come to witness the grand opening of the newest museum to grace the streets of London. The advertisements in the papers had worked a treat, bringing crowds of people, the street was amassed with activity, the pavements lined with excited folk on both side of the arched entrance. Men, women and children all dressed in their Sunday best, top hats on top of polished boots and bonnets with shawls that covered pretty downs that swept the floor as they walked, the women drawn around the waist like an hour glass, the children's faces scrubbed clean.

The building itself had been many years in creation, a proud and magnificent structure it could rival any cathedral in splendour, the construction was exquisite with the use of spiralled columns, perfectly patterned brick work, doomed windows at regulated intervals with gothic inspired towers supporting the two longs arms that spread from the grand central doorway. Hours could be lost viewing the exterior alone for it had carved into the stone work ornate patterns as well as many creatures and flora with sculpted beasts looking down, ready to pounce into action should a breath of life be blown into their stone hearts. The testament that the city loved to while away their time looking at relics from long lost eras or to be reminded of the history that brought the city to its current point was evident in the masses that had congregated.

I climbed the steps that lead to a giant M and entered the natural history museum through one of the large double wooden doors that was supported under each arch of the letter. The room opened into a large open space, a large staircase was at the furthest end and swept to the left and right, taking the traveller on a journey into the upper floors. The archways ran in unison leading to treasures of the past, the excited whisperings and gasps echoing of the walls, a great ceiling of painted plants, some familiar and some exotic, not native to our own fields and gardens topped the room, glass panels provided the light that fractured of the stone work.

There was something to please every taste, paintings from

arts resident to England or from across the globe chronicling animals of the land, sea and air with colours as bright as flowers or so fanciful that they could have come from the artist's imagination. There were still-life's, landscapes, portraits of important figures, unknown figures, un-proportioned males with painted skin, beautifully drawn animals from around the world as well as creatures that looked like they should exist and some that did once but now only exist on paper.

Case upon glass fronted case lined the walls of the zoological gallery containing the caresses of birds, not rotting but arranged as if they had been suspended in time, atop the cases were antlers of animals which once proudly roamed the land, the only testament to their lives. A solitary pair of buffalo horns, each the length of young child was a jewel in the collection. Hidden in draws were fanciful insects pinned behind glass and lifeless pigeons, stretched to form feathered cylinders.

There were shells in varying shapes, sizes and colours with patterns so intricate they were mesmerising, jars with creatures suspended in time, encapsulated in fluid with inscriptions of their species inked onto labels and a gothic display of hundreds of tiny hummingbirds posed mid-flight or nestled upon branches which drew looks of horror was well as pleasure. Fossils of long dead creatures, preserved as rock or embedded in it like a pattern in a cardigan, evidence of a world that existed before recorded history, the impressions left by their fossilised remains trapped by nature, immortalised for the world to see.

The precious stones were laid out in accordance to their properties, draws of persevered rocks sliced to reveal their inner compositions and jewels of every colour, embedded to form jewellery, sculpted into representations or presented in their natural state. The light refracted off them, a hypnotising twinkle shone from their polished surfaces, some translucent that their colour was vibrant yet impregnable, others pale in tone, some a deep striking mass of colour and others with plumes of varying shades and colours, as intertwined as the feathered birds. They were so exquisite, how I longed to wear one, to parade around in the glory they would bring.

I was whole heartedly impressed with the grandeur of the place and should very much like to return, it was easy to lose oneself, conjuring imaginary tales to accompany the exhibits.

McHogg, for that is how I came to refer to it, released all its worker at four o'clock in the afternoon on Christmas Eve 1881, which fell on a Saturday, the majority of adult workers heading straight to the closest pub house, the New Globe, although we lost many on the way to the enticement of establishments further from the factory but closer to their own abodes and fistfuls disappeared around the corner to seek their satisfaction at the Bancroft Arms. The Globe was an impressive building of three stories occupying the spacious corner plot located at Canal Bridge so could be accessed from either side of Regents canal from the main drag or up the footpath and across the bridge, patrons coming from both directions in a bid to get their hands on the first festive refreshment.

I was more than happy that the factory frequented this public house as Father sought refuge in the Anchor and Hope at Duckett Street, so I was safe in the knowledge that I wouldn't unwittingly be caught out and humiliated in front of my fellow workers. Even though we were under-age Leeny and myself accompanied Matilda, using our generous bonus of a penny, for we were classed amongst the adult workers, towards a quart of beer for which we would have to sacrifice the whole penny if we were to consume the entire quart alone.

It was different from the alcohol that I had previously sampled, a tot of gin taken from father's secret stash that he kept hidden in a simple wooden box underneath a pile of discarded newspaper and cloth that was used to wrap food and make modest repairs to clothing. The translucent liquid had burnt my throat as it descended into the pit of my stomach, leaving a warm sensation in my torso, centralised heating but it left a lingering taste in my mouth, the flavour repeated on my tongue as I brushed it over my teeth. The beer was free flowing in large pitchers of undetermined size or jugs containing the twelve ounces of intoxicating liquor, I felt bloated and giddy after the consumption of the first pint and half, but I was eager for more and for the inebriated worry-free feeling to continue.

By the time nightfall had arrived the evening was in full swing, some of the party had passed out due to intoxication, others were slurring their speech, bouncing off one colleague and into another, one push away from a punch in the eye or a visit from the local constabulary or from joining their unconscious friends. Still more were dancing a merry uncoordinated jig accompanied by singing, of sorts, although a room full of cats being strangled would have better described the sounds escaping from the black toothed uneducated mouths of the factory workers.

Outside the cold had settled its icy grip over the city turning the muddied streets into a perilous impromptu skating rink for those that had departed the Yule tide greetings being drunkenly shouted at friends, acquaintances, strangers or just at the night sky. As Leeny lived down from me we left the globe together, staggering and laughing our way down the canal footpath, it was a miracle that neither of us ended up in the murky water, for I wasn't treasure hunting and had lost much of my desire to do so now that I was earning a regular reliable wage.

We parted company at the East end of Maroon Street so that Lenny could continue in the direction of home while I veered off to my own, only the short walk of Maroon Street to sober me up and allow me the opportunity to conjure an excuse for my tardiness. It mattered not for the house was deserted, no explanation as to where the family had absconded, but I seized the chance to taste a little more of Fathers hidden gin before retiring to the cramped room I shared with my siblings. I was asleep when the rest of the Wheeler household returned from their excursion to Midnight Mass, a family tradition that I had forgotten all about and cared little for once the ale was flowing. A kick from Lottie alerted me to their presence but I rolled over, pulling the holey blanket over my head and was left alone until the excited murmurings awoke me before dawn, eager to commence the day's festivities.

I was reluctant to wake from my slumber, I opened my eyes and let them adjust to the darkness of the room, the previous evenings revelries came crashing into my mind like a nightmare as I stirred, accompanied by the backdrop of several drums beating a steady rhythm somewhere within my brain. The nausea took hold as soon as I stood, my cheeks burning with the need to expel the beer that had been consumed, my stomach feeling like the drummers had used it for practice. Eager for Mother and Father not to become overtly suspicious of my new-found associations I gathered myself and proceeded downstairs to the front parlour that we used to congregate as a family. The Buckley's were yet to rise but I suspected that they wouldn't be for sleep for long with three eager Wheelers clod-hopping on the floor below. It would be late morning that the first of the carol singers could be heard droning outside the window, singing their way up Maroon Street, the tuneful lyrics of Come all ye faithful drifting through the window pane to serenade us.

I walked into a room transformed to reflect the festivities, the traditional holly, ivy and mistletoe hung in sprigs around the room, mother had dutifully made a string of bunting that weaved its way around the room like a multi-patterned snake and on the table stood a sparse tree top which had paper decorations precariously balanced on its near naked branches. The tree was a feature that had adorned the room since I can remember but this is the first time one looked so withered and sad despite mothers attempt to make it cheery before it ended up on the fire.

A few years ago, after the death of Mills mother had created us a stocking, a Frankenstein creation of mismatched material in an image that roughly resembled a sock which she placed around the tree. Every year it had contained a few pieces of fruit and a chestnut, this year brought the expected apple and orange with the addition of a handful of nuts as well as two hand carved wooden animals. This brought a rapturous chorus of excited gratitude from my younger siblings but also secured their attention as they created a menagerie under the table. I got a crudely carved bear and a petite bird that looked as fragile as the real thing but sat snugly in the palm of my hand, smoothed like the stones polished by the sea. The dinner served was a veritable feast and the best ever to my recollection as mother had more than ever to spend due to my contribution to the household. Each plate had a generous helping of potato and crunchy season vegetables and a turkey the size of father's head sat in the centre of the table, crispy skin bubbled above a layer of succulent meat, a Christmas pudding warming in the oven for dessert.

The only cards to adorn the mantelpiece were hand drawn creations produced by the Wheeler children at school, decorated with garish colour and misshapen imagery of the festive season. For the first time we had a cracker each, produced by the infamous Tom Smith, it consisted of a small sweet wrapped in tissue which was enclosed inside a tube covered in red paper wrapper secured with a green ribbon. I got a small horseshoe inside mine, Lottie got a miniature penny whistle, as well as a printed motto embossed with a cherub upon a lily pad ready to stab a fish with an arrow. In addition, it contained a delicate paper hat that ripped as soon as I tried to put it on, all of which arrived with an unexpected ear popping bang as we pulled the cracker apart which gave my siblings a start followed by incestuous laughter although it and the accompanying excitement it caused only accomplished making the banging in my head worse.

I could not have been certain at the time, but this Yule was the last one of any innocence and expectation for me, not quite the last that I would spend under the roof of Maroon Street, but it was a certainty that it was final for my childish whims and wishes, no more anticipation at the nightly arrival of the bearded Santa Claus or prospect that my stocking may contain more than usual.

In all the years that I spent as a seamstress for McHogg I never once saw the arrival or departure of the boats that brought the cotton thread from Lancashire, sparing us from the respiratory disease that the damp conditions caused, or as far afield as Scotland for weaving and sewing up Regents Canal that ran adjacent to the factory, perhaps this was due to the buildings in front of us but was most likely due to the amount of time we were incarcerated within the building.

Hearing the tales from workers in other factories and trades about being fined for idle talking or vacating their position without permission made me realise that I had a reputable employer and to be thankful for this small mercy. One evening I overheard some sour faced toothless crone in her fifties claim that the clocks had been altered so that she could be justifiably fined for lateness but had no way to prove the accusations so would have to tolerate the reduction in wage or join the ranks of the unemployed in the workhouse.

Another evening brought the story of a young whelp who suffered broken fingers after a vicious session of strapping whereby he was repeatedly whipped across the knuckles with a leather strap which made the caning at school seem child's play in comparison. Another told about the regular practice of hanging iron weights around the children's necks, a cruel punishment but perhaps some would have benefited from such harsh discipline for most were merely orphans from local workhouses, apprenticed to the factory as labour, many of which only received a meal as payment. Occasionally one of the smallest workers were required to crawl into the machine to dislodge a blockage of cotton but McHogg ensured that the particular machine was temporarily suspended from use whilst the child cleared the obstruction and returned unharmed, a grace that was not afforded in many of the neighbouring factories resulting in serious injury or death on a bi-annual basis.

A year after I started at the factory the business opened up a fine new warehouse in Basinghall Street. I remained at the Spa Factory in Mile End alongside Leeny, but Matilda choose a change of scenery and moved with around a third of our floor to the new premises, I never saw her again.

We were half-heartedly offered the opportunity to relocate but I chose to remain due to the proximity of the factory to our house in Maroon Street, the new warehouse was only 3 miles away with the magnificent St Pauls Cathedral as a backdrop, but I had had enough of travelling miles to work and the reputation of Whitechapel was a disconcerting factor as it would have been one of the possible routes back home. The fact that I had my eye on one of the young men who worked on the ground floor, responsible for maintenance on the machines if the permanent smudges of oil and dirt on his muscular arms, hands and handsome face were anything to judge by was another reason for remaining.

The lad that had captivated my eye and thoughts went by the name Fergus, an immigrant from Ireland with hair the colour of a carrot, pale skin and a splattering of brown freckles across the bridge of his nose spreading to his cheeks that could be seen from a distance emerging under the stains transferred from his hands as he wiped the sweat from his face. His accent was a thick droll, his words came tumbling out in a cascade of Celtic history but only fragments were decipherable to the cockney ear.

Despite my longing looks I seemed to repel those steaming from a different county for my feelings were not recuperated so I set about finding a suitor worthy of my affection from a stock closer to home that would led me into the next chapter of my existence.

5

I had all but abandoned the search for a mate when William literally walked right into my life. Thankful no ale suffered as a result for I had developed a liking for the sustaining substance, it tasted nothing like what we were given at home, a pale imitation yet still safer than the water, mothers also lacked the numbing sensation that was derived from drinking a pint of London's finest.

Whilst enjoying a quick tipple in the Globe we collided as he hurried in the direction of the water closet as I returned from relieving myself, slipping into the facility between male patrons, the landlord uncaring that only the male clientele were specifically catered for, only installing it as the persistence of urinating on the wall had caused him to finally reach the end of his tether. The task of urine management usually befell the unfortunate George French, the fifteen-year-old barman who had the height of one of the many patrons but an intelligence that fell far below even the simplest of the factory workers.

I had been enveloped by a swarm of drunken locals despite it only being early evening. The public house was at its capacity, bursting at the seams with revolting smells and faces all eager to consume the last drop before their pockets ran dry and they would have to return to who or what awaited them. Or else find a suitable spot that would accommodate them for the night with only a prayer that they would make it till morning and not be dispatched by the harsh temperatures of a cold February, the blade of a killer or the ever-eager medical students so desperate for a cadaver on which to practice their chosen trade.

A hand snaked through the throng and gripped my right shoulder. I jumped from the unexpected deliberate contact forcing me to spill an amount of my quart eliciting a look to kill the dead on my part which softened as the perpetrators face came into view and I recognised it as the one I had been momentarily close too as our paths crossed.

As my visits to the Globe, the inn we had adopted as a refuge, increased so did the frequency in which I encountered William. By this point Mother and Father had little care where I found my pleasure or spent my time providing that the money I brought into the house remained unchanged. Although the romance that I had first lusted for failed to develop we found in each other kindred spirits and forged a bond that secured our friendship.

By the time my seventeenth birthday arrived I felt that I

had known William for a lifetime. It was following a somewhat lively discussion that the landlord was having with a fellow patron over the validity of the make-up of the alcohol that I decided malt would be an appropriate name for William to be sired with, lovingly named after one of the ingredients that formed part of his beloved dark froth topped tipple which smelt and tasted like smoked wood, my face a contorted picture of a grotesque beauty when I had sampled it, choosing to remain loyal to the golden ale that provided me with comfort and escape.

Unbeknownst at that time that the name I had christened him with would have a duel meaning.

He was open and frank about his aspirations to become a surgeon, his secrets and desires. At twenty years of age he was four years my senior and had been gifted with the impressive name William Emanuel Clive Pearcy by his butcher father. He wasn't classically handsome but had a roughish charm and piercing blue eyes that would have been at home in a foreign country sparkling like the crystal waters but an accent that was dripping with the cockney influence of his upbringing, East End born and bred but with a determination to escape the slums that was echoed in few as most were resigned to fate and their lot in life.

Due to Malts association with the medical profession I would met him on occasions at The Bancroft Arms which was situated opposite the Alms houses of the same name up on Mile End Road, an impressive building with a columned entrance that was neighbour to an equally beautiful cemetery that was littered with large yew trees and grave stones that displayed the emerging skills of the local stone masons and their apprentices. Due to the area being home to large pauper and Jewish settlements the alms houses were two a penny and the addition of the workhouse meant that there was ample opportunity for experience and the construction on the new infirmary was already under way, the corner stone having been laid over a year previous.

I would listen to the tales of blood and gore that the medical students discussed over a drink, some drinking into oblivion to blot out the hideous injuries and disease that were presented to them.

The decision to progress Williams prospects happened over several weeks, it started out as a whimsical idea, just a notion that gained credence and practicality the more we debated the advantages that it could deliver to Malt upon the ability of his fellow students. The practical knowledge and first-hand experience would be more valuable than a library of anatomy books for seeing something in reality, in its true colours, trumped the flat illustrations produced in the weighty tomes.

The outline of our plan was solid, each being an alibi for the other should law enforcement seek to find the unfortunate soul that would fall into our trap, after all William belonged to a reputable family and neither of us appeared to be of questionable character. From our wages, we saved a little each week so that the volume of gin needed to capacitate the victim could be obtained for our venture at several sources. As the Globe was still our usual haunt we had decided that we would implement our plan at the Bancroft where we were less familiar to the patrons and landlord Mr West.

Our target departed the Bancroft shortly before midnight, plied with enough alcohol to floor a small elephant, it was a wonder that he could even stand let alone find the exit and walk away but it meant that our plan could be executed without any patron making the connection of seeing us all leave as one. We finished the remaining dregs in our own glasses having had to ebb out the portion so as to remain relatively sober for the task at hand as we could ill afford to be caught in the act or fail to achieve our goal.

Approximately half a minute and several customers elapsed before we left the Ban, arm in arm, discretely walking in the same direction as our mark, following at a distance so as not to avoid detection but close enough that we could easily see the direction he took, praying that we could intercept him before he reached his abode or stumbled on a populated area.

After about ten minutes of deteriorating coordination his pace slowed, staggering uncontrollably, the alcohol finally taking control of his senses, his feet crossed causing him to stumble into the nearest building resulting in him sliding down the wall to form a pile of foul smelling rags. His breathing was heavy, his speech undecipherable, he raised his arm in protection, his eyes out of focus as we approached, ready to evolve him into a human text book.

The suffocation was the easy part, the work of only a few minutes exertion, Malt lay upon the stranger's ample frame, pinning down his limbs so that he couldn't escape or make any moves that would delay the process of death. A loose-fitting garment that hung conveniently around the unfortunate souls' neck made the perfect weapon in which to hold over his nose and mouth preventing any air from re-inflating his lungs. I felt the last gasp exhale into the cloth, a final rush of hot air absorbed by the material.

There was noticeable decrease in Malts tension as the body below him released its hold on life, the muscles relaxing as the signal for them to work was terminated. I kept my hand in position, my fingers straining from the effort, locked into a deadly hold, until I was sure that the life had been extinguished. I looked into the grimy bearded face that moments before had been struggling beneath my grip, his lifeless brown eyes tinged with blood pooling in large spots beside his pupils, an eerie echo of a life that once was but will be no more. Otherwise it looked like he had fallen into a slumber, his mouth in an open gasp as if mid breath, his greying beard cascading over his chin, his skin turning a shade of grey against the dark smudges of dirt that littered his skin.

For most the hardest part of the plan would have been to make the pre-meditated decision to deliberately bring an innocent life to its conclusion but the logistics of transporting the body, now a dead weight, was the part that we had under-estimated, it was a test of our strength and resilience for he was harder to move than we had anticipated.

We hauled him to a standing position, I pushed against his chest struggling to hold him upright against the wall while Malt positioned himself to bear the brunt of the weight, the cadavers body precariously balanced against Malt, substantiated with an arm around the waist while an arm was slung across Malts shoulders. I provided a supporting shoulder although in reality I had neither the physical height or strength to be of much assistance and was used to steady the body preventing them both from collapsing in a heap. As Malt concentrated to hauling the weight I doubled up as a look out, alert to the presence of others.

We encountered a few folk, most too inebriated to take notice of us let alone make enquiries with the exception of one individual who not only eyed us with suspicion but asked us what our business was. Our joint reply was that we were assisting our drunken uncle home like dedicated family concerned for his well-being which seemed to fulfil the stranger who moved in the opposite direction at a speed that would indicate he feared he may be cohered into helping, he had no intention of interfering with our business beyond the simple interaction, satisfied that his conscious was appeased.

Thankfully Williams father's business was located on the corner of the crossroads of Duckett and Alfred Street, so we only had to drag the body a short distance for he had unwittingly staggered the majority of the way himself. The entrance to the rear of the shop were the butchery was performed was accessed through a narrow doorway that lead into a small cobbled yard, lined with ruts to allow the blood from the meat to drain away, mixing with the household wastage of the street before being washed into the Thames. We had to walk sideways like crabs as the width of the door could not accommodate all three of us and we did not want to raise any of the residents by over exerting ourselves.

The majority of the tools of Mr Pearcey's trade were housed in the outbuilding attached to the shop where the animal caresses would be stripped for sale to the public.

The premises were small and only had one window for display, so was unable to accommodate a multitude of animal carcasses hanging from hooks to entice custom, the interior taken up with the serving counter that stretched the length of it which housed trays of produce, his fathers' raw meat jostling for space with the pies that his mother baked. Malts position in the family business was primarily cutting the deliveries down to size for none of the customers could afford, or would require, the whole animal allowing him to practice his surgery skills and incisions whilst earning a small wage to contribute to the hospital fees for training and examinations. He was used to the practice of cutting meat into small sections as his mother baked pies with the offcuts to inconsequential to sell as a side line to subsidise the family income and reduce wastage.

It wasn't uncommon for Malt to complete his tasks at night by the light of candles so that the meat would be cut and hung ready for the day's trade allowing him to pursue a career in medicine without hindering the family's commitments and it allowed Mr Pearcey to stay for extended periods at the public houses knowing that he would not have to rise before dawn. Due to this reason, we were almost guaranteed to remain undisturbed until the first light of the day when Malts father Thomas would grumpily descend from the accommodation above the shop to prepare for the day's customers.

With me at his shoulders and Malt at his heels between us we managed to manoeuvre the body onto the thick wooden table, the weight a struggle for us but no issue for the table which was accustomed to the weight of half a cow being hauled onto its surface however the victim's legs flopped over the edge dangling freely like flags in the wind.

For Malt to be able to dissect his unwilling assistant the first job at hand was to strip him of his clothes and return him to a natural state. His skin pale and mottled in the chilling environment, his ageing skin sagging, gravity pulling it to the side with his insignificant member lying on a nest of black, a striking image that imprinted itself into my mind as I had never seen one that was not erect, the pathetic deflated object as lifeless as its owner.

Malt had memorised the section in his text books regarding the internal layout of a human body so decided that that is where his practical lesson would start. With trembling hands, he took the smallest sharpest implement that he had at his disposal, a sticking knife with a wooden handle and freshly sharpened blade and made the initial incision. He started at the left side, sliding the knife in at the point where the collar bones joined the shoulder and made a clean straight incision that followed a sharp diagonal angle to the centre of the donor's chest stopping opposite the nipples. His movements were measured and precise and the only sound that could be heard was the shallow breath that escaped Malts lips as he concentrated on creating the symmetrical incisions, a perfect V, a necklace of exposed flesh adorned the naked man that lay exposed on the butcher's slab. Next William ran the knife down the length of the mans' torso, from the bottom of the V he had created all the way to the first curly hair finishing the carving into a Y on the hairy body. He ran on old stained rag over the knife several times so that the blade was clean and dry before returning it to its allocated position in the rack that protruded from the wall behind the table.

Malt took the large metal bone saw from the rack and proceed to crudely hack off the arms and legs, giving no attention to precision as speed was of the essence, carelessly discarding them in a heap. It was my job to hold each limb outstretched in turn so that Malt could sever it and too separate the meat from the skin as well as strip it from the bones so that we could discreetly dispose of the remains by mixing them with the animal meat and spices, that Malts mothers baked into the pies or put through the mincer and turned into sausages, in the hopes that the texture and smell didn't raise suspicion.

Malt flexed his fingers whilst stretching his arms in preparation for the next stage of his lesson. Malt sunk his fingers into the incision he had made with a squelch that reminded me of the sound that escaped from the mud of the Thames when a scavenger was trying to remove their boots from the ground that had attempted to swallow them.

Taking a hold of the right side that ran parallel to his V he slowly lifted the skin and peeled it back exposing the pink and jumbled insides which made a suction sound, reminding me of the childish tricks we would play on the crabs we found, trapping them under a bowl which would glue to the mud then quickly raising it to release them before the capture, a biased game of cat and mouse. He did the same on the left then pulled the remaining skin upwards securing it by stabbing a roasting needle forcefully through the layers of fatty tissue, penetrating the face, a human notice board of anatomy.

The final element of the preparation was to remove the rib cage protecting the lifeless organs, gently Malt sawed at the frames, breaching its integrity before brutally snapping the bones, with a sideward glance it looked like a giant putrid infested mouth, stubby teeth protruding from lips formed by thin lining of skin sliced perfectly.

Even before I had time to register fully the exposed site before me a foul odour filled the room, the concentrated metallic scent of blood tinged with a musky hint that was hard to define and an unexpected sweet twist that brought me close to expelling my guts. I had to leave the building as the assault on my senses was momentarily overpowering, I silently exited the outbuilding and breathed in the night air, washing away the smell of death. After I had composed myself I returned to our secret, determined to remain diligent to the task at hand.

Looking at the slaughtered man I was repulsed yet transfixed at the same time, the wonder of how a human body could function with a seemingly insane jigsaw of parts was beyond comprehension yet the sight of it wasn't far removed from that of any butcher's window display, it was just housed in one package and I was a little disillusioned that I did not feel greater empathy. The tissue that formed the triangular frame was a mottled effect of an array of feminine colours from red to yellow, the inner point was a spiral of tubing to a quarter

121

way up leading to a dark expanse before dividing into three, two equal light masses on either side with an assortment of shapes running through the middle, it would have made for a revolutionary masterpiece had not the subject not been considered to macabre.

Malt was engrossed in his study, texts book lined out in front of him, propped open on pages showing diagrams of the human body, he muttered to himself as he began to dissect the helpful fellow, holding up the real-life example against the illustrations, making blood stain notes of his discovery's. I let him work and turned my attention to my part in these proceedings.

The sharpening steel was used greatly so that we could keep the implements sharp, aiding our work but putting increasing pressure on Malts already sculpted arm muscles, I watched the candle light as it danced across the colliding metal in the repetitious back and forth movement.

Malt wanted to retain one of the arms so that he could study the appearance and make-up of the muscle structure as well as fathom the intricate workings of the tendons, fascinated with the complex procedure that occurs for each finger to work either independently or as part of a team and associate them with the movements that can be seen happening under the skin when a finger was moved or flexed in any direction.

Whilst Malt toiled away removing and inspecting organs I

sat compliantly on the floor, my dress rolled up to avoid becoming stained by the blood that seeped from the limb that I was currently dissecting.

A wooden slab had been placed before me as a makeshift chopping board of my own, a selection of tools neatly at my side. I began by making an incision from the centre of the wrist, forcing the blade towards me as I cut down the length of the arm, a small line of red forming but not gushing as it lacked the heart to pump the blood around. I hummed a nonsensical tune in my mind, unwillingly to be a distraction, to distract me from sounds that the corpse produced as it gave up its remains one by one.

A wave of nausea hit forcing me to urge as I pulled in opposing directions revealing the intricate structure of muscle and bone, the sucking sound that I heard as the skin was parted from the fatty tissue underneath made me feel faint, but I persevered. Taking the curved skinning knife tightly in my right hand I began to slice away the long thin strips of meat that formed the forearm, stripping them of the cartilage and bone before moving onto the upper arm which vaguely resembled a skinned rabbit in appearance.

The legs were a greater task due to their size forcing me onto my knees to get the leverage needed for momentum I used to de-flesh the bones, the individual parts on a larger scale so the removal was swifter. It took me several hours of diligent work, performed in silence, but when I had finished I had a pile of flesh that was reminiscent in colour of any cut of beef, a myriad of red and pink with veins of white weaving throughout. The smell however did not resemble that of any meat found within a butcher's establishment, a distinctive coppery metallic scent could be detected and would have raised doubts in the authenticity of the meat. We placed our hopes that the spices would disguise the smell and prayed that the cooking process would not release an aroma to betray the contents. We had had no time to drain the blood from the body as the abattoirs did, not that Malt would have as it would have interfered with the dissection process, altering the appearance of the internal organs.

Malt had already gained a working knowledge of joints and how they worked from the animal caresses that he stripped for the meat, examples of which hung from hooks in the corner of the room, stripped clean of flesh and boiled to prevent disease. He used gelatine from a sealed jar that he had concocted from the animal's bodies to lubricate the balled joints when he wanted to study the movement. The principal was roughly the same as in a human skeleton without the added risk of being caught and possibly hung for the possession of human bones which would raise questions about the identity and death of the owner.

The distinctively human bones that remained once the tissue was removed were sawed carefully into pieces, so they did not splinter and placed in a boiling pot along with simmering bones which had been gutted from delivery that day. A ladle lay beside the pot so that Malts mother could spoon out the stock once it was cooled into jars for sale in the shop. A regular visit for one of the numerous rag and bone men would take care of the disposal of the bones on our behalf who would then sell them on top one of the many industry's that utilised the bones in manufacture.

There was an old burial ground tucked away behind the row of houses that faced the shop which could have provided a refugee for the bone but that would have required disturbing the dead and it was surprising how vigilant the neighbours were, which came as little surprise as the graves had been robbed on numerous occasions to satisfy a need or want from the living.

We were fortunate that the sawdust used to cover the floor of the shop in-case of spillages or blood seeping from the meat was swept into the yard for reuse in the outbuilding until it had absorbed it's fill and would be disposed of. This provided us with a convenient hiding place in the event that Malts mother or father would come into the building to remove more meat for sale, safe in the knowledge that it was part of Malts responsibilities so would remain un-tampered with whilst we were about our usual daily activities. I wrapped the chosen arm in the rag that I had used to suffocate the possessor and hid it in the corner inside a pile of sawdust.

As the night sky began to take its leave we could vaguely detect the ringing of church bells which heralded the arrival of a new day and an urgency came upon us to ensure that the meat was prepared for the day's trade and that any evidence of our crime was assimilated into the expected imagery of a butchers or hidden from view, so it could be retrieved that evening and disposed of.

I tasked myself with the duty of disposing of the clothing that we had stripped away, bundling it into a package of cloth wrapped in cloth, the least distinctive comprising the outside layer. Before I had gathered them, I had meticulously checked them throughout to ensure that no identifying objects could be found. I removed two sixpences and a farthing which I hid inside the pocket of my own overcoat.

I left Malt finely chopping up the last of the remains and took my leave. I trudged the weary trek towards McHogg for a day of needlework I prayed that I would not fall asleep and betray the activities of the previous evening and that I would happen upon one of the many rag and bone men that frequented the streets and dispose of the evidence under the pretence of being a generous citizen who was disposing of her dead fathers' clothes for the upset caused in seeing them was too much for mother to bear.

I happened upon a weasely looking man, complete with a shabby horse who looked like it would eat him given half a chance and a cart already breaming with a mixture of items. I quickly dropped the bundle to the floor and proceeded to drag it across the ground, pretending that the burden was too physically and emotionally heavy for me to bear in the hopes that his pity would assist me. My plan worked like a charm, the devious enterpriser eager to unload me of my burden took possession of the bundle in heartbeat. With a relived smile, I watched as he disappeared around the corner in a clip clop of hooves, my guilt vanishing with him.

As I wearily ambled the remaining distance to join the line of mostly woman waiting outside for the doors of McHogg to open I recalled the story that I had heard many times over my childhood which reminded me of the events of the evening just passed. Fifty-four years ago, in 1828, an enterprising duo named William Burke and William Hare started a unique but illegal business of selling the bodies of people they had murdered to medical students desperate for a fresh cadaver. They had cornered a market for the demand was high and the lucrative sums that were paid to tempting, the two Bills taking advantage of an emerging intellectual age thirsty for knowledge and advancement.

The Scottish neighbours of the two business men were their undoing, with the execution of Burke happening the following year by order of the courts, Hare escaping punishment by renegading on the friendship and turning turncoat before disappearing into oblivion never to be heard from again.

So as to keep with our regular routine I meet up with Malt inside the Bancroft Arms for a quick tipple when my day at the factory had come to an end and Malt had completed a day of learning, a particularly gruesome case of syphilis having been presented.

The conversation between yawns was strained for Malt seemed preoccupied, the short walk to the butchers one of contemplation but he shook off the sombre mood for a second night at the dissection.

After repositioning what remained of the body I retrieved the bag of skin and bones, all that remained of the man's legs and arm and set about the task of slicing the skin into unrecognisable sections, tenderising it beyond recognition so that it could be disposed of alongside the pig hide that was sold onto the tanners, the resemblance to human skin a close match. I made sure that I removed any identifying markers such as the small patches of freckles that congregated on his arms and the poorly applied naval tattoo that was branded into his forearm, chopping them into small pieces so that I could discard them around town for they would bring the arrival of police constables to investigate for sure.

I had already wielded the blade of the cleaver the night before to separate the hands and feet from the limbs, securing them in a sack full of sawdust and stones. With my assistance Malt used the saw to easily slice through the flimsy neck and remove the head which he placed on the floor, so the sawdust could perform its magic and absorb the fluid which oozed out.

It too was added to the bag of appendages after I had rammed a few large rocks into the flaps of skin. Before tying the sack with a cord, I added more stones that I had collected on my walk from McHogg to the Ban in preparation for this very task.

I had reached the point of exhaustion, having been awake for the most part of forty-two hours so headed home, still one more day of work ahead of me and one more task to accomplish before my part in the slaying came to an end. Unbeknown to myself Malt had taken a portion of the mixed meats and wrapped it in paper, he handed it to me as a gift for my services to his education, one that I would use to appease mother and avoid the interrogation that she would conduct over by absence the night before for I had never stayed away the whole night.

The sack was heavy with the combination of the body parts and the stones that were required to weigh the sack down allowing it to sink to the bottom of the river, hiding our secret in its murky depths. I heaved the sack over my shoulders, using both hands to steady the weight as it pressed into my back. I trudged down the length of Edward Street before making a sharp right and onto White Horse Street which I followed until it spilt at Salmon Lane which I proceed along until I reached the bridge that spanned over Regents Canal. I had deliberated on where I would dispose of the remains and had decided against the Thames itself for the tide was unforgiving and the sack may be discovered as well as it being a populated area, so I stood the risk of being seen in my late-night activities.

I waited on the bridge for several minutes to make sure that there were no fellow Londoners on the prowl and that my deeds would pass un-witnessed. Sure, that I was alone I used the last of my strength to swing the sack from my shoulders over the bridge, it's decent quick but the result an almighty splash that I hoped would not raise any of the residents. Again, I waited for several minutes to ensure that the coast was clear for my escape, my heart hammering a rapid beat in my chest. Confident that I had completed my task without detection I walked the remaining stretch of Salmon Lane before doubling back across the canal using the small footbridge which joined onto Henry Street which would lead me back up to Maroon Street and the welcome knowledge that I would soon be asleep.

Within days the mysterious disappearance of Alfred Ford was the talk of Mile End. He was regarded as a gruff ex-naval officer who had three dependants' due to having taken a young bride when his long-suffering wife shuffled off her mortal coil. From the general consensus, his personality would not be missed but his termination had a detrimental effect on his young family. His grown-up brood had disowned him following his relationship with the woman young enough to be have been conceived by him leaving their half-siblings to face a childhood in the workhouse. The unskilled wife and mother had placed her faith in her husband's reliance but with no knowledge as to his whereabouts she was faced with little option but to pass the care of her offspring to the institution.

I never heard about the fate of the mother, whether she had chosen a life in the workhouse alongside her children or had found a new suitor was as mystifying as the final resting place of Mr Ford. After a month with no word the interest in his whereabouts was dwindling with the waning of the moon and he was soon forgotten, except perhaps by those that had loved him in life.

The secret that we shared between us did not change our friendship, but it did alter the dynamics a little. It was not possible to maintain the pretence that either of us were innocent youths struggling to survive in this climate of industrial and cultural upheaval. We had in fact embraced the depravity that was so rampant and set our fates on a path that many had trodden but few had circumvented successfully. Whether our paths would remain parallel or one would branch off taking us in a direction that the other was unwilling or unable to follow.

The map of my life had become one of twists and turns

having started on even ground, an open expanse of potential. Some paths had led to dead ends, others arching in a circle, my progress often stunted or obscured with the feeling that I could not see the wood for the trees. The potential in my future as elusive as the woodland sprites.

Life in London continued to rumble along, the industrial revolution the making of some whilst being the destruction of others, businesses came and went, lives were created and lost. Every walk of life was represented in some way, the growing Jewish company mixed with the Londoners, the rich strode with their chins up whilst the poor grovelled, begged and toiled. The docks were awash with activity, every man in hat, be it flat, peaked or bowler worn at a jaunty angle, perched upon their pompous foreheads or crammed onto their noggins for fear of it becoming dislodged. They worked alongside those from far reaching countries their origins evident in their dark features, their scalps also shrouded in a spiral of fabric, their speech fast in their native tongue and those that had mastered the queens English did so with an exotic tone.

People were earning a crust at every opportunity and on every street, crowds huddled around the street performers, a cap extended in the hopes of being filled with farthings. I happened upon a group, made up of mostly well-presented school boys in matching tailored uniforms and flat caps, who had gathered around to watch a street artist. Eight pastels pictures, that would be washed away by the morning light as if they never existed, had been brought to life by the expert that had created them. The boys were intrigued with the skills on show, intently watching as the artist, sat upon the hard ground, added colour to build the detail except a few who had directed their attention to me as I observed the scene.

One boy in particular wore a look of disgust upon his face, a look of disdain for the world as well as the street artist was etched upon his features. My mind, riddled with guilt and sin, had cause to believe that he knew my secrets for why would a woman draw such a look from one so young that was unknown to them? Perhaps my appearance, in contrast to the woman at the opposing end of the rails which forged the backdrop to the artist's scenes, one leg raised upon the low wall whilst she held the rail for support, her jacket open to reveal the shirt underneath was less appealing, my hat was certainly not as impressive, a simple green felt offering in contrast to the feathered monstrosity that sat perched upon her head.

The large black street lights that stood tall in the middle of the thoroughfare were circled with woman and their large wicker baskets full to the brim with flowers. White pinafores or over-coats unofficial uniforms of the flower trade, the woman's faces rarely as beautiful as the flora that they peddled. The ever-present boys would shout the headlines as they peddled the day's news, enticing customers to buy a paper.

Off the main streets woman of ill repute would smile and

batter their eyelids in gowns that were once fine and vibrant but were now tattered ghosts of the garments they once were. Windows with lace curtains ripped and yellowed through age offered limited coverage against the smeared windows to the unholy activities that were carried out within. The distorted candle light gave apparitions of the occupants and glimpses could be gleaned by peeking through the holes of the unloved net that was hung over the window.

Posters faded and peeling peeking out beneath freshly applied adverts were plastered across the walls and laundry hung from the upper windows, off shades of white and stained with humanity.

Public transport was flourishing with horse dawn tramways and open top carriages, the roads were seldom free from the sound of hooves trotting over the cobbles and the trains

had made moving around the district a rapid ease for those that desired it, their steam adding to the smog that hung over the city and the noise to the general soundtrack of a municipality in the grips of modernisation.

Another year slipped by, the factory remained the mundane prison of employment it had always been with the exception of one harrowing accident that broke up the endless stream of identical white cotton that passed from one woman to another.

The word "clear" echoed around the room that was uncharacteristically silent due to the machines being shut down but, as we prepared to recommence our employment, it was swiftly followed by an ear-piercing scream that reverberated off the walls of the factory and penetrated us to the core. It transpired that the machine was in fact not clear of the small body that had crawled inside to dislodge a thread that had come lose and wound around one of the mechanisms. Whether the accident was the result of an over-zealous leader eager for the industrial machines to ignite again or the careless actions of an under-skilled workhouse delinquent I was unsure, but the outcome was devastating for the poor soul involved. Although I saw neither the invalid nor his subsequent removal to the infirmary I did get a glimpse of the blood splattered floor and adjoining work benches and a graphic if not exaggerated version in the Globe after our day was brought to an unexpectedly early end. It was generally believed that the loose-fitting garment the lad wore had snagged on a cog within the machine which had proceeded to rip his tiny dirty arm straight from the socket, sucking it into the rotating spindles in a spray of red, his clothes as ripped as his skin. Little sympathy was extended as we had lost pay due to the early closure of the premises and the increase in workload that we would all suffer.

The friendship between Leeny and myself had begun to wane as I found her idle musings over love and Prince Charming coming to rescue her unrealistic and infantile having chosen to walk a path of shadow, the coarseness of life a vivid contrast of colour in comparison. We were still allies and drank many a quart together but the confidant that I had hoped for could not be entrusted with the life ending truths that I had locked away for they were not all mine to share.

The increasing lapses in my sobriety did little to foster positive relations at home, my siblings were mostly seen in their sleeping state as I tiptoed into and from bed and my parents were content with the knowledge that I was part of the great London workforce.

My refuge became any of the public houses that littered the Mile End region of the expectant city, the amber liquid, discouragingly resembling the colouration of urine, sliding down my throat in the crowded stale atmosphere that provided anonymous comfort and feigned pity. I had never developed a liking for the burning sensation that occurred when drinking spirits, so I tended to stick to the ale that slid down like mother's milk although a tot of rum did help to warm me on the cold nights.

As the bells rang to herald in a new year the rapturous merriment spilled into the streets, strangers embracing strangers, lovers locked in passionate embraces and landlords celebrating their bursting tills. Lost within the moment, my body heavy with the weight of the beer sloshing around my insides William took me by the waist and turned me to face him. His smouldering eyes locked onto mine and the innate draw of human emotions pulled us together, our lips meeting with a soft instinctive impact. A war was waged inside me, the initial closeness that I had once so desired conflicted with the incestuous feelings that the kiss was inciting in my mind. However pleasant the feel of his lips were on mine I could not shake the feeling that I was kissing a brother I had yet to meet, so was the strength of our kinship. I was the first to break the connection, pulling back but not away unsure of my next move. Heartfelt repentances were exchanged in hushed tones from both sides. A sad acknowledgement registered in his eyes as I took my leave, hopeful that the dalliance would not harm the platonic bond that we shared.

William was with me when I suffered a particularly debilitating attack that left me with a deep gash down my right shin that I obtained when I fell to the floor, like a child's discarded rag doll, which required a visit to the infirmary to have the wound stitched shut. The sharp needle stung on every stitch and was a monstrosity in comparison to the work performed by the cities seamstresses. The gin offered by Malt numbed the sensation and his generosity in a horse drawn carriage ride home secured his position in my heart. The lifelong reminder of my sporadic condition was an ugly raised scar that carved a vertical path down my calf.

March 1883 brought the completion of the freshly erected Queen Mary University Hospital, William being among the first of the students to apply and be accepted, his staggering knowledge of anatomy would lead him onto a prestigious path that would eclipse but not neglect my own and eventually result in him taking leave of the country to convey his skills over the vast sea.

We spent a perpetually increasing amount of time at The Bancroft Arms due to its proximity to the infirmary, the Globe becoming less frequented every month until it was a rarity that we returned to my oldest haunt.

Williams twin brother John had moved away when he was apprenticed to an uncle who had a carpentry endeavour over in Gravesend, Kent and had returned a fully-fledged carpenter ready to ply his trade alongside the established businesses and sole practitioners in the hopes that the volume of people would constitute enough work to be divided amongst all the men. John was a man of strong build but reproachable morals, taking less than half a year to seduce me to a wanton whore, desperate for his approval and touch. Another chapter in my life was about to start.

6

Since our practical assignment utilising Mr Ford, I had unwittingly become drawn into the Gothic movement that had London in its grasp, absorbed in the influence that was evident in all aspects, from great works of art and literature to the fashion that paraded the streets and the beliefs that infiltrated the home.

The living were no longer afraid of the dead, great monuments to the lives of ordinary folk were being erected across the city and the trade in post-mortem photography of the recently deceased was alive and thriving. The architecture of the cemeteries was outstandingly ornate, the high standing Mausoleums of Highgate were not only novel to the city but were a wonder to behold, set in a maze of pathways with a backdrop of tombs and grave stones designed to every specification set in austerity and dedication. The funerals proceeding the internments a mourning sea of black, a celebration of a life that once was complete with all the finery of a wedding.

There was an ever increasing need to make contact with the dead permitting the custom of attending séances to become as wide spread as the dead themselves. This in turn resulted in a network of charlatan's eager to exploit the heartbroken widow or devastated parent with falsified messages from dearly departed loved ones, genuine practitioners vying for trade among the tricksters. Many an eccentric individual was declared a practitioner of the dark arts, some revered but others hounded into submission or subjected to the very fate they were accused of manipulating.

William and I were still thick as thieves although I had developed an ulterior motive for his company, eager to spend time with his replica brother John and convince him that I was a viable candidate as a lover. His prospects were increasing at a rapid rate for he was becoming a successful carpenter in his own right having obtained the commission on a few pieces that had allowed him to secure the lease on a property that he could call his own. Remarkably he had yet to be snared by any of the volume of vixens that stalked the affluent of the city bidding me time to stake my own claim.

Secretly I had reworded the lyrics to an old nursery rhyme and would idly hum the tune, the first verse went thusly-

Jack and Jill went up the hill

to fetch a deserving victim

Jack blew down and broke their crown

and Jill stabbed them after.

Up Jack got and home they'd trot

as fast as they could scarper

He went to bed, alone she slept

with images of blood all over.

Due to Williams standing in the infirmary he had arranged for me to attend a post mortem examination which further fostered my interest in the macabre. I stood in the gallery amongst the fresh young medical students as eager as them for the surgeon to make the first cut and provide us with a running commentary that would explain the function and appearance of each fleshy organ, an element that I was denied by William due to his silent practical study.

The body of a deceased male was laid on the reclined table in all its glory, the mortician stood at the head of the specimen in a white long-sleeved gown, that almost swept the floor, with matching un-styled hat and apron tied at the waist. A bow tie nestled underneath his chin and a pipe hung from the corner of his mouth. His hands were clad in gloves and a scalpel was held expertly in each hand waiting to demonstrate their scholarly ability.

As I watched I couldn't help internally drawing parallels to the night of the butcher shop dissection, with the obvious distinction that I was now standing in an accepted environment for medical investigation.

The sterilised gleaming walls and floors reflected the metallic gleam of the equipment, similar in appearance to many that William wields for his family's livelihood, saws and steel in varying degrees of size from delicate slight blades to lethal amputation knifes although the arsenal of the surgeon was greater than the butchers with an assembly of forceps and other fanciful instruments all laid out in order on a pristine trolley that could be wheeled into position to accommodate the needs of the user.

At first the smell of cleanliness was alien and suffocating but the familiar smell of death still infiltrated my senses keeping my attention focused on the lesson at hand. An influence imparted through the knowledge of a pioneering woman by the name of Florence Nightingale who broke through the confines of a male dominated profession to improve the sanitary conditions of infirmaries and prevent the spread of disease within the confines of the sick. The smell emanating from this corpse was be far fouler than that of Mr Ford for this chap had had the time to ferment and the organs were beginning the process of decay for the dissection was not performed as rapidly after death as ours had been.

The metallic smell from the blood masked with the odours of decomposing flesh and bodily fluids secreted after death. The sensory overload was too much for several of the young ladies to bear and they ejected themselves in a blur of white as they ran from the room, hands held to their faces to prevent the intrusion of any further smell and to keep in the rising bile that was waging an expedition from their stomachs.

We were given a lengthy introduction to each organ as it was removed from the donor, its functionality within the great organism that is the human body and the colour we should expect it to be as well as its place in relation to the other organs.

The prospect of becoming a surgeon was appealing but beyond the reach of any female yet midwifery was within our grasps, the whole feminine scene of childbirth being dominated by females from the expectant mothers to the attendants who assisted the men that brought forth their precious bundles and to the mothers solely once the delivery had been performed. The father being present only at conception and begrudgingly thereafter once the child had entered the world providing a wedding band had anchored him.

As my eighteenth year approached little had improved in my prospects although I was still earning a respectable wage for an East End factory worker and residing with my family, when I made it home during daylight hours. I was still not a regular feature at the side of John Pearcey, a mission that I was determined would be a success. The rations to sustain me at work were dwindling, mother not permitting wastage by preparing food that may not be consumed that day, preferring instead to encourage me to purchase food from one of the many traders operating in and around the markets but failing to take a reduction in the contributions I made to the Wheeler household.

In a matter of weeks my world had been turned upside down, John had finally seen the woman that I was, the veil that had previously masked me as just a friend of his brothers had fallen. That or my prospects as a potential nurse had made John see me in a new light, a viable candidate to be swooned, not that I needed any persuading of our suitability. He had uncharacteristically joined Malt and myself in the Ban for celebration drinks in honour of my birthday, the free-flowing liquor seemed to loosen his spirits and taint his eyes towards my dark features, unsure what beauty he could derive from my shapely figure and jumble of teeth that forced my lower lip into an unattractive covering that protruded almost as far as my chin.

John chose the moment of his assault on my heart to commence when Malt had taken a trip to relieve himself, the coincidence that I had met him in similar circumstances was not lost on me.

John casually leaned across the table that was littered with the debris of half consumed quarts and ash from the mounting pile of tobacco on the pretence that he was to talk with a little privacy over the din of the pub. He indicated with a curl of his index finger that he wished for me to meet him half way for the exchange, so I stood in order to gain enough height that I could lean across the table without sending the contents flailing across the floor with my ample bosom. Our faces meet towards the centre of the small round wooden table, he maintained eye contact which at first felt a little disconcerting as I was yet to be aware of his change in feelings towards me.

Unwilling to break the contact that I had dreamed would prevail I reluctantly began to turn away so that he could fully access my ear to impart whatever he felt couldn't be overheard. His actions were quick, catching my lips with his own before I had turned my head. The stubble of his week-old beard was coarse against my skin, I felt like the wood he sanded down as a daily chore, and his kiss was passionate and urgent. He wasted no time in the gentle pleasantries or teasing peaks of courtship but went straight to the unbridled desire that I thought him incapable of towards me.

The embrace is how Malt found us on his return from the privy, a flash of betrayal evident yet fleeting across his features but no words of his disapproval were ever uttered. We finished our drinks and made our preparations to depart the thriving establishment, Malt checked into the Butchers, suspicious of his brother's motives, John promising to see me safely to my door. We walked a little further in the direction of home when John grabbed my hand and doubled back through a warren of streets, leading me by the hand we weaved silently amongst the night workers and the debris of an over-crowded growing community towards a destination unknown to me. Through the excitement and discarded inhibitions, a niggle of apprehension crept up my spine.

I managed to nervously enquire for an explanation as to the manner of his behaviour, but he just simply smiled at me, winked and continued on his way, dragging me in his wake.

He stopped outside a property in an area that I was unfamiliar with, he fumbled in his pockets for a key, never releasing his grasp on my hand. Once over the threshold John released his grip, my arm stayed in position, frozen like the rest of my body, I felt like a pose-able doll. John reached out and raised my chin so that my eyes would be forced to meet his gaze. As I looked into his mesmerising eyes they told of his intent, I was too captivated to move.

John finally broke the silence by saying that he had a birthday gift for me, he smiled as he unbuttoned his breaches to reveal an erect salute in honour of my special day. He bit his lip, averting his gaze to take in the length of me, breaking the spell that had me anchored to the floor, my eyes widened as the horny brother of my dearest friend advanced, his shaft the lance of a knight in shining armour. Our lips meet in a passionate exchange, hot, wet, his hands concertinaing my dress until he had accessed the location of his hidden treasure. John swept me onto a rough wooden surface and with a salutation of Happy Birthday John penetrated me, pulling me into his rhythmic movements. The room swam inside my head, a whirlpool of dizziness against the waves of euphoria that pulsated from my laycock. Satisfied with his gift John withdrew his lance, his lips claiming a victory kiss that was full of promises and anticipation.

Once our breaths had returned John offered a night cap which I eagerly accepted. We retired to his bedroom and spent the night in a state of erotic embrace. Owing to the good fortune that my birthday had been celebrated on a Saturday I was not required to attend work next morning. I was awoken by the sensation of a force tracing the length of my torso, dipping at my hip and following the fold of skin before brushing across my laycock, tender from the repeated penetration, and travelling up to the dip of my throat before gracefully sweeping back down again. The arousal had worked for both parties as he slyly slipped inside me again. He lay above me, encasing me with his arms, slowly employing his magic and working up a fine appetite.

I did not leave until the following dawn when the urgency of the impending reprimand for tardiness pursued me to depart.

Begrudgingly I hurried along, praying that I correctly memorised the direction that John had given me to the factory but once I had reached the populated central road that ran through Mile End I had established my bearings. I ate a pie for my breakfast, most lost to the floor in my haste not to be late.

I arrived in the nick of time, joining the back of the line as it disappeared inside.

Leeny commented on my sombre mood, but I was too lost in the possibilities and consequences of my imminent future to muster an adequate reply. I left the factory in a daze, blindly following the herd, my head still a thousand miles away having been taken on a journey of hypothesises.

At first, I didn't hear him call my name, but his voice penetrated my trance, he had come to meet from work, escort me to the Ban. He also escorted me home after, like an honest gent.

It was two days before I saw John and Malt again, mother had requested me to grace them with my presence, so I obligingly submitted to her request.

The next time I found myself in the company of Malt and John it played out in a similar fashion as my birthday, John 'escorting me home' for a night of copulation.

The morning brought not the merging of two bodies that I had expected but the merger of two households. Casually, as if talking to a customer, John asked me if I 'cared to move in with him', barely a hint of interest in the reply was etched on his face. There was no grand gesture, no bended knee, no ring, nothing other than the invitation to bed down with him on a permanent basis.

My heart told me to say accept his proposal, but I hesitated in my reply, what would mother and father say? What would Malt say?

Time slowed down as I thought about my answer, this was everything that I had dreamed, all I had to do was say yes and it would be mine.

I said "yes".

The deal was sealed with an act of the most intrusive nature, kneeling on the floor in facing him, he took his continually ready horn in one hand and the back of my skull with his other. Gently he pushed into my mouth, my teeth scrapping across the raised veins. He rocked softly, mindful not to push too hard and choke me. He released his hold on my head and withdrew from my mouth, moving silently behind me, positioning me into a pyramid, my head buried into the mattress.

He placed his hands firmly on each buttock, parting them causing an involuntary spasm to shudder through me. Without warning his member was pressed against me, the oozing fluid aiding his intention. With an increased grip, his fingers embedding into my skin he forced his engorged tip inside me. His grip tensed against my strain as pain spiked through me, but he persisted, slowly working his way in until the head was swallowed forming a plug. The pain intensified as he flexed inside me, exerting force to keep me still he withdrew after only a few minutes had passed. Shaking from shock I easily found myself on my back, staring up at the man who I thought had the utmost of feelings for me.

Like a snake he slithered up my body, his member impaling me halting his accent. As before he slid his own human snake slowly inside me, pausing as the head was consumed, feeling the throb as my own muscles flexed against him. He inched his way inside, burrowing deeper until our bones met, his chest pressed against me, the wiry hairs on his chest brushed my firm nipples, using his hips and legs in unison to grind into my matching motion, maximising the penetration.

John arched his back in the finale as he exploded within me. He lay upon me, his weight pressing uncomfortably, as he removed himself he said, "now you are mine all over".

The closeness that had formed between John and I was orchestrated and well played on my behalf, although I had been unprepared for my reward and the next chapter in my life would be one of my making. I had was already ingratiated with the Pearcey brotherhood and acknowledged by the family as being an enforcer of Williams resolve to become a surgeon which could be my saving grace.

7

The house that John leased was located on Little Collingwood Street, over in Bethnal Green, it was a little over a mile away from Malts families place with a walk of around twenty minutes, often hindered by the cobbled paths that weaved their way around the streets of London, a trap waiting to snare the heel of any good woman's boot. His was the end plot that backed onto the row of houses that ran adjacent, a curved archway framed the front door that faced an open patch of cobble that swept away to another street and the downstairs window was accompanied by two wooden shutters that stood sentential at either side of the thin glass, shutting out the world when they were closed on a night.

The property was constructed of brick, tarnished black from the fumes of the industrial era but rendered smooth of the front. Sturdy metal bollards that stood five-foot-high having been placed in the centre of the road to prevent access to horse and carts meant that the exposed space opposite was invaluable to John for the operation of his business and the delivery of supplies. He had it all to himself.

It was small in comparison to my own home on Maroon Street, the downstairs was divided into two rooms, a tiny gallery kitchen which miraculously contained a small stove, a table and two chairs, which John had built from salvaged wood as well as a floor to ceiling cupboard. The room to the front had been transformed into a workshop where John would sketch his designs and construct most of his pieces, his larger work was done in the yard of his father's butchers. The master bedroom overlooked the street and was bear with the exception of a large bed, a night stand and a sturdy looking wardrobe, it was devoid of any character or decoration.

I did not hurry home in a charade of joy, instead carrying on with my life under the pretence that nothing had altered. I continued as before toiling over garments at McHogg, meeting Malt at the Ban, and laying my head to rest at Johns whilst still paying mother a portion of my wage, my share to the Wheeler income. It would be two weeks before I found the courage that had so far eluded me.

I was apprehensive about breaking the news to mother and father that I was going to be taking up residence with John. They were mortified that I would be living in sin, without even the promises of a ring. I had out grown the family home, I'd stayed longer than most, Joe had long gone from the street and two of the Buckley children had departed to pastures new.

Losing my contribution to the family's income soured mother but Lottie and the boys were now bringing in a few pennies a week to add to the pot.

To appease the situation, I informed them that I would adopt his name, if anyone was to ask, so that the stigma of her shame would not reflect badly on the Wheeler name.

It took only 10 minutes to remove all traces of myself from the room that I had shared with my siblings for a lifetime. I'd rarely been without their company during the twilight hours, their peaceful breathing a symphony to my dreams. Although I would not be sleeping alone as there was only 1 bed in the house in Collingwood Street. As a gift John had constructed a wooden box that he had attached to the outside of the window sill of the upstairs room that fronted onto the street and filled with soil, a sorry looking cutting that had withered in the chill. The romantic notion being that I would be able to look out at something beautiful every morning, but John had forgotten to lavish it with any care or attention.

With the exception of the fees owed for my education I used the last few shillings from my McHogg pay to purchase a small art set consisting on a range of coloured pastel, the brand of the infamous Conte company of Paris stamped into the length of each one, as well as several pencils and brushes to advance my skills in observational drawing.

I was good but no master yet. I was determined to add a

sparkle of femininity and colour to the otherwise drab and masculine surroundings of my new abode. My first commission, as such, was to inscribe the words that made up the advertising for Johns carpentry – J. Pearcey, in bold white letters outlined in yellow followed by the wording 'repairs and commissions taken for furniture, handcarts, wheelbarrows' and finalised with the invitation to 'enquire within'. The board was as tall as me and stood outside the front door, propped against the wall.

My resolve to learn and the payment for a period of study, cobbled together through meticulous strategic financial planning on my behalf and from a portion of Williams wage now that he was classified as a junior medical practitioner, secured my escape from McHogg and ingratiated me with the doctors but did little to foster positive relations with the students of a higher breeding status.

I was saddened to be leaving behind Leeny with whom I had shared hundreds of days of sweat and toil but elated at the notion that no more would I hear the dooming echo of the wooden doors as they closed behind us, a pang of jealously stabbed deep inside that Leeny would likely befriend my replacement and I would soon be forgotten, it would be as if my existence never was within the great industry.

The illusions of grandeur that I had been imaging were not forthcoming. On the surface I was accepted amongst the ranks but in reality, I was at the bottom of the heap, the last to be chosen for the interesting and gruesome but first to be volunteered as the skivvy, an echo of my time at Kenwood ringing in my head. I was forced to secure a small job within a sealskin Alaska factory that was even less appealing than McHogg, for it was our trade to de-hair and dress the skin before it was dyed then transported to be crafted into an item of clothing. The work was hard, smelly and exhausting in conjunction with my attempts to become a medical practitioner. I lasted the princely time of three weeks and four days.

After working the rounds and shadowing the midwives of Mile End, attending the homes of the high born as well as the working-class mothers on their fifth child and the whores who bore children as a side-effect of their trade, I came to the conclusion that I was not destined to be amongst their personnel. After my rapturous sexual encounters of the last month and those in my early adolescence as well as the traumatic visit to Dr Lee I feared that I would never bear a child of my own. The act of birthing a joyous mother, delivering a hapless soul who would be destined for a life of poverty and servitude or even pulling the lifeless miniature corpse from the warmth of the womb only served as a constant reminder of what had been stolen from me.

I hadn't thus far decided if I wished to bring a new life into this hellish world but to have the right ripped out of you was incomprehensible and had caused irrevocable physical and mental damage that I was yet to admit to myself.

Over the space of a year I had become increasingly disillusioned and my mood was one of depression, my fits had increased and the feeling of being sober was becoming alien to me.

Having returned home for the umpteenth time in a state of anguish John had suggested that I reconsider my decision to pursue a medical career like his brother and instead turn my hand to a womanlier pursuit. In the meantime, he could sustain my lack of employment and in return I provided everything a dutiful wife would, a clean house, a warm meal and a welcoming bed every evening.

Johns existence was turbulent, and we had already moved from Collingwood to a dismal dwelling at Piermont Street before being moved on again to Bayham Street. Johns commissions were successful but sporadic, so rent was not always paid, and the landlords had no tolerance to wait for their money.

John gifted me with a beautiful cardigan of a rich red wool, it was fitted to the womanly figure, tapered in around the waist and full in the bosom. The sleeves were as long as the body of the cardigan, straight tubes that ran down from inflated shoulders, the collar weaved high to sit under the base of my skull with identical triangles forming a frame to my exposed throat. The pattern of the tailoring was an intricate lace design, a variety of skills combined to create one piece that was finished with five shinning buttons and topped with a brooch style fastener that had flowers embroidered onto the surface. It was the beauty of the bodice that first drew the eye and instigated a conversation between myself and the gentleman that I would finally know as Mr Frank Hogg. I wore it daily until I noticed that it was losing its shape from over use so made the decision to retire it and only wear it on special occasions.

Even after a whole month had elapsed John was infeasibly accepting of the situation pertaining to my lack of employment, allowing me to serve as a wife figure within his home. I dutifully prepared and served his meals daily and thrice weekly I would venture to the markets to purchase fresh produce from some of the hundreds of costermongers that lined the streets plying their wares from barrows, donkey-cart or baskets that they held or had positioned on top of a conveniently placed crate. As a child I would scan their clothes for any pearl buttons, a sign that they were on top of the selling game, most had none but one wizened old woman had a whole host of shining buttons, a beacon of success and pride proudly displayed.

I had settled into a life without work as if I was born to it and

I adored visiting and perusing the market stalls. The mixture of scents from the variety of food stock was a nasal delight but had to contend with the industrialised fog that often settled over the rooftops and the scent of the unwashed that mingled with the aromatic scents of the foods and flowers as well as the distinctive smell of tobacco that hung in the air. Birds hung by their feet awaiting their fate in the pot, their souls long departed adorned carts, the vendors less appealing with gruff attitudes and dirt so ingrained that their nails were tinged with black. There were often wonders to be beheld, my favourites were the dainty and colourful birds housed in ornate cages who sang sad songs of freedom. Many an hour could be whiled away observing the human nature that was displayed in all i's glory for the world to view, men, women and children shouting their wares to potential customers, the pick-pocketers sly fingers working the crowds, a stray mongrel sniffing out abandoned scraps, a destitute mother with a tiny babe in arms begging for their supper, a thin woman collecting waste to sell on in exchange for a few coopers.

London itself was undergoing a change in the direction of its commerce, already fashion was readily available at a more affordable cost due to the mass production of the industrial revolution that had swept across the country, merchants plying their trade to the population of the city and the visitors that flooded to the great capital.

Although the overcrowded and unsanitary slums of the East

End housed the most destitute and desperate of the city it was not short on character and was a constant hive of activity, from the traders earning a living to the labourers out of work hounding the factory's and docks for work to avoid a stint in the workhouse. Groups of women on street corners carrying out domestic and servitude chores, their offspring working the streets was a constant staple.

Initially Johns sexual appetite was exhausting. We were at it like proverbial rabbits, it became our night time ritual. His desire to ensure that I was as equally satisfied died off as quickly as his libido. Our nightly exercise dwindled by the month until we were intimately sharing a bed only once a week, John pounding away unemotionally until his ejaculation then falling into a deep sleep beside me as I pondered the life decisions that had brought me to this point in my life, lying awake, sometimes into the small hours, waiting for sleep to claim me.

The honeymoon period had run its course on our relationship, with every passing week the animosity between John and myself grew. I was not privy to the knowledge as to why our relationship was unravelling, I could not tell if his heart had found lodgings elsewhere, but I refused to allow it impact on my friendship with his brother whom I still met with, alone, on a regular basis. We would reminisce over a quart or two of beer, exchanging memories of our days together and listening to tales of the current events that were affecting either party.

Perhaps, after all, we were the more compatible match but that was a ship that had sailed so long ago it was certainly lost at sea, if not a wreck festering at the bottom of the ocean. Our friendship was sealed in blood and bound in secrecy.

John was making a habit out of disappearing as evening approached, choosing to spend his time in the company of his drunken associates to return around midnight when he was sure sleep would have come for me. He was not yet ready to render his hold over me, preferring to retain me as a live-in whore, serving him like a wife without the commitment, occasionally instigating or submitting to the love making that quenched his limited needs. I had no grounds for complaint as John was still allowing me to manage his household although he was unaware of the creative measures I took to with the weekly budget, usually coming in at fourteen shillings and six and a half pence.

I choose to make my own entertainment when I was free of Johns influence and without Malts company. Having served as the dutiful good lady during the day I served as accommodating mistress on an evening.

It started as an ale addled one off, a beer-soaked session at the Globe with past acquaintances. Several of us left together, initially all heading to our separate abodes but strolling in the same direction, leading us on a merry precession which terminated for me at the heavy wooden door of Bayham Street. There were still several people in tow and with the house decked in darkness it was clear that John had yet to return from his nightly excursion, being only around ten I doubted that I would see him for several hours to come.

In my inebriated state I felt it a worthwhile experience to open the door and invite the rabble inside to partake in a small glass of gin from the bottle that I had hidden in the pantry. John rarely ventured into it for it was my domain to provide for him as a wife would.

The bed was warmed that night but not with the heat of Johns body. The proposal came from the negro that had attached himself to us, which resulted in all four of us urgently stripped of our clothes, standing uncomfortably in our under garments unsure of the next move as I suddenly became aware of what we were about to embark on. The chill that was rising from the floorboards, alongside that nakedness of our bodies had caused our nipples to become erect, four hard buttons pressing against the fabric of our slips, goosebumps rippling up our arms as we stood hand in hand, nervous anticipation racking our bodies as the two men drank in the images of our figures that were silhouetted in the candle light. From the erect members that stood to attention it was obvious that the men were ready to move the evening along, the thin fabric covering their manhood did nothing to disguise their excitement, thick veined flesh urged to be released. Acting in unison the men had moved forward and taken us in their arms, forcing sloppy open-mouthed kisses across our own mouths and down the nape of our necks whilst simultaneously manoeuvring us onto the bed.

The first act performed was a stimulating expression of oral invasion, their lips working down from our necks, taking the vast mounds of flesh that formed our breast into their own mouths, flickering and biting the rock nipples sending ripples of desires to my laycock, an internal yearning causing me to become wet with animalistic need, his penis tickled and teased the entrance as I longed for him to fill me.

The pleasure was ecstatic but tinged with shame as I battled with my conscience over Johns whereabouts. Before long a path had been traced down our torsos with their tongues and the men were working the moist entrances into a damper environment, lubricating the doorway to their enjoyment sending waves of pleasure across my public bone.

The men ploughed away, lapping up the juices produced by their conduct a soft delicate hand found my exposed and recently departed nipple, still hard from the pleasure of the manipulation under the dark and experienced hands. A sharp nail flickered across my nipple, tweaking it like a knob causing me to pant with delight, the touch smooth and caressing. I turned my head to meet the entrancing gaze of the young female who lay bare and open legged beside me on the bed, her eyes as green as the grass locked onto mine, her lips parted in an expression of lust, inviting them to be kissed. As the progress of the men slowed we gravitated towards one another, our lips meeting in a unison of red, hands beginning to explore the surfaces of each other's body. Not to be ignored we were soon separated, the instigator of the others pleasure now transferring the bodily fluids that hung on their lips, the taste of another woman pushed into my mouth.

Time passed in a haze of sweat and limbs, eight arms and eight legs intertwined in an abstract moving sculptor. At times I could not tell who I was touching or who was touching me, the muscular arms and hairy legs an identifying feature of the males but the fondling of both sexes was involved, hands were placed on my breasts and cupped my bottom as I placed my hands over the bodies of the individuals, my nails digging into flesh and caressing skin.

Despite the mixture of bodies, I could feel the difference in the shafts of the men as they rode me, one filled me to the brim, rubbing against the inside of me but the other was lost inside the cavern of my desire, a gentle pressure as the length pushed against me. As the larger of the two members worked me, changing the speed of his thrusts keeping me begging for more his lesser associate found its way into my mouth, the salty taste stung my tongue and I gagged, the owner to lost between the thighs of my counterpart unable to hear my protesting murmurs which fought against the gasps of pleasure. The mountain of bodies shifted again, and I found myself moulding into a different position. The tight black curls tickled my nose as my tongue explored her, flicking back and forth, up and down, her body shock with the orgasm that I induced.

The night ended in a show of gratitude, our bodies glistening with the sweat that covered them. The men removed themselves, hands instinctively covering the areas that moments ago were pressed against another as the force of what had just occurred sunk in past the beer related delusions. Good nights were murmured as the three lustful partners scrabbled around to retrieve the clothes that had, until an hour previous, adorned their bodies. They scurried around the room, limbs were placed back into the breaches that housed them and the magnificent breasts of my counterpart were secured within a filthy blouse hidden beneath a dark coloured hole ridden shawl. Soon the only one still naked was me, as bare as the day I was born. As they took their leave it was suggested that the candle remain in the window to alert them of Johns absence should I wish for a repeat episode of the evening antics. I pulled on my nightdress and climbed into the bed that was still warm from the indiscretions it had hosted.

I was asleep when John returned that night.

The guilt was eating away at me like the diseases so rampant in this country that ate away at the flesh and humanity of their victims, the events of the orgy, the unrestrained indulgence flashing through my memory.

On one hand I was still desperate for the relationship with John to succeed but the flip side of the coin was my own personal stimulation. John's attention was not forthcoming, and I had glimpsed the pleasure that could be derived from the touch of another.

The notion of displaying my availability through the plain and effective means of using a purposeful household item of a candle was simplistic and afforded the cover that it was simply being used to light a room and extinguished when the user was no longer in occupation or had settled down for a night's rest.

How word spread of my window in Bayham Street I am unsure but the few selected gentlemen that I choose to spend time with soon multiplied from familiar faces of regular callers with a handful of strangers thrown in. I made no charge for my pleasure, but some left me a small deposit of coins, others nothing more than compliments. The candle had become my calling card.

I frequently encountered a gentleman that lived a stone throw away, he was handsome and carried himself well. He was often in the company of a younger woman. Having struck up conversation through the familiarity of seeing one another I became friends with the young woman. Her name was Clara Hogg and the attractive gentleman was her brother. We meet each other often from then on and talked, as women do, about men, babies and a future when we were whisked away for a life of riches. Never did she suspect that the basis of our friendship was orientated around her older sibling.

I first met the gentleman, who would become my saviour, in this fashion. He was a fine wealthy fellow who was some twenty years my senior and was always immaculately turned out in a tailored suit and hair that was swept across the top of his head from a parting that started above his left ear. The finishing touch to his appearance was the tie that was fastened around his neck, expertly tied without the aid of a mirror and positioned as if it had not been removed at all that day. I made no enquiry into his personal history or the events that had led him to seek my attention and not that of one of the many ladies of the night who were in the business of providing an accommodating sheath for a man's appendage. He failed to offer personal information which I made no effort to uncover, instead it resulted in my imagining of a family, a wife to withdrawn from the birth of his hordes of children to welcome his touch and conform to her wifely duties or he was descended from nobility explaining why he had an air of importance about him or he was a fraudster on the lam from the law plying a trade of deceit or he was an international jewel thief on the hunt for a rare cut diamond or he was nothing more than a working class man with an aptitude for tomfoolery.

After several months of weekly visits Charles informed me

that he wanted exclusivity and was uncomfortable with the notion that other men, with the exception of John, lay their hands on me and touched me in areas and ways that he wanted to control. It was a request that I was not prepared to honour at the present time. The refusal of his offer had caused offence for Charles left as soon as he could button his trousers. When his routine visit was not forth coming the following week, I assumed that I had wounded his pride and that he was seeking his pleasure from another source which was mores the pity for me as he treated me like a lady and not like an object and it pained me to admit that it grieved me so.

The following day I woke in a state of despair, a black cloud had settled over night and a melancholy mood had taken me that morning. I walked into the front parlour room while John was discussing the requirements with a customer to be confronted with a nodding Charles, as John sketched designs, talking through his suggestions as he went. My heart was suspended in my chest at his presence alongside the man that I had taken as my own, but Charles betrayed neither by voice although he could not disguise the longing in his eyes, fortunately John was ignorant to this due to his focused attention on securing the commission.

Charles used the claim that he had amendments for his order to feign reasons for visiting Bayham Street in daylight hours, which worked for our arrangement as I could pass over his presence as an enquiry about his commission for his London lodgings.

The influx in custom could have been my undoing for it was certain that John had discovered my secrets and he would remedy the situation. I had been courting John for the best part of three years, the anniversary falling on my twenty first birthday which was only a month away. Glimpses of the man that I had been so eager to secure as mine all that time ago occasionally surfaced, and the odd night would be spent in each other's company as opposed to the company of others but the strain between us was evident and the gap in our emotions as wide as a broken gate, any fix just temporary before a change in the wind would rip it open again. My own actions would lead me into the most unpredictable chapter of my life so far.

8

My birthday was only a week away and, although I wasn't a child any longer, I was secretly excited about what it might hold. Internally I was fostering the hopes that John would make an honest woman of me and present me with a ring. For two days he had been attentive and kind, laying a trail of false hope that I followed as blindly as Hansel and Gretel.

It was Charles that made a declaration of his heart. He stated that I had unequivocally taken possession of his heart although the previous claimant still held it through the sanctity of marriage, a bond that Charles would not sever, his suggestion being that I was to act as his mistress, solely. An escort to his desires and perversions that a respectable wife would not allow to even be uttered, let alone performed, in her presence. He left without an answer for his proposal had left me in a quandary.

Charles must have been waiting for John to leave as his timing was impeccable, no sooner had the door been closed he was knocking on it, his gentle tap as soft natured as the proprietor, and no candle stood lit in the window to instigate a visit. I ushered him through the door in haste, keen not to be seen by a neighbour or for John to turn and see another man at his door. I knew he had come to retrieve what I was not yet ready to yield, his answer.

My mind was still split for I understood that John would not be amenable to willingly share me and I placed my current accommodation and association with the Pearcey's in jeopardy if I choose to accept Charles offer, a part of me still hoped that John would muster the strength to make me his lawful wife.

Much to the annoyance of Charles my flighty indecision could provide him with neither an answer nor a solution to the predicament, so the agreement was reached to continue on the existing basis for the immediate duration, but it was clear that I could not continue in this manner. His body left contented, but his mind did not.

I had only made three visits home since I had left in disgrace, a dog trailing its tail and bowing its head in disgrace, a bundle of possessions dragged in its wake. Mother was awaiting my arrival, Lottie and the boys in attendance but father notably absent from the family portrait, called away on work mother had said. Mother had joined forces with several of the neighbours to produce the silk flowers that the elegant ladies wore on their hats and upon their coats. Once weekly they would receive a box containing all the elements to create beautiful arrays, farmed out by the factory's on the cheap. The depression had affected a great number, thousands out of work yet those close to me had clung to work for their lives did depend on it. You had only to venture into the street to hear a tragic tale of woe.

A pleasant afternoon was spent in the company of my siblings and the woman who had born me into this world. It accumulated in the giving of an extravagant gift, a simple pen with interchangeable nibs that would alter the style of the writing produced as well as a glass ink well full to the brim with black ink and a few sheets of parchment of which to become accustomed with my new writing instrument. I thanked mother wholeheartedly for the thoughtful and costly present, exchanging warm embraces as I took my leave, eager to return to Bayham Street and the gift that John said would be waiting for me on my return. I couldn't help but anticipate what form the gift would take, how I longed for it to be the long-awaited proposal.

On entering the abode that I shared with John I observed a wooden crate beside the door, it's familiar contents spilling haphazardly on to the floor. An ice-cold chill of dread took my heart in its grip as my mind identified the possessions as my own. The jumble of cloth was crowned with the remainder of the candle that once served as a welcoming beacon in the window of the room that had seen me the lover of many a man.

John was stood at the foot of the stairs, his arms defensively crossed against his chest, his stance awkward, a look of anger tinged with sorrow plastered on his handsome face, his unforgiving eyes as hard as stone. There was no joyous air of celebration about his person and no hint of a birthday endowment or drink on the horizon.

I took several nervous steps towards him, hoping that my eyes had been deceived and I had misinterpreted a message that was not there. Johns reaction confirmed that I was indeed correct and should be in immense fear for my future.

John did nothing to disguise the look of revulsion that he painfully felt at my approach which stopped me in my tracks. The lover that once felt warm and excited at my touch was now repulsed by my presence and I realised that I would never feel his hands upon me again.

I made one more attempt to placate the spiralling situation, but he took measures to avoid me by retreating onto the first step of the stairs before exploding in a cruel tirade of venomous filled accusations, laced with truth that to deny would make a liar out of me. He called me out as the whore that I am and challenged the world to take on my sins for he was washing his hands of me, I was to never again darken his door, he stripped me of my home and his love but did not strip me of the Pearcey name that I had been peddling for near on three years. My demons were my own to tame and control, he would no longer take any part in restraining them.

He only just held the discipline to physically expel me, his knuckles white from the clenched fist that hung defeatedly at his sides. I could feel his eyes burning into my back as I followed his instruction and left his home for the last time. Heaving the crate into the street I imagined how the morrows talk would surround my expulsion, the echo of the door slamming shut shook the building and rattled my senses. Where would I go, the security of my immediate future consumed me for several moments, leaving me on the street contemplating my next move as the world continued to live around me.

Malt was sympathetic to my situation, he had known me through the most informative and developing years of my existence and we shared experiences that sealed us together like no other and Malt appreciated the temperament of his twin could leave much to be desired although it did produce a little animosity as it was evident that I had been the sole cause of his brother's displeasure, despite Johns reputation for his caddish behaviour. Malt displayed the depth of his friendship by allowing me to make transitory lodgings on the floor of his room for the duration of two days and provided me with a protected place to store my belongings, alongside his tools and the memories that were housed in the outbuilding of the butchers.

The despair that was ever only a sorrowful day or conflicted dilemma away was rooting deep into my soul, threatening to consume me and carry me to a crossroads grave. The advantage was that I cared little for the plight that I found myself in, only concerned with how I would find payment to hand over to the deep pocketed landlords. Where I lay my head brought me little bother, be it bedding down with an accommodating patron or huddling in the street, it mattered little to me. The search for employment was as forthcoming as my ability to secure lodgings with no means to pay the rent. Malt was oblivious to the escalating burden that I was morphing into as I refused to abuse his good nature and plead for the charitable donation of accommodation or finance. I had after all caused this, along with the catalogue of failures that I had so far chalked up in my stay on this earth.

Malt had convinced his brother to take me back, to act in the husbandly manner that he had aligned himself too, which he did although it grieved him to know that he did not possess me fully. My eyes had already been captivated by another, an Adonis of a man, immaculately turned out and well-bred he seemed destined to become embroiled in my life for he seemed to be present at every turn, in the shops that I visited and upon the streets that I walked. An onlooker would have been mistaken but we were not yet antiquated with one another's company. Despite the promise to his brother, John was unable to commit to me and our relationship ended, broken beyond repair.

I took my anger out on an old cardigan jacket that John had left behind, the inanimate object had done nothing to deserve my retribution, but it paid for Johns hostility, mutilated under my own hand. The once fine apparel was now button-less, the sleeves hacked off and the left-hand pocket ripped, the stitching frayed, hanging limp and useless from the severed material.

By now my palette was so accustomed to the flavour and consistency of the ale that I no longer paid any heed to the taste, not bitter nor sweet just a little tingly as it washes over the tongue. Even after the last drop had been drunk the taste could still be detected as it clung to my mouth and even in my nose as I inhaled. The trouble that I had encountered with this particular drink is that it left me thirsty for more and I liked the way in which my pudding-house felt happy, full, and warm which meant that I spent more valuable coins than I should to keep my feelings numbed and my inhibitions dulled.

Near on three months had elapsed since my departure from Bayham Street, London's shops had transformed for the festive season with teasing extravagances on display for the world to envy, the rich parading their finery, the poor parading down trodden jealousy. It was however a welcoming period when the population were generally more jovial and accommodating to the needy and the atmosphere held an air of generosity.

My status of homeless wench still held true. The cardigan that John had gifted me with was almost unrecognisable, the vibrant red had withered through continual exposure to the elements, holes had grown through neglect and the reminder of happier times ensured that my disposition remained sullen.

Boxing day 1887 arrived in a downpour of rain that looked set to flood London, making my gratitude to Malt and his family ever the sincerer for he was permitted to allow me to bed down for the night, on the condition that I was a spectre by the time John arrived to make merry with his mother, father and siblings.

I was hauled up in the Globe by noon, a poultry filled pie in one hand, a quart of ale being nursed in the other. I continued in this fashion until the sun had long set and the moon was riding high and glorious in the night sky.

The woman at my feet was dead by my hand.

Her fair hair was turning the colour of rust as the blood seeped from the fatal wound on the back of her head, her skull caved in with the solo powerful blow that was unsuspected and unwarranted. The pent-up fury that I was unaware had been building inside me like an unexploded bomb was released in a torrent of blows that were rained down on the lifeless body of an innocent woman, guilty of no other crime in my eyes than being in the vicinity.

I was half way through the act when sense battled its way through the drunken haze that settled on me, like a gentleman's top hat, my mind as insulated from the blood as the brainpan from the rain that bounced from the brim of the said hat.

She had no worldly possessions about her person other than the bloodied clothes that she had died in, not even a penny to pay the ferryman who would transport her to her final destination.

I abandoned her lifeless body where it lay, a deathbed of cobbles in a filthy alleyway that led onto Commercial road, taking no steps to hide the body from detection, instead fleeing the scene with as much composure and haste that I could muster. The blood-soaked metal pole, a weapon of convenience, dripping my guilt in a trail of red which was washed away by the rain that pounded the street, as forgotten as the victim would be. The usual throng of daily activity that left barely a passable space of cobbles during the daylight hours was eerily quiet, gone were the carts of produce, the flowers, the noise, the smell. The sounds of the drunks and the promise of a gruesome discovery waited under the moonlight.

With a mind half driven mad at the notion of my callous actions I found myself passing through the stone archway of St, George-in-the-East Church, a place that was alien to me. Having been the centre of such celebration and displays of worship over the last few days it was eerily silent, exhausted from the faithful in prayer and the faithless searching a Yule miracle. With the last remaining sanity of the night I stumbled my way through the recently reclaimed Wesleyan chapel burial ground that ran adjacent to the flat and open ground of the church, searching for a spot in which to conceal the evidence of my crime. I was forced to be content with entrusting my secret to the roots of a tall yew tree, thankful that the rain had softened the ground I was able to work the pole far enough into the earth that it was somewhat undetectable amongst the uneven root infested surface, for the respectful markers that stood alone and silent in memory of those inscribed on their surface now stood as a decorative fence, mourning the ground where they once stood prominent and admired.

I took shelter that night in one of the arches, inside the down-turned mouth of god, the splendid house of the lord a vast white structure above my head. The landscape was barren due to the creation of an open space some two years previous, much perturbing the permanent residents who suffered a desiccation of their final resting place. I was moved on the next morning by a harassed looking rector, conflicted by his duty to the parish and his duty to his God.

There was no article to commemorate her untimely death in any newsworthy publication, nor any talk on the streets of her dire end, it was as if it never happened. She was aptly named "Fairy Fay" for an identity was never attributed to the fallen soul and her appearance in death was angelic, soft and peaceful.

Malt had known me long enough to discern when my mood was suffering from the influence of the dark plague and was persistent, the following evening, in his attempts to draw from me what had vexed me so.

I disclosed to my confessor the details of the slaughter of the young Fairy Fay, relieved to unburden myself but shamed that the deed was carried out alone. Malt and myself couldn't share the intimacy of sexual encounters so we shared the thrill of killing instead and I had omitted Malt from this one.

He was silent for an uncomfortable amount of time before casually noting that the murder had gone unannounced, so it was unlikely that the constables were exasperating themselves to find the culprit and bring them to justice. The fact that there had been little interest in the death despite the circumstances of how she was found was encouraging and a tantalising challenge to commit another murder and repeat the pattern of evasion.

We had been unsuccessful and unmotivated in the search to send another to meet their maker, no suitable candidate had been forthcoming, so life mundanely rolled by.

This time it was myself who registered that Malt was rather perturbed. At first my questions were deflected with counter interrogations about the deteriorating state of my appearance and the validity that I had a roof to shelter under, of which I still did not, the untruth against Malt a stab in my heart for I detested deceiving him. It was my turn to be persistent and chip away at Malts aloof exterior until his composure began to crack and he succumbed to the pressure to reveal his deepest nature to me. I think he found it so troublesome to share his darkest desire as he had been reluctant to admit to even himself that his heart and appetite did not sing from the same hymn sheet as other men and the implications if he was discovered would destroy his career and the reputation that the Pearcey's had built in the city of London.

Malt believed himself to be unnatural, an abomination of humanity, a freak of nature that should be punished for the feelings he harboured for others. He had tried to find pleasure and happiness between the warm shapely thighs of a woman, but they did nothing to provoke a reaction in his heart or head. What did stimulate a reaction in his groin was the close company of another that matched his sex, the rippling biceps and sizeable package that made me wet and hungry had the same impact on my dear friend, although society, and the law, prevented him from acting on his whims. I could sympathise as I thought back to the night that I had sampled the delights of a woman's body. I reassured him that his disclosure had no impact on our friendship, in fact it bolstered my confidence that should he have been so inclined I could have snared him as I did his kin.

The news of the attack on Annie Millwood was the main topic of conversation amongst the traders, buyers and patrons of Mile End on the morning of the twenty-sixth February. By all accounts an attempt had been made of her life, the assailant disappearing before the job was complete, leaving a partial description that the attacker was male and the injury to her lower abdomen and legs had been inflicted with a clasp knife, a weapon more associated with the military than the medical profession. A suitably matching account was portrayed the following week in East London Post that reiterated the fact that she had in fact been stabbed but made no attempt to discover the perpetrator.

It crossed my mind that the attacker was Malt, but he assured me that it was not, and that he would have completed the job, leaving no witnesses alive to testify against him, or us. Whitechapel was a hunting ground that we had not considered, it was close enough to be viable but just far enough that we would not instantly fall under suspicion.

We had to act with diligence in light of the botched assassinations. The perfect specimen found us, a petite brunette with an accent that placed her descending from the south. She sat alone, her appearance startled and nervous, inviting the tender care of a welcoming citizen. Happy to oblige I used my womanly wiles to elicit trust, a few compliments and the offer of help were the winning combination. As we were preparing to execute the final stages of the abduction the felicitous victim was unwittingly saved from death by the fortunate arrival of another who secured her attention so fully we were relegated to our own troupe.

The vigilance that had been warranted in the aftermath of the failed attack had vanished as the world had returned to business, Annie's plight as forgotten as Fairy Fays. It made a brief resurgence with the attack that left Ada Wilson close to death from a frenzied assault, another opportunity squandered, but Annie's name was only mentioned in the reporting of her death which had claimed her a mere three days after Ada had been victimised. Ada had been alert enough to provide a more in-depth description of the short fair skinned man as well as his apparel but the potential killer had likely been a common thief as robbery was reported to be the motive. For several days the men of Mile End were viewed with a suspicious eye, but the trappings of life soon buried the two attempted murders, the need to survive prevailing over the need for justice.

So that suspension did not fall on our own doorsteps the idea of heading to an area a slight distance away was appealing and we seized the moment. We trawled the inns in search of the perfect target, each quart adding to our determination, the opportunity presenting itself in the shape of a middle-aged whore who already bore the marks of abuse, a swollen eye that was turning a combined shade of black and purple and a demeanour that invited the company of others. There was plenty of trade for us all as Easter had brought out the tourists as well as the locals, but she stood out against the crowd. It later turned out she went by the name of Emma Elizabeth Smith.

We stalked our prey for a lengthy period as she drunkenly weaved her way down to Fairlance Street in Limehouse, on a course that was ignorant to all but herself, a chance encounter with a dapper gentleman who wore a long dark overcoat topped with a pale coloured scarf forced us to bypass the couple as if we were heading to a premeditated destination. Disappointed that we had lost our unfortunate we headed back to the bibulous population. Fate was on our side for we happened upon Mrs Smith as we converged onto the dirty, narrow entrance to brick lane, her entering from Wentworth Street.

I recognised her immediately as the woman that we had marked for death, the assault instigated when Emma arrogantly barged past me, instinctively my hand shot out and grabbed the length of hair that cascaded down her back, one purposeful pull brought her crashing to the floor like a sack of spuds. Before she could process why she was on her back I was raining down a torrent of blows, my fists pummelling into her body in an orchestrated beating, her screams snuffed out by Malt who plugged her mouth with his fist. As she pleaded to be saved for the sake of her children the red mist of being baron fuelled the need to punish the unworthy for squandering the precious gift of motherhood. Malt used a small wooden handled blade that resembled a skinning knife to remove part of her ear lobe, the delicate pierced skin a memento of his involvement as I committed the ultimate invasion on her person. Using the wooden handle of a broom that I had fashioned into a pole I violated Emma in a way akin to her clientele, a hole ripped through her scant stocking as I forced the pole into her.

What we hadn't factored into the equation was the activity of the gangs of young men that patrolled the streets of Whitechapel exacting their protection, at a cost, upon the districts prostitutes, their boots beating down the mud that served as a floor in some of the streets, cobbles not reaching past many of the main streets. Before we could complete our task, we were interrupted by the sound of several people heading in our direction from Osborn Street, forcing us to abandon the badly beaten woman where she lay, blood seeping from the various cuts to her face and arms and from the penetrating wound that would destroy her trade, an ultimately her life.

What the others did to her upon finding her spread across the ground would be known to only them and Emma, we had taken nothing from her but her ravaged dignity and the blood that painted the street and she had been violated by nothing other than the blunt wooden pole that I had left inside her in our hurry to evade capture, but it was those that she recalled from the attack, not Malt or I.

The papers took delight in publishing the detail of the 'wilful murder and dastardly assault' of Emma flagging the inadequate police investigation and casting aspersions on the way that Emma conducted her life prior to being 'barbarously murdered'. Suspicion fell on a knowledgeable pickpocketing showman character that was known locally as Freddie Fingers for he conveniently disappeared from the scene, aiding to the speculation that he had an involvement and, coupled with the reluctant testament from Emma herself that she had been attacked by a group of three or four youths we were beyond the realms of dubiety. We had escaped justice again.

Malt developed a nervous disposition following the death of Emma four days after our failed attempt on her life. I was unaware of the reason for his sudden change in demeanour, no evidence had been left at the scene and I am sure that the gang members would have no reason to identify us for they operated above the law and we had hidden at the scene to avoid detection and any skirmish that would have resulted through interfering with their racket of protection. Nothing I did or said seemed to ease his nerves. He could not have been aware of the dossier that the Whitechapel constabulary were to compile on the succession of deaths.

The night that Malt broke the news that he was to leave me and the city to embark on the fortuitous opportunity to take up a position in an infirmary abroad was crucifying. My heart split in two, I was inconsolable with grief and self-pity, but I could not argue that it was a chance to change the direction of his life and escape the stigma of the killings that hung over him like a grey cloud, his disposition detrimentally effected by the knowledge that his deeds may be discovered. We had discussed what would happen if this possibility was on the horizon, but I had hoped that the sun would never rise on the notion and it would remain always just a dream. I would have relished the chance, so I feigned my excitement for him and acted as if I were as excited as he. It vexed me to see my friend apprehensive in the presence of the law, scared of the power they had to end the life of another in the full view of the public for he had witnessed the execution of another by the length of a rope and it had remained imprinted in his mind since his childhood.

The ship that took my best friend and co-conspirator away was a locally built fully rigged steam and sailing vessel by the name of S.Y "Ceyon" that was moored at Billingsgate Dock and would sail Malt to his new destination and a life of freedom that waited him in the exotic Malta on its cruise around the world.

I arrived with Malt and his mother, who tolerated my

presence for the benefit of her son, in a horse drawn carriage, he had managed to cram all his possessions, his clothes and text books into two large trunks. Each was just manageable through the determination of us at either handle, but the combined weight called for the need of a carriage. They were loaded with the other cargo into the bowels of the vast vessel alongside similar trunks and matching sets of luggage, all the classes mingling together in the guts of the ship and loaded by the ship's crew.

He took with him a small case which contained some of his own personal tools, a reminder of our times and crimes an echo on the blades surface, as well as a few private possessions that would grieve him deeply to be parted with. In his pocket he carried the sealed letter written by my own fair hand with a plea that he writes to me when he was settled in addition to a pastel drawing of the Ban with an exaggerated back drop of a sea blue sky and a portrait to remind him of the ally he was leaving behind.

I wasn't bitter that he was abandoning our shores for a climate of sun as he would be imparting his learned skill on those less fortunate and securing an escape from any justice that maybe served in penance for the atrocity we had inflicted on the doomed.

A warm embrace and a promise of communication was my parting gift from Malt, that along with a parcel that was awaiting my return to Priory Street.

I stood, rooted to the spot, watching the ship as it grew smaller and smaller as it sailed away into the distance. The other well-wishers and relatives had long gone, returned to get on with their lives and fill the hole that the departed had left, or rejoice that they would no longer be a concern. Malts mother had returned on the carriage, content that her son was embarking on a prosperous adventure, leaving me abandoned to make my own way home.

I felt bereft stood alone at the dock, ignored by the men as they performed their duties, the incessant caw of the gulls and lapping of the tide against the harbour wall were the accompanying tunes to Malts departure. The empty feeling that had my heart in its cold grip tightened as I contemplated life without my partner in crime, my confidant, my friend.

With no employment to distract me I took up residency at the Bancroft Arms, arriving in the early afternoon, a tummy full of pickled whelks obtained from a trader at the docks and eyes red from the descent of my tears, my feet throbbing from the walk back, the furthest I had walked in the whole of my twenty-one years on this earth.

I stayed, falling progressively deeper into a drunken stupor until the landlord's bell signalled I was to be ejected from the sanctuary of my haven to the cruel mercy of the world outside the shielded doors.

This behaviour persisted for the entirety of a week, each day blurring into the next, a continuing routine of drinking to blot out the pain of my loss, sometimes returning to the security offered in the arms of Charles in our forbidden hideaway in Priory Street, other times waking up beside a stranger in a bed that was not my own. The anger that I was feeling over Malts departure was bubbling beyond control and I was struggling to retain my resolve and not unleash my emotions on the unsuspecting degenerates of London.

It was a pity that I received no fees as an assassin of the unworthy. The duty had fallen to me alone since Malt had taken his leave, but I was determined that I would continue in honour of his legacy to me. This chapter of my life was going to unfold without the strength of any other to support and encourage me.

9

I used the sparse allowance that Charles afforded me to purchase some essential items from the market, the day was dreary for late July, a steady drizzle of rain fell from the grey clouds that filled the sky as far as the eye could see. I was still exploring this part of the city, investigating the streets and characters, discovering delights and perversions. The usual route that I had carved out back to Priory Street was blocked due to the demolition of an old building, an eyesore I'm told that had blighted the community for an age, the crumbling walls and broken beams not even an attractive refuge for the desperate, pigeons and rats the only occupants.

My journey found me idly strolling along the streets that separated the slums of Whitechapel from the marginally less impoverished neighbourhood of Camden, committing the sites to memory. I was initially attracted by the gilded writing on the beautifully painted sign, reminding me of the board that I had crafted for John, that informed the public that a family by the name of Hogg could remove their furniture, for a fee. Intrigued as to the exact nature that this employment would involve I took it upon myself to make a feigned enquiry, on behalf of a non-existent elderly relative.

The door had a bell that alerted the owner to my presence as soon as I pushed the door far enough ajar to enter, making my retreat an impossibility.

The gentleman that answered my calling stood about six-foot-tall, his broad shoulders topped a belly that had been well fed and nestled for space in a tailored suit. His up turned collar supported a silk cravat which cradled his neck, his handsome face was framed with a moustache and beard that hide a strong jaw line. He must have been my senior by some twenty years, specks of grey evident in his beard and tan mane, his knuckles had a splattering of dark hair that matched that which protruded from his cuff-linked shirt sleeves. He was the man that I had met on many an occasion and flirted up a storm, acting like a smitten giddy school girl in his presence.

He presented me with a printed business card that bore the name 'S.H.Hogg' and invited me to make contact if my 'relative' required his service or should I have any other need that he could fulfil. His affluence impressed me greatly, I thanked him and took my leave already concocting a scenario that would engineer another meeting between us. It would be many many months before I had any knowledge that the business belonged to his brother, his employment dependant on the generosity of his kin.

I lost count of the amount of times that I looked at that card,
the address as imprinted into my mind as it was the card. I had
decided that I would go to Mr Hogg on no other pretence than
offering myself to him, the worst he could do would be to spurn
my advances, the best would be to accept me and take me as
his own. I had no intention of surrendering my hold over
Charles for he had proven to be a life-line, a float to my sinking
ship.

I dressed in my best skirt with the red cardigan that John
had gifted me, my hair drawn into a tight bun and my face
adorned with a lip stick as red as a poppy. When I reached the
threshold that I had crossed days earlier the door was firmly
shut, no movement could be detected from within. My plan
had been thwarted by the absence of the object of my desire.

My flattering appearance was still in place when Charles
came to call that evening, his weekly offering had almost been
forgotten in my urge to become integrated with Mr Hogg. I was
thankful that Charles took it as an endowment for him,
spending longer working me into a frenzy leaving me begging
for him to fill me, any desire for another forgotten in the
moment.

By morning the longing for Mr Hogg had returned so I
resumed my challenge, this time finding Mr Hogg available
and in an agreeable mood. Once inside I took the liberty of

closing the door, my heart thumping in my chest as I deliberated my course of action. Without a word I walked towards him, unbuttoning the cardigan as I advanced, my breasts exposed and erect, his gaze falling from my face to rest upon the two mountains that signalled my intention. There would be one of two outcomes, he would eject me from his premises in disgrace or he would reciprocate my affection. He chose the latter of the options; my plan had been executed to perfection.

Mr Hogg was an accomplished businessman, the sole driver of his own destiny but he was a gentle man. We stood for some time at an impasse, his gaze transfixed upon my breasts but his body as unmoving as a statue, only a stirring in his loins as proof that he had not petrified on the spot. It was clear that I would have to act further to secure my prize. Tenderly I took his hands in my own and placed them upon my breasts, his course skin rough against the sensitive nipples that pressed into his palms. Through my guided touch he kneaded my bosom, his breathing increasing as I vocalised the pleasure I was deriving from him, panting as a dog in the summer sun. The swelling that had formed within his breaches was as unmissable as the sound of the street traders plying their wares but obtaining his seed would prove a harder task than bartering with the best of the mongers in town. Mr Hogg showed great restraint and chivalry for I left wet between the legs but with the promise that he would desire me to return that very evening, he had an appointment to keep and would be perturbed that his reputation could be impaired should he not attend so could dilly-dally no longer.

I doubted that a man of his calibre who possessed such dominating features had gone through his life without the touch of a woman, but his tentative nature would indicate that he had been impervious to the charms of a woman's beauty or sampled only the joys of a meek mannered individual.

I returned that evening as the sun began it's decent from the sky, a fiery glow consuming the cloud speckled blue.
We consummated our newly established connection on a bed of freshly laundered linen.

My mood sunk lower than the sun at night but did not improve as the sun rose to its' peak, a relentless cycle that was akin to my life, the sun's daily appearance a certainty unlike the path that my future would take. An eternal frost infiltrated my hardened exterior, a cold hand gripping my insides, any joy frozen solid like the icicles that hung from the pavilion during the icy winter periods. The rainfall that fell from the sky a stark contrast to the desserts that had become my eyes, devoid of tears, a lifetimes' worth shed as Malt had sailed from my life.

I had taken liberties with Johns affections and brazenly flaunted my desire for another by being seen with Frank out and about in Camden Town, some meetings were carefully contrived on my part, others were genuine statements of his feelings. Mr Hogg frequented the busy King street for professional and personal reasons. It housed a working men's Club and institute where he would while away hours in the company of other industrious men while I would often browse the shelves of the free library, tinkering with knowledge of herbology or broadening my horizons with the intellectual works of such classics as Frankenstein or Gulliver's travels with the giant and tiniest folk, my favourite being the dark story of Wuthering Heights, the brooding Heathcliff and the fateful Cathy.

I could also engineer meetings at the St Pancras Baths and Washhouse under the pretence that I was laundering clothes and was afforded ample opportunity to flaunt myself in my swimwear whilst using the swimming pool. There were dozens of shops lining the street, a fried fish shop with a window of nine panes and a wooden counter from which the monger sold his fish, the shop lit into the night by a modest chandelier of two candles that hung down from the ceiling. The local shops that served King Street was a veritable wealth of produce from food to clothing and I would often see Frank in the bakery as they offered a staple of food from bread to pies, the open fronted premises did nothing to conceal the patrons inside. Mr Hogg favoured particular establishments over others which made it favourable for me to be in his presence though I could not determine what, if any, connection he had with the proprietors. It was an idle remark that let slip his associations had been formed whilst he manages the provisions business that his mother operated from a small premise located at number eighty-seven.

The first letter of many that I wrote to Frank declaring my undying passion for him was left on the counter, a practice that I would come to repeat. I was always keen to retrieve my love notes once they had been read to ensure that they were witnessed only by the eyes they were intended for.

It took several months of self-pity, a barrel of ale and my twenty-second birthday passing in oblivion for me to find any resemblance of the person that I was before my Malt had left me and the shores of England for a life devoted to medicine and devoid of guilt. The fainting sickness had claimed me many times, I woke in various predicaments, alone and abandoned in the street, slummed under the table in a nondescript inn and once under the weight of a hairy sweating beast that was rhythmically pounding my unconscious body with his minuscule apparatus.

I could hardly feel him inside me but was unable to break free of his lusting as my strength ebbed away with each fit, taking time to return. He had expelled himself, leaving me on the unfamiliar bed, retreating to partake in a session with his tobacco pipe. I heaved myself off the bed, pulled up my stockings and adjusted my dress to a semblance of normality, any evidence of the violation hidden beneath an exterior of dirty clothing and unmoving expressions. I left without exchanging a word, the stranger satisfied with his spoils didn't give a second thought to my departure.

As I wondered the streets, seeking a place to bed down I heard my name being hollered through the air, an echo ringing down the road. The voice was familiar, a gruff tone that held the notes of desperation and relief, as I turned I recognised the owner as they emerged from the shadows that had clocked their presence.

Charles Creighton, my former lover, must have frequented every pub in Mile End for by the time he had happened upon the chance encounter under the fume filled night he was red faced from the excursion of trailing from establishment to establishment, from street to street. It took him a moment to gather himself, his great chest heaving with the effort of sustained movement, his breath escaping in gasps, his eyes locked onto my body, afraid that I would vanish from his life if I was no longer in his sight.

Charles again declared his intention to have me as his own and expressed his melancholy since John had evicted himself from the dwelling in Bayham Street, leaving me with rent I could ill afford to pay rendering me of no fixed abode. On account of being unable to trace my whereabouts, his insistence to embed himself inside my warm body spared me from finding my own accommodation that eve. I gracefully accepted, walking arm in arm we trawled the district until we found a lodging house with a vacant room.

My body was consumed for a second time that night, this time with mutual compassion. As the morning rays turned the room from dark to light Charles whispered his hearts desires, pleading that I meet with him the following Sunday when he would next be visiting this depraved area of the country's vast city.

A meeting was arranged for seven pm, he would find me waiting for him in the Globe, the solace of my old haunt a comfort to my degrading set of affairs.

Charles was consulting his pocket watch as he entered the Globe, the glass panelled double doors swinging closed behind him. I observed him as he fanned out his overcoat and smoothed down the ruffled waistcoat that attempted to constrict his ample frame. His eyes scanned the patrons until they came to rest upon me, the look in his eyes akin to a child being reunited with a lost toy.

I was rewarded for my supposed loyalty to Charles with a permanent roof over my head, his fleeting chance encounters not enough to sustain his need for my company. He had rented rooms at two Priory Street, Kentish Town, I was to be his mistress hauled up in lodgings of my own. Despite the anticipation that this would result in regular meetings Charles maintained his once weekly visits to me. His timing predictable and appetite unchanging. Unbeknown to Charles the man that shared the bed he paid for had helped to move it in, both working in unison for my benefit.

My disposition had positively improved since I found stability at the hands of Charles however boredom as hovering in the background and the anger that I felt bubbling under the surface was released in small bursts of cruelty or acts of wanton prostitution, my nails ripping into flesh under the guise of passion. Why had Malt chosen to leave me, to start a new life away from all that he had known, no mistrust had befallen him, he was a free man.

I still made infrequent visits home, whenever the desire caught me I would find myself walking the familiar cobbles of Maroon Street, the environment as bland as when I resided there. I was mostly greeted with the strained civilities from mother, genuine affection of my siblings and a gruff response should father be home. I was delighted that on one visit mother had in her possession a letter that had been addressed to me and travelled across the vast ocean judging from the stamped marks, but it had been prised open, its contents revealed to another. Mother begrudgingly handed over the envelope with no explanation as to why the contents had been riffled.

The letter was in the fair hand of my Malt, I recognised his scribble from the anatomy notes comprehensively complied. The contents were informative, leaving me with a pang of jealously that he had escaped the clutches of justice, no reference to our past was made. His success in Malta had been recognised by the neighbouring country of Spain and he was to be dispatched for service in Madrid, an address to follow in due course.

My thirst for ale would find me partaking in a merry tipple most days, I alternated the bars that I frequented so that my presence would not become customary in any establishment, determined not to repeat a pattern of behaviour that would lead my suitor onto a path of suspicion that would end my reign as his chosen lover and find me with no place to lay my head, left with the prospect of a life lived in one of the many workhouses that blighted the landscape.

A chance series of fortunate events transpired to bring me into contact with the man that would truly steal my heart. I was to know a devotion that superseded any that I had known so far, with the exception of my dearest Malt, the childhood closeness of my family, the young love of Alastair Ramsey all paled in comparison to the rhyme of the beat that my heart danced to when his eyes fell upon my person.

My relationship with Mr Frank Samuel Hogg was passionate and all-consuming on my behalf, I craved his attention and pined for him when we were apart. I wholeheartedly believed that true loves kiss had been planted upon my lips. I bequeathed him with a latchkey so that he could gain entry without raising the house, keeping his visits shrouded in secrecy so that our immoral intercourse would continue undisturbed and I could leave letters for him should I be absent when he called.

To alert Frank to my availability the candle reappeared in my window, a calling card that I knew to be an effective means of communication. Mindful that this practice was my downfall with John and the means in which I would inform Charles that he was permitted to visit.

Frank's business was as impressive as his cards, he also had printed stationary of a receipt book that was embossed with his name, address and trade and it featured a tiny intricate horse and cart piled high with furniture, a picture aid for those impressed with the finery or illiterate to transcribe the wording. His cart was of a strong construction, the wheels as tall as a man with lengths of ropes coiled like snakes ready to wrap around another's belongings, a sheet of material forming a parasol to protect the objects from natures interference.

He kept the cart at the livery where he housed the magnificent beasts that pulled his livelihood. There was no indication of maltreatment, their coats were as smooth as silk with a shine that glittered in the sun, their manes groomed, a feathering of hair cascading down each hoof. Both were a chocolate brown with a white blaze down their long noses, their mouths as wrinkled as an old mans with white whiskers in a bristly beard.

The two horses in his employment were named Rusty and Harley they possessed more decoration then any woman I had yet to encounter, polished silverware made up their bridles and was studded along the straps that connected them to the cart, leather blinkers hid their eyes, dark whirlpools of terror staring through long thick lashes, glimpses of white as they surveyed their surroundings. Their powerful thick necks supported a harness that was coated in leather and weighed that of a cumbersome child. The creatures stood as tall as me, petting them reminded me of the horses up at Kenwood House, of Cookie, of Alastair, of Dr Lee.

Despite an upturn in my fortune the blackness was only ever an upset away, hovering just behind me like a shadow. I was not always strong enough to show the restraint that I used to keep the shadow at bay and it would rear its ugly head, striking out at an innocent bystander or trying to drown itself with a gallon of ale. Malt had abandoned me again; no word had been received since his relocation from Italy to Spain and the request that he had made for me to secure passage to his newest destination was a future that was beyond my grasp. I had not the saving to purchase a ticket nor an address to seek once the ship had docked.

A rather curious sight met me on an early July afternoon as I gazed out of the window of one of the many taverns, a great gathering of women, consisting mostly of adolescent girls, moved like a flock of gulls towards the heart of the city. Curious as to the cause of the movement I necked the remaining liquid in my glass and went outside to better observe the proceedings. From the tone of the conversation as the woman passed, their numbers must have been several hundred, the protest was centred upon the ill treatment of some fellow workers, the conditions at the Bryant and May match factory had been condemned by a radical female journalist of whom the women were seeking out for further help in addressing the deplorable conditions in which they worked. The term 'white slavery' was banned around by many a woman although I'm sure the strike would only serve to anger the exploiters and place their employment in jeopardy. The outcome was played out in the papers for those that wished to follow the trials and trepidations, the ineffective plight of previous strikers as well as the eventual victor.

I was still enamoured with the idea of using an unfamiliar area of London in which to seek out basic pleasure or to carry out devious deeds as I would not be recognised with ease and could pass unobserved by most should I choose not to draw any attention to my direction. Whitechapel held for me the briefest of memories of Malt without the painful sting of everyday encounters to trigger my recall that were littered throughout Mile End.

I was not grieved to leave behind the streets of my

childhood, nor was I concerned with the distance that had grown in miles and love between myself and my family. I had settled into the life of Kentish Town with great ease, the markets flourished with an abundance of wares and the community was not as closely packed as that of a few miles East, the conditions a slight improvement on the slums that bred children and pestilence. Besides, I cared little for the trains, that hurtled both above and below the ground, there painted wooden carriages and black engines speeding through the city although it did offer a speed that could not be matched by the legs of a human or a horse and the hustle and bustle meant that I could anonymously travel great distances in a short period of time and provided an insight into the key features of human nature for it was all on show for those that looked deep enough.

By the rule of thumb, I would board the train at the Midland branch of the Great Northern Railway and ride the rails as it carved a sweeping path, departing at the Broad Street Terminus off Liverpool Street. The carriages were lined with panels of glass through which the world past in a blur, rows of seats allowed over two dozen to ride in any single carriage which were illuminated by candlelight, the rhythmic rocking motion of the engine hypnotic but sickly. I had chosen this destination as it afforded a comfortable walk from the sights and smells of Whitechapel to the East, the financial heart of the city to the South, the affluent Finsbury with buildings as tall as a tower and streets wide enough to accommodate five horses and carts abreast with monuments that honoured past deities to the West but little to interest a person to the North with the exception of the police courts which could be rather entertaining.

The day stated as any other with the exception of the presence of another in my bed as I woke. It was a rarity that Charles stayed the duration of the night, often being gone before my senses had been aroused, returning to whatever manner of living allowed him to keep a mistress housed and feed. As a parting gift I rode his erect member for the few minutes that it took to bring him to the point of ecstasy, his hips throwing my balance as he exploded inside me. A content Mr Creighton whistled his satisfaction as he glided into the bright morning sun, I contemplated what I would do to pass the day away.

After perusing the market stalls that lined the streets of Camden Town I decided to venture away from the area, my intention to stop and explore the offerings of an area I had yet to discover but I found myself disembarking at the now familiar terminus of Broad Street. The weather in my mind was changing, the blue sky was diminishing, the rain clouds blowing in to eclipse the sun and darken my mood. The splendour of Finsbury was not enough to draw me, and I had no desire to act as imposter amongst the elite, so I ventured into the barely familiar territory of Whitechapel, settling on a public house named Two Brewers which was patronised by whores, drunks as well as many infantry personnel. I could find no peace so moved on to the White Swan which stood tall and proud on the High Street of Whitechapel.

I was left to my own devices for the most part, a few hopeful men dispatched with a flea in their ear for it was my heart and mind that needed tending, not my flesh. I could find no peace, the ale offered little healing to my soul and the dreadful caterwauling from the two whores attempting to seduce a couple of uniform clad officers was grating my temper.

The wretched old whore Martha and her degenerate associate who referred to herself as Pearly Polly had given my ear little rest and I was in no mood for their shenanigans. The time had come when she should be remedied for inflicting upon us her reproachable character and diabolical scent, a sweeter smell had been breathed from the banks of the Thames.

As I formulated a plan for her demise they sat about a jug of beer like two haggard old crones around a cauldron, formulating their own plan, one to secure the temporary affection of a willing participant with enough coins in their pocket.

My plan was simple, to follow the drunken whore with the intention of delivering her a thrashing for her insolence and vulgarity. I was hindered by the fact that she left in the company of both Polly and the two uniformed officers.

A discussion ensued where by the woman haggled a price

for their laycocks, departing in opposing directions, a solider per whore. Martha disappeared, giggling like a child, with her meal ticket into the shady area known as George Yard. A filthy alley inhabited with the dredges of society, rats and waste had stolen my prey. Content to bide my time I concealed myself in the shadows in the event that an opportunity may present itself before the night came to an end.

I could detect the distinct groans and feigned pleasure of a man relieving his natural tendencies as Martha earned her keep right there in the alley, against a stone wall already stained with urine. The intercourse lasted as long as the negotiation that proceeded it but her client would detain Martha for some time yet, she would end the solicitation on her knees, her body ravaged by flesh and blade. I was considering abandoning my task as it seemed the soldier's appetite was insatiable when I was alerted to a struggle, the tone had changed from satisfaction to distress, a scream of pain echoed around the yard but brought no attention to her plight. Before the echoes had died they were matched with the ringing of heavy footsteps as the solider made a hasty retreat. I stayed hidden for the most part of an hour, but the arrival of the constables did not prevail and no person residing in the buildings made any attempt to discover the source of the shriek.

My feet had gone numb from staying in the same position for such a period of time, I shook them out whilst deciding how I would proceed. Curiosity drove to me to the site in which Martha lay, her body slummed against the wall, a kick of my boot against her own informed me that she was not yet slain, there was still life in this aged hussy despite a wound that had penetrated her breast bone for blood that stained her dress from an incision that penetrated through the fabric and into her chest. My plan could still be executed.

My plot spewed out of mouth in a web of deceit, first the offer of help, to assist her into George buildings where a friend would provide a tipple to numb the pain whilst I sought help from a medical practitioner so her live may be spared.

The worthless bag of flesh was heavy with ale and the burden of injury and the struggle to bring her to her feet almost defeated me, but perseverance saw her on her feet, waddling at a cripple's pace to the door that she thought would be her deliverance. To ensure that Martha was suitably away from prying eyes we negotiated the wide stone steps that lead to the first-floor landing, the hand rail a convenient aid that allowed me to reposition my strength to just the one side of the great bulk giving leverage to propel us up the rock mountain. I had no need for fear as the lights had been extinguished some hours previous and the sinister surroundings had been plunged into darkness. Martha was struggling for breath, her ample size and the wound in her chest making her progress painfully slow.

As we evened out onto the flat surface of the flagstones I took the opportunity to retrieve the blade I had hidden and lodge in her belly. The hunched position I was in due to her weight bearing down on me and the angle in which I held the blade, the handle clasped in mine as a baby would hold a rattle, made for the perfect motion in which I could deliver 6 orchestrated incisions.

I had managed to incapacitate her, as Martha's grip on my shoulder loosened and she slid to the floor, with a loose grip on consciousness from the initial attack she was now rendered quite senseless. In a simultaneous movement I pushed her backwards resulting in the used four-penny knee trembler resembling a position in which she spent much of her working life, on her back with her legs spread eagle. As I stood back to admire the scene that I had prepared a gurgle of breath escaped her lips, her eyes desperate to focus on the angle of death that stood forebodingly above her. A frenzied assault would put an end to the wretched beast and it would take a further 15 repetitive blows that I concentrated on her torso before she released her deplorable grip on this world. A final slit in her throat completed the task, her dark hair a bed for the river of blood that ran over it. I took quite a fancy to Martha's worn, but attractive black bonnet but thought better of the notion to retain it for fear of being identified, the clothes were too ample for my frame and the boots were as worn as the owner, but it did grieve me to leave behind the bonnet.

I found it surprising how easy it was to penetrate human flesh, how little force was required, the fabric a more obstinate obstacle than the skin. It was different from stripping the bones which was a detached experience, little different from that of a joint of meat and the attack on Fairy Fay was not a premeditated murder of which I had prepared myself, this time it was planned, colourful, exhilarating.

I was quite exhausted by the time I halted my unprovoked attack and the position that Martha had fallen gave me the notion to arrange the body so that suspicion would fall upon the male of the species, the murder would look like rape should much of an investigation be instigated. There would be no reason to look for a woman, besides we had not exchanged a word and scarcely a glance and I had used the cover of shadows to move from the pub to the yard.

I was again stranded and homeless in the streets of Whitechapel. The apron that I wore so that no trace of blood would fall upon my person was folded and held beneath my dress and the murder weapon, the evidence of my guilt was nestled snugly back within my boot, the cold blade pressed safely against my skin. I would wash the stains from the apron when I returned home, blaming any residue on a cut that I could replicate if the situation called for it. My preparation in place to avoid detection and a chapter of evasion about to commence in my life.

10

By the time my deed was done I had missed any possibility of travelling home by train, so I sought out an old refuge to sleep away my inebriated state and wallow in my actions. The arch of St. Georges which had once been my salvation. Next time I would have funds enough to secure lodgings for the night. The morning brought the arrival of the sun but also the stains of blood that had transferred from victim to perpetrator the previous night. My presence had not yet been discovered so I pounced on the desertion to ensure that my appearance was consistent with an attack, of which I survived but could offer no details for prosecution should I be asked. The slash from my wrist to elbow of my left arm, made expertly to avoid any major blood loss, was my alibi, the source of my blood-soaked clothing.

The morning also brought the news of a murder in Whitechapel, a night worker had been brutally slain, and the perpetrator had evaded capture, no suspect was in custody, the murderer was at large to strike again.

I ambled past the entrance to George Yard, the menacing archway a portal to an alley that last night saw acts that would bring both the start and end to life, mindful that I carried on me the proof of my crime. In the light of day, it was teaming with constables dressed head to toe in black and topped with a hat that resembled a woman's stimulated breast, broken up by the eager monocle clad journalists that would sensationalise the murder across the papers that littered the city. They confirmed the date of extinction to be 7th August and that the victim as one Martha Tabram of Marshall Street, estranged wife of Henry Samuel Tabram. The residents of George building had been cornered like rats, being asked questions that nobody could provide an adequate answer for, collaborating their own alibis or reasoning that Martha resembled that a homeless drunk who had sought shelter within the building so was aptly ignored by those that encountered her motionless form. The mystery of Martha's demise would remain, my act and her passing chalked up to a dissatisfied punter or a creditor who took his payment as a pound of flesh.

The universal sticking knife formed part of the gift that Malt had left behind for me to discover. I had given it a cursory wipe over with the apron to remove Martha's blood, but the blade was turning black, Malt had told me that it had some connection to the oxygen within the blood reacting to the metal of the blade.

As it happened I made the return journey to Priory Street without any person making an enquiry as to my appearance, two well dressed women did happen upon my person, exchanging notions as to the source of the blood, stemming from a woman of ill repute to the victim of an assault but settling on the assertion that I was the deliverer of offspring, a midwife, the blood the only piece of evidence to support the proposal, no bag of instruments, no clothing consistent with medical care but with funds enough to travel by rail. The apron had not proven as discreet as I had hoped that it had. I would put their idle chat to good use in the future, a plausible career that coincided with my skills and determination to deliver a scornful retribution on the undeserving, it was just unfortunate for those that would be in the wrong place at the wrong time. Besides I had learnt from Dr Lee that a position of power could hide horrendous crimes in plain sight, so the guise of midwifery would benefit the adulterous men as well as offer me a modicum of protection from detection.

Life returned to normal, as if nothing had happened. The murder was discussed little, if at all, amongst the people of Kentish Town, the likes of such a crime reserved for the hovels and unlicensed brothels of their neighbouring kin.

I had nobody at home in which to answer too so my staying out all night passed as unnoticed as the murder.

Charles continued to visit once a week, like clockwork, no

number of pleas could persuade him otherwise.

My love for Frank was as bottomless as the deepest well, a melancholy ache would descend when I had not been in his presence and I longed for him to make me his fully, but he was reserved in matters of the heart, not as eager as I to see it joined in union with another, or so it thought.

The intercourse was still as passionate as the day I presented myself to him, but his advancing years laid pay to the lengthy sessions that I enjoyed at the hands of the much younger John. His strength depleted after a day of physical labour.

As we approached the end of the August Franks mood had altered to the point that I could no longer ignore that change in his demeanour. A coolness had come upon him, the source I could not put my finger on. When we were alone he was the Frank Hogg of my dreams, the man that I yearned for above all others.

I had been dissuaded from seeking him at his address, instead being forced to orchestrate chance meetings or wait for him to acknowledge my flaming signal. He did not deny that he had feelings for my person but had not returned the gesture of love that I had worn upon my sleeve.

The day that Frank informed me he had another was devastating, I was crushed more than I thought humanly possible. The departure of Malt from my life paled in comparison to the gut wrenching feeling that was running amok inside my chest. I learnt that the betrayal involved a woman by the name of Phoebe, but I was prevented from venting my frustration on her for fear of losing all connection to Frank, as it stood I still had his body if not all his heart, both I would have to be content with sharing until I had formulated a fool proof plan to remove her from the equation. Frank took what was on offer, my tears dripped into our mouths as we embraced, the taste of salt upon my tongue was mixed with the bitter sweet scent of cologne and sweat that added to the appeal of Frank. With a heart that had been as trampled as the mud under the hoof of a horse I saw Frank to my door. I watched his back as he walked away into the arms of another, a backward glance was the glimmer of hope that all was not lost for me, that I still had a part to play, a space to fill.

Stewing in my own self-pity the sadness that hung about my person soon changed to anger, my temper was frayed and my nerves fraught at the disclosure that Frank had laid at my feet. I set out, apron and knife in hand, to exact my revenge and to vent my wrath on some worthless blight on our society.

Without hesitation, I boarded the train on the now familiar route, to the destination that had provided both prey and anonymity, the sway of the carriage as it hurtled along the track moved my body, but my mind was unmoved, set on the course of action that would end the life of another. As before I would target those that would not be missed, as common as rats there was an abundance of unfortunate souls who would either join the angels in heaven or consort with the devil in hell.

In my search I passed the archway that lead to George yard, no flower nor memorial marked the place that Martha departed the Earth, her memory already forgotten. I called into the Two Brewers public house as I knew that it was frequented by the despicable degenerates. I was not disappointed by the patrons, one of which was Pearly Polly, the demise of her friend a distant memory, the knowledge of her fate no deterrent to those who used their bodies to eke out a living. Although the pickings were high I felt an unease at Polly's presence so decided to find another haunt. I made my way up the wide pavements of Whitechapel Road, the awning on the buildings hanging over the shop fronts like the peak on a corduroy cap topping the head of a young boy.

Even though the hour was late there were still carriages being pulled through the streets, clusters of women made the most of the last hour of light, huddling beneath the street lamps with thread and garment in hand to make an honest living, the night workers at the start of their day lurked in doorways, smiling at potential punters.

I had been fraught several times when my prey had been intercepted by the offer to relieve their impending money woes, forced to watch as they disappeared into an alley or through a doorway to pleasure the gentleman that had paid for the privilege.

At the Earl of Warwick, a bar of polished wood and mounted bottles offered a reprieve to the challenge of the night. Two women who were deep in conversation had noticed my solo status and taken it upon themselves to involve me in their lives. I would learn that they went by the names Mary Nichols and Ellen Holland. Mary, my name sake, was once a picture of perfection, an attractive woman with the love of a good man and the gracious gift of five healthy offspring but her love of alcohol had stripped her of her family, and her front teeth, the precious life so desired by many was squandered for the sake of drink. The remnants of her beauty and a life that once was were still evident in her demeanour for she held herself upright and talked with an air that screamed educated and she still retained the porcelain complexion beneath the lines that pitted her face, the scar on her forehead from a childhood accident a striking identifiable mark.

Ellen was a cockney born and bred, her accent as thick as the mud of the Thames, every hard year of her life was etched on her face for the world to see yet she had a manner that was maternal and affectionate. Her ill fortune had led her to living in the same lodging house as Mary, the unpredictable earnings enough to secure a bed for the night in the common building at Thrawl Street, one of hundreds that served the touring causal workers of the East End, working when and where the money pulled them.

No matter the ploy I used I could not separate the two friends. By Mary's own admission she had spent the evenings doss money on the drink that had flowed into the night so took leave to earn the pennies she would need to pay the landlady. My chance had finally come, as not to appear too eager and raise the alarm the following day I remained in the company of Ellen, half listening to her stories of growing up in the slums, parallels to my own life passed me by as my mind was preoccupied with how I could extract myself in a timely fashion. A few quarts later provided me with the opportunity to take my leave, hopeful that I would encounter the other Mary on her return journey. Ellen's bladder was the ticket to my departure, using her biological need to expel the liquid I thanked her for her courteous friendship, ensuring that the knife was secure in my boot I wrapped my shawl over my head and headed out into a street that was relatively deserted, save for the usual passage of people, now in darkness.

Although I was becoming accustomed to the street names and layout of Whitechapel I was still a stranger to the area and was not privy to the locations that could hide an illicit act from prying eyes and I knew not where this lodging house was that Ellen and Mary had talked off. I was considering calling time on finding Mary, disgruntled that the idyllic candidate had escaped my justice.

All was not yet lost, I could change tack and take another in Marys place, but a familiar voice rang through the street. At first, I thought that I was made, my name screeched into the humid autumn sky but before I could answer another replied. The owner I also recognised, it was Mary, the woman who I had searched the streets. The shadows hid my person, my dark clothing abetting the illusion of invisibility. The two women argued, their voices raised, Ellen pleading with Mary to return with her to the lodging house, but Mary was insistent that she had no money to her name owing to her having "pissed it all away" and would not return, for she had earned her four pence at least twice over but had none left. Ellen, defeated, threw her arms in the air and watched as her friend drunkenly stumbled away up the road. I too left Ellen alone, subjugated, on the corner of Osborn Street. Like a cat stalking its prey I pursued this silver haired vixen waiting for the moment to pounce.

Mary was not only drunk but agitated by her own irresponsibility, ale steering her directions.

It was child's play to coax her on the pretence that I had accommodation that would cost nothing for the night, the groundwork of an introduction already achieved.

I took the nearest road that ran parallel to Whitechapel Road, heading towards the Great Eastern Square which would be too populated for my deed to be carried out, so I veered off along a darkened street that I would later find out went by the name of Bucks Row. The houses that lined one side of Bucks row where similar in appearance to that in which John Pearcey lives, two stories of blackened brick, a bland row of uniform fronts that gave rise to tall warehouses, a gated yard separating residential from industrial, the lights in every window extinguished, the inhabitants asleep or away on some errand of business or pleasure. The imposing factory buildings were as deserted as the street, quiet as a church mouse and idle before a day of trade would breath life and noise into the dismal structures with the exception of a few trades that worked through the night, the men in the slaughterhouses as bloody as the scene outside would become.

Mary was beginning to make protest that she knew of no lodgings in this vicinity forcing me to act, exposed to any that may blunder into the street. The gated yard provided an appropriate opportunity for I feigned a fainting fit, falling dramatically into the railings of the gate, using it as a support as well as a prop in which to snare my prey. The small but lethal blade camouflaged against the bars of the gate pointed towards the sky like Cleopatra's needle. Mary played her part well, she fell for the trickery and came quickly to my aid. Like a noble stead she bore the weight, my left armed draped across her shoulder, as we made to move away from the gateway I swung my left hand down. With a sweeping circular motion, the blade came heaven wards and slit the throat of the whore that held me. The incision near ear to ear, the wound opening in a yawn as a choker of red swelled to the surface. It all happened in an instant that could not be undone, a fluid motion that lasted mere seconds.

I was already hunched from the burden of supporting her, the body fell in a natural inclination, twisting towards me as I aided her release to the ground. Her grey eyes held the haunting look of shock as they locked onto mine, widening as she gurgled her last bloody breaths. The incision in her throat rendering her speechless, her dying screams only heard in her own mind. Scarlet blood trickled from her mouth and leaked down her chin to join with the river that flowed from her throat. Having learnt from Martha that it required exertion to penetrate the tightly woven fabric of clothing I pulled up her loose-fitting dress and grey woollen petticoat to expose her ample abdomen with the intention of displaying her internal finery for all too see, exposing the warm insides that had cradled her five children of which she had rendered custody to her estranged husband. I would show the world the workings of this cold heartless harlot. Her black knitted stockings required the expert handling of a fellow female to part them as they had been already on several occasions that night.

Using both hands to grip the smooth handle, one clasped around the wood, the other clasped around i's twin I sunk my weapon into her flesh. It sunk in as easily as penetrating an apple, the skin parting to expose the fatty tissue as I ran the blade down, exiting her body as it fell away between her legs. It felt like what I would imagine slicing open a sack of grain, albeit the insides did not spill out as the grain would from the sack. The blade was almost blunted on the hard stone floor for the extreme force that I used must have penetrated to her very core, her gullet a wet body of flesh cushioning the bony snake of her spine. The cuts that lined the stomach were jagged and not as smooth as I would have desired, the skin ripped open like a ladder in stockings, my frustration taken out in a childish tantrum as I stabbed at her laycock before concentrating my efforts on her abdomen.

Spooked by a noise in the distance I froze like a thief caught red handed, the blade in my hand dripping red droplets onto the floor. Footsteps came no nearer but it was enough of a scare to take my leave for I had no desire to meet with any of the workers or carriage-men that would soon use the thoroughfare to commence a day in their mundane lives. I pulled down the dress, smoothing it out so that the concealed incision would be a surprise for the inspector or mortician and biding me more time to abscond in the hopes that she would be mistaken for a drunk sleeping of the effects of the night before. The true intention to expose the tart for an undeserving existence known only to myself. Casting one last glance at the woman that lay silent on the dirty floor, in death she looked different to in life, I had known her no more than twenty-four hours but the brief time that I had spent in her company her foul features had been etched into my mind, every wrinkle committed to memory.

Essentially, she looked the same, in a troubled sleep, retaining the same characteristics she had taken on a surreal appearance, an unrealistic colour had invaded her skin, her face lost all animation but was neither sunken nor puffy but altered from that which I knew.

I escaped unseen, the thrill of the kill coursing through my veins I found no pull to the world of sleep so instead I traced a path down to the docks, content to linger among the mongers as they began to organise their pitch, the smell an assault on my senses that stimulated my feeling of vitality. The cold of the steel blade pressed against the thin stocking that separated my ski from chaffing on the leather of my boots, the apron, which I had no time to secure in place now provided the cover for the evidence that stained by dark dress, the dark fabric adding to conceal the blood that had flowed. I could pass as any number of professions from servant to nurse, invisible amongst the throng of early morning hustle and bustle.

The body would be found and removed before a group of spectators who would retell the vision of the murdered woman for days to come, the blood washed from the paving stones, but a stain left on Whitechapel like the bloat of ink on a parchment. Women, and men alike, would talk in hushed tones about the murder, a few already making comparisons with the bodies that had been discovered to date, but most was idle gossip about the brash nature or mental integrity of the perpetrator, never an accusing glance was cast my way. A slight smile would tease at the corner of my mouth as I revealed in the knowledge that I was the one that held the knife that was beginning to grip the fear and imagination of the residents of the Eats End. My wayward ways were spiralling in a direction that I was reluctant to be pulled but would follow with a determination to rid the world of my adversaries.

The newspapers carried varying details of the murder, printed amongst the reported crimes of day but I was yet to make the front page. I would have to try harder if they were to become as notorious as Mary Ann Cotton, Burke and Hare or Mary Bateman, the Yorkshire Witch. Some papers attempted to convey the squalor through descriptive writings so that those who had not the pleasure of a first-hand experience could derive some of the seedy and dangerous conduct amongst i's streets. The name Mary being perhaps doomed for a life of depravity and outlawed behaviour for many a Mary had fallen from grace, myself included, the burden to bare for a name that was two a penny to come by.

I found the East London Gazette to be a monger for stirring up the public, attempting to instil a feeling of insecurity amongst its readers, pondering on how women could be "foully and horribly killed", that the villain had disappeared without a trace and that the women were victims of a 'wilful murder by some person, or persons, unknown'. The Star newspaper tarnished the Jews with the murder providing a truly frightening description of a sadistic killer with shifty eyes, a repellent grin and an ancestry distinctly Hebrew for no

Englishman could commit such atrocity. They even went as far as to accuse a local racketeer who was given the moniker "Leather Apron" as being the murderer. His practices were certainly deplorable, and he was a despised character among the prostitutes that he hoodwinked but he was not responsible for the Whitechapel slaughter.

I did make my mark in the black printed front page of the police news albeit I had to share the space with four other murderers, their images illustrated for the whole of England to peruse but I had the wait of a whole week. The artist affording Mary with a beauty that she did not possess in life, the inquest played out like an illustrated play set in the Whitechapel mortuary, the moustached characters drawn with an ornate background of swirling detail, educated gentlemanly folk discussing the gruesome details of the slaughter, attempting to establish facts from the witnesses and derive clues the body.

Franks affections for another had bitten at my insides, I felt cold internally just thinking about him touching her, my feelings of hurt and inadequacy would be defeated by anger, the fiery tentacles fuelled the jealously at the root of my predicament. I was being kept at arm's length for I did not know where he lay his head at night, he had access to my home and my heart, but I knew not where he resided.

I was aware that the dark illness had crept upon me, yet I felt no inclination to improve my mood and my actions only served to hold me under the dark stream of despair. The whole experience was not the same without Malt, it lacked the joint enterprise of selecting a deserving victim, the thickening of the bond that occurred with each kill could not be derived from a solo act and I could share with no one the thoughts that it stirred, the glory was sour without a kindred spirit to share it with. The notion of finding a new partner had crossed my mind on several occasions but there was none I could think of in which my soul was content to be placed at their mercy. An assumption from a journalist that the supposed the killer was a male gave me the idea that I could don a male person. It would be a work of ease to obtain a gentleman's coat and hat so any eavesdropper to the crime would suspect it the work of a male for why would a female masquerade in a gentleman's clothing? It would be an ode to represent my dear Malt, he could be at my side in spirit if not in person.

I had not ventured home for several days instead finding temporary lodgings at a common house situated at twenty-nine Hanbury Street, just off of Old Brown's Lane in Spitalfields, a hovel run by a portly woman by the name of Mrs Richardson who cared little to whom the rooms were let provided that the fee was paid, and no nuisance was caused. The house in appearance was the grandest residence, with the obvious exception of Kenwood House, that I had stepped foot in. It was arranged over four floors and had more souls in residence than mice, every square inch inhabited, even the roof had been made into living space. I must have seen some good twenty people pass through the front door that was never locked on account of the frequent comings and goings of the lodgers.

I was spared the cost on one night as I shared the bed of Mr John Davis, a man that was as short in stature as in his manhood. All I had to do was part my legs to save the cost of my lodgings and I was pickled from the last few days of drinking to excess to offer a care. All it took was a few minutes of puffing and thrusting on his behalf to satisfy his need, his face pinched with an expression that looked more painful than lustful, but he finished in the usual spray of warm. It was an uncomfortable night in the small bed, his balding head nestled into my breasts was more of an inconvenience than a comfort and he rose before the sun although he did not turn me out of his bed.

Mr Davis rented the front attic room and dressed as quietly as a man trained in stealth, his footsteps hardly audible as he descended the four flights of stairs that wound through the house. Under the cover of darkness, I sought out the Pearcey butchers, creeping into the yard I unlatched the door to the outhouse that Malt had used for his medical practice and to store the tools of his family's trade. I stole the sharpening knife from its hook, the long-pointed metal hard to conceal but the theft essential to ensure the weapons of my trade did not become blunt.

A lack of funds and a personal aroma that had become intolerable forced me back to Priory Street where upon I discovered that Frank had visited and, in my absence, left behind the letters that I had written to him. Although grieved that he had not retained them it had been our agreement that they be returned to me after he had digested the contents so in his defence he was only honouring my wishes. He had written no letter in return.

William Butler from upstairs expressed his dismay that the light in the hall had remained unlit in my absence and that he had suffered an injury to his foot that he blamed me for due to the passageway being in darkness. I was in no mood to be spoken down to and informed him that, although the light had been put up to my expense I supplied the oil and would light it if and when I choose but would try to inform them I was to be absent. The simple work of a flame had been both a calling card and a means of communication, each location offering a different meaning. The flame that flickered in the back room alerted Frank to the fact that I was out and would not be expected back shortly.

After I had washed and dressed in cleaner clothes I went on the hunt for my love but could not find him. He was not in any of the shops in King Street, nor was he at any of the public houses or venues that I searched. With a heart heavy from failure I returned home and lit the candle that illuminated my window in the hopes that Frank would find me instead. He did not. The following morning proved to be a fruitless endeavour, Franks presence in Camden was still non-existent which only served to anger my already melancholy mood. My temper led me to my now familiar stomping ground, everyday a chance meeting could seal my fate or perhaps I would encounter some demon who had made his lair in Whitechapel and I would become a victim as stone cold a poor old Mary Nichols.

Mr Davis found me in a stupor, barely coherent and knuckles bloodied from an altercation with a fellow drunk who had desires on my person which were unwarranted and unwelcome. I had a vague recollection for being dragged up the endless steps that led up the heights of Hanbury Street, my bed again paid for by the kindness of another. My intoxicated state no deterrent from Mr Davis taking his payment, his small cock wiggling like a worm inside me. I woke before John was due to rise for work and contemplated what I should do next. The room was as dark as my mind and had I brought with me the tools I had wielded with such voracity I should doubt that Mr Davis would have turned up at his employment, today or on any day. I extracted myself from his clammy grip causing him to stir but not wake. I had no idea of the time, but the sun was yet to rise, and the streets were absent from the sound of carts and hooves, so the merchants were still hold up in their beds for the time being. I was not as gentile in my negotiation of the stairs, my head was afire with last night's alcohol and my leg ached with a bruise that I must have sustained whilst ascending them the previous evening. My knuckles throbbed from the battering that I had inflicted upon them and my scalp was sore under my bonnet from the clumps of hair that had last night been in the fists of another.

As I came upon the first floor landing I could hear a hushed conversation from the ground floor, but I could not hear it in its entirety, the male voice did not possess a local dialect and the female voice carried a pleading tone. From my vantage point I could see a short, plump woman standing in the doorway, her hair a mass of wild curls, her body racked periodically with convulsions of violent coughing. I could not determine her age, but she spoke with the tone of a woman in her forties and from her profile she had a bulbous nose that extended far from her face. I could not see clearly the gentleman that she was speaking with, but her pleas seemed to be falling on deaf ears for he did not permit her past the threshold.

I tried the door nearest to me and it opened with a slight creak. Frozen to the spot as I listened for any sign that the occupants had awoken I kept an ear on the murmurings from the lower floor as I observed the contents of the room, lit golden with the flame of a small candle. The room was sparsely furnished, and the bed seemed to contain the mounds of two bodies, a cradle with a sleeping infant an arm's reach away. The crockery stood by the basin, stained with the food from last night's supper, the silver blade of a carving knife catching the flame as it danced from the draft from the open door. The floor creaked under my weight as I moved as silently as possible, praying that I could retrieve the makeshift weapon and make my exit before my presence was detected. I closed the door, concealed the blade and descended the final set of stairs.

By the time I reached the narrow passageway that led from the front to the back of the house the woman was alone, using the doorway to prop herself up. It looked like she was suffering from an aliment and her face was potted with bruises, she was a sorry sight and looked worse than even I felt. It would be a mercy to put her out of her misery, one that I would be happy to oblige. With a kind word of a room I offered to assist the woman in her moment of need, she begrudgingly accepted though insisted on making her own way which only served to be an advantage as she unwittingly headed in the direction of the backyard.

With the suggestion that the back-door lead to another room she was easily fooled until the door was opened and she realised that she had been duped. She spun around, her face twisted in rage at my deceit but before she could utter a word I grabbed her by the face, my fingernails digging into her chin then planted a foot squarely in her abdomen propelling her though the doorway. Her ample frame brought her onto the flagstone like a sack of spuds and her head hit the ground with a thud but did not spill onto the ground. No curtains twitched, and no movement could be seen from any of the windows, so I dragged the body by the ruffles at her collar into the corner and set to work. The blow to her head had rendered her senseless so I knew that she would not alert anyone by screaming but time was of the essence and I had not a moment to lose.

I could tell from her shallow breathing that she was alive, so I positioned myself at the base of the steps and slit her throat. It was as easy as cutting through a pie crust. As I had done before I lifted her dress to expose her sagging flesh, I felt for the ribcage then sunk the knife into her, ripping a jagged line from her stomach to her privates. Blood immediately swelled to the surface of the incision. I placed my hands back to back and pushed them into the cut quickly pealing the skin apart to lay open the jumble of insides. I wiped my hands clean on the exposed underside of her frock, the warm blood smearing across my own skin. A moment of childish fancy came upon me and I began pulling out the organs, scattering the tube parts across her shoulders as if they were confetti. My mood snapped in an instant and the anger that seemed ever present, bubbling just below the surface erupted. I tugged at her womb, but it was held fast so I propped up her legs in the fashion of child birth to give the leverage I needed to extract the very organ that had nursed her unborn children.

As a final insult I tossed it over the fence and into the beyond. I left her there, lying beside the fence, her left arm resting across her chest, the other laying limp at her side and a ghastly expression of fright in her soulless eyes.

When the job was done and her life extinct I contemplated my next move. I could retreat through the house or make my exit through the backyard but choose instead to return to the top floor of Hanbury Street and reclaim the sleep that my body craved from its early morning exertion. I crept like a spook through the narrow passageway, each creak of a step making my heart pound harder, every second I took brought me closer to being caught but I made it undetected. My next task would be to hide the blade and return to my position in Mr Davis' bed. My boots made a suitable place to conceal the bloodied blade and my alibi was snoring soundly, unaware that I had absconded for any period of time. The bed moved undeniably as I repositioned myself beside John which caused him to half wake, but I was quick to ensure my eyes were closed, snuggling into him as if I were in a state of dream. The heat from my body and the thundering of my heart passed unnoticed as he was in a state of semi-conscious himself.

I had just started to fall asleep when John awoke and readied himself for a day at work, my mind contemplating the fact that I did not know what he did for a living and I had paid little attention to the man in general that I would have difficulty recalling what he wore or any information he had imparted upon me. He kissed me tenderly on the forehead before taking his leave, quietly exiting the room unaware of my true nature, my acting so good I could portray sleeping beauty on stage.

My peace lasted only a few minutes before a blood curdling cry echoed through the house, my handiwork had been discovered. Within half an hour the house was teaming with police and nearly every resident had been raised from their beds by the raucous. Desperate to escape justice I wiped the blade clean and set to washing off the blood that had dyed my hands scarlet, the underside of my frock a convenient and discrete towel. The bowl in which I had washed away my sins was now as bloody as the stones in the backyard. I disposed of the water by releasing it through the floorboards underneath Johns bed praying that it would not alert the occupants of the room below.

My challenge now was to escape the house itself, the only exit being the front door. I made my way precariously towards the lower stories of the property, passing appalled and senseless tenants as they made their way back to their lodgings, tearful that such a crime had been committed in their neighbourhood and thankful that they had not been the unfortunate soul who now lay cold and lifeless. They were too consumed in their own thoughts to question my presence and I passed as if I were a ghost. Upon reaching the first floor landing the door of the room in which I this morning snuck was ajar. I paused for a few seconds and listened at the door, all was quiet, so I seized the moment to hastily return the incriminating knife to where it belonged and crept back out, nobody any the wiser.

As I came to the tight passageway that ran the length of the house I gave a cursory glance towards the police and lodgers that were congregating at the back. A torch had been lit to illuminate the proceedings casting shadows across the walls. Most had their backs to me except one elderly and distinguished gentleman, his snow-white hair merging with an equally white beard that clung to only the bottom of his jaw. Before I could enquire as to the source of the commotion I was ushered out by a fledgling police constable concerned that the site of the body could cause a woman to falter and suffer sever shock. Lady luck had blessed me for I found myself on the street outside with not a single interrogation.

I took the earliest train on its weaving course back to Camden before retiring to my residence only to encounter Frank metres from my doorstep. The relief in his face at seeing me was evident, my heart lifted at the thought that he must care for me. Once inside he berated me as if I were a school girl for my flippant attitude in reply to his questioning of my whereabouts this last week then confessed that he feared I had become a victim of the uncaught perpetrator of the recent murder, and soon to be murders. I assured him that I had simply been assisting my mother with a sick relative who was now on the mend, so my services were no longer required.

He buried his thick yearning manhood into me, slowly savouring the feel of me as he expertly brought me to a heightened desire. He lay with me afterwards, his hot breath blowing across my neck while I ruffled his luscious mane of hair. He took his leave to commence a day of labour and return to *her*. I fell into a much needed yet fitful sleep, raising shortly after noon.

Refreshed from my slumber and satisfied in body I set to the task of securing myself some manly attire to dupe any potential witnesses and sway the blame. Camden was flooded with market stalls. Row upon crammed row were spread out across the town, I had my pick. Charles still afforded me a small allowance and Frank had left a few pennies so that I may fill my belly. Even though there was considerably more fabric and stitching the coat was the least costly of the two items I was to purchase. It cost me just shy of a florin as it had seen better days and would require a little handiwork on my part to return it to a resemblance of its former glory.

The vendor had not even questioned my purchases, no care for the destiny of the fabric, just consoled with the knowledge that he had money to take home that evening. I don't think he would even recognise me should the need arise for he was suffering from some aliment that rendered him poor of sight. I scurried home with the coat folded into a black parcel, trying to draw as little attention as possible and explain why a single woman had possession of a coat belonging to the opposing sex. I made the short journey uninterrupted and even managed to pilfer a pie from an unguarded cart, the merchant too distracted by a beautiful upper-class woman strutting by, her attire as fine as any peacocks, to pay heed to his livelihood.

I had hardly the time to hide the coat under my bed when an urgent rapping on my window startled me, causing me to let out a small cry. Through the curtains I made out the distinctive form of Charles. With a sigh, I went to admit him, his relief at seeing me as sure as Franks although he did not receive as enthusiastic a reception as I bestowed upon Mr Hogg. He too showed his relief in the form of taking me in my own bed. Unlike with Frank poor Charles stirred in me no feelings of wanton passion, I was simply going through well- rehearsed motions, my hips raising to meet his, my nails running a bored path down his back, releasing moans and groans on cue whist examining the texture of the ceiling. I could not deny him is gratification whilst I lived rent free at his doing. Leaving him exhausted in my bed I went to King Street to purchase a tea of fish and chips which I laid out on the table and a meal was had as if we were man and wife.

I returned to Hanbury Street on the arm of Mr Davis just a little over a week since the murder of the part-time whore whose name transpired to be Eliza Chapman although she was commonly known as Annie. I was in awe as well as disgusted that a charge was being made, and paid, to see the site of the infamous murder, the second Whitechapel slaying, it was profitable to house a crime scene, to earn a crust from the demise of another, such a deplorable characteristic! The temptation to turn over the profits paid by the grisly sightseers was strong, but I could not risk bringing any attention on my own person, nor could I dishonour those callous enough to set up such an enterprising business opportunity.

When Mr Davis was through with my company I ventured onto my original home turf as opposed to returning immediately to my residence in Priory Street. On the way, I encountered many young boys shouting about the recent murder, it's week long draw still attracting morbid curiosity. The campaign to arrest the assailant had been amplified from Mary's slaughter with the presence of more uniformed constables stalking the streets and posters plastered on walls and posts calling for the capture of Leather Apron and for everyone to be vigilant in the wake of the backyard murder. It did little to deter the trade in woman's bodies for the back streets were still littered with harlots dangling an exposed leg to entice the weak minded and candles shone from windows that I knew to be brothels.

My former home in Maroon Street was silent, not a soul was in residence, all must have been out working. I hung around for a while in the hopes that one of my family would return but boredom overcame me, and I found myself wandering a well-trodden path towards the Globe Inn. I was on my second quart of ale when my name rang out in a voice that was vaguely familiar making me splutter on the mouthful I had just swallowed. The voice belonged to my old friend from McHogg, Louise. It had been five years or so since I had last laid eyes on her, yet she had changed little. Now a woman with a figure that supported her age her face barely looked older than the adolescent that I knew, and her voice carried all the trademarks of the Londoner that she was.

We wiled away several hours reminiscing over our former exploits, Louise filled me in on the details of her family, one husband and 2 young children while I gave a rather abridged and jaded description of the life I had led since we had parted ways. Sense saw us leave before the sky became impenetrable to light, Louise heading home to her family, me heading to the Cambridge Road station to board the train back to Camden.

The journey provided me with the opportunity to secure the toppings of my disguise when the intoxicated gentleman in my adjoining seat became over whelmed with a belly full of beer combined with the motions of the train leading him to fall asleep. His head bobbed up and down like a float in the Thames, a particularly violent judder from the train caused the shinning black top hat to become dislodged from his head and roll under the seat. Lady Luck had again dealt a winning hand to me for the carriage had dispelled many of the occupants at the previous station and those that still inhabited paid little attention, consumed in their own thoughts. Despite the fact that I was not yet at my stop I did not squander the opportunity that fate had laid at my feet.

In preparation I removed my over coat in a display of being overcome by heat should I be observed more than I anticipated, exaggeratedly wiping non-existent sweat from my forehead. In a dramatic stretching gesture, I retrieved the hat from under the seat and placed it on the seat beside me covering it with my over coat. As the train chugged into the station I stood to make my exit, the hat on my arm and covered with the coat, I only hoped that nobody paid any heed and the owner did not rouse before I had departed the carriage. He did not, and I escaped the station without suspicion. The hat joined the coat in its hiding place under my bed and a new chapter with a novel persona was to begin.

11

The momentum of social reform that the killings had triggered was escalating with the public calling for common lodging houses to be locked up, their doors barred, and residents protected. Even the Queen had been quoted as calling for the dark and menacing areas to be well lit and free from shadow where these heinous crimes are being committed. Whilst I had unwittingly succeeded in highlighting the depraved conditions in which the residents of the East End lived, I also highlighted the inadequacies of Scotland Yard's finest. Every time I set foot outside I would hear some dramatic retelling of the killings, be it speculation or children re-enacting the deaths it would seem that the autumn of terror had transfixed all of London.

Life continued to rumble along, the boredom of a mundane existence niggling away. Frank and Charles made sporadic appearances and each time managed to avoid one another. Frank had let slip that the predicament he had caused himself to become embroiled in could be solved by the selfish act of fleeing the country. I could not let another man leave England to escape me, the wounds that Malt had caused by fleeing were still raw with emotion and would leave deep seated scars if they ever healed. As I sat by candle light writing Frank a note to request an overnight visit I happened upon the idea of taunting the police. They were already at a loss as to who the murderer was so perhaps I could throw them off the beat with a letter and antagonise them into action.

I must have drafted seven or eight attempts, all of which burnt to a crisp on the fire, before settling on an angle that amused me and I am sure would provoke the citizens of London and the law enforcement to further mayhem. My birthday gift had provided useful now in several areas and I would always have a debt of gratitude to mother and father for allowing me to attend school and acquire the skills that escaped so many.

I wanted to be as far removed from my own person as possible so as not to attract any undue attention or inadvertently lead the blundering police force on a path that would end at my own door. I initially addressed it directly to the police but thought that if they suppressed it then it would have been a waste of my time so decided to insight further panic and send it to a medium that I am sure would make it public knowledge, the papers. To be honest I was rather proud of myself.

As we had been taught at school I first dated the letter, of which it was the twenty-fifth of September, then addressed it. I had no clue as to the name of any newspaper personnel so titled it Dear Boss in the hopes that the top dog would be enticed enough to bite at my bait. I wrote:

"I keep on hearing the police have caught me but they wont fix me just yet. I have laughed when they look so clever and talk about being on the right track. That joke about Leather Apron gave me real fits. I am down on whores and I shant quit ripping them till I do get buckled. Grand work the last job was. I gave the lady no time to squeal. How can they catch me now. I love my work and want to start again.

You will soon hear of me with my funny little games. I saved some proper red stuff in a ginger beer bottle over the last job to write but it went thick like glue and I can't use it. Red ink is fit enough I hope ha. ha. The next job I do I shall clip the ladys ears off and send to the police officers just for jollys wouldn't you. Keep this letter back till I do a bit more work, then give it out straight. My knife's so nice and sharp I want to get to work right away if I get a chance. Good Luck. "

My dilemma was how to end the letter, obviously I could not sign it Mary. I remembered the song that I used to sing with Malt and had the perfect ending. I would sign it Jack the Ripper.

The city-wide sale of stamps made for anonymity, it was not uncommon that a woman would seek such a purchase or be remembered for it and it meant I had to involve no other. I just had to simply slip the letter into one of the designated boxes and it would be delivered on my behalf.

The letter had its desired outcome, a resurgence in the interest and fear of the Whitechapel murderer. Even though I sent only one letter to the Central News Office every major newspaper would carry the story, reiterating all the gruesome details and spreading suspicion though the citizens against those in their ranks that originated from different beliefs than those held by the majority of true Londoners, the Jews being targeted as the scapegoats. I could revel in the notoriety without suffering the indignity of a cramped diseased jail cell.

As I requested they did indeed hold on publication until I had set to work again. I had planned to tease them further and make them wait but I had received devastating news that sent my mind into a murderous rage. I could not release the torrent of rage on the one that deserved it, so I would take my pain out on another. I had left the house early to purchase a loaf of bread and happened upon Frank who was on an errand to buy a sample of arsenic to assist his lover who was suffering from a sickness. He did not tell me direct, but I was aware that it was used as a remedy for treating a woman who was nauseous due to being with child. This combined with Franks mind seeming preoccupied I knew that she had accomplished the one thing that I could not, and I loathed her for it.

I shoved the dark coat and hat into a large holdall, the scalpel into my boot and set out, my mind fuming and my body tense with the anger that was coursing through my veins. I left the bread abandoned on the kitchen side, my stomach to knotted with fury to consume a morsel. I could have walked past the Queen and would have paid little heed I was so determined to dispel my pain. My mind focused on the target I barely registered the journey to the station or even disembarking, the cold blade against my ankle the only comfort in my bleak outlook.

Whitechapel had gone to the dogs this last month past, there were more people drinking and folks seemed to care little for the danger, in fact they seemed to be inviting it. Violent altercations were on the influx, brawls were happening on almost every corner, shouts and screams rang through the streets but the whores were being avoided for fear of being fingered as the murderer. They had to work harder and were prepared to risk everything for their money, dolling themselves up and taking their chances where they were offered. Honourable men prowled the streets as vigilantes whilst others prowled the streets to extort money from those that would have benefited from their protection. Innocent men were harassed, and communities targeted by the fearful.

My stomach rumbled from the lack of substance, but I

ignored it as I poured more ale down my neck. I was still smarting from the news of *her* pregnancy that my mind was an unfocused mess awash with hatred, I reluctantly acknowledged the comings and goings until one overly joyous woman brought me back to a semi-conscious state of reality. I caught her eye and indicated a spare seat with the nod of my head, she shrugged but joined me anyway. We shared a few drinks as she informed me of her circumstances in an accent that did not originate in this country. Long Liz, as she called herself, seemed content in my company and divulged her dull life story to date for which I produced few feigned facts about my own. Bored with her tales I prepared to take my leave but as I rose Liz grabbed my arm. She begged to come with me for fear that she would meet the night killer. I obliged, and we walked out into the rain that was pouring from the sky.

We had only gone a few metres when the rainfall got worse forcing us to take temporary shelter in the doorway of the Bricklayers' Arms Pub. Huddled together Liz looked down upon me, for she was of a thinner but marginally taller stature. She kissed me. I was shocked by her action and took a moment to compose myself before a truly diabolical notion itched within my mind. Whispering my plan in her ear I removed the coat and hat and promptly put them on over my own clothes. Assuming the role that my clothes portrayed I moved upon Liz, holding her in an embrace whilst we kissed, her soft lips delicate yet experienced upon my own. From behind I heard the call "Watch Out, that's Leather Apron getting round you" causing me to jump and break away.

In a panic I grabbed her arm and pulled her into the street, hurrying in the direction of the less populated Berner Street. The rain had stopped but our boots splashed in the puddles that had congregated in the grooves of the cobbles stone floor. We walked from one end to the other, Liz taking up the antidotes of her past, spewing out information that I had no interest in knowing but adding to the illusion. The rain which had ceased came down again in a torrent forcing us to again seek relief. An arched gateway that separated the row of houses provided a convenient resting place to allow the down pour to pass. A little down the street a man stood outside a shop renowned for its beer, smoking a pipe, his back turned to us for the meantime.

Under the pretence of addressing an untied shoe lace I slipped my hand into my boot and retrieved the blade. We resumed our affair in the darkness of the gateway, a tunnel of darkness leading to Dutfield's Yard stretching out behind us. My lips ran a wet path from her mouth, over her cheek and down her neck causing her to moan in pleasure. Her head lolled backwards giving me ample access to her neck which made slicing her throat a work of ease, she did not even see the blade coming as her eyes, albeit closed, were angled towards the sky. I wielded the blade fast and strong, her body falling to the ground, blood running down her chest as footsteps approached. I had been caught, my deed discovered.

I had no idea of the identity of the figure that hovered in the street but based on the vicinity likelihood would suggest that he was Jewish, so I screamed "Lipski" in my deepest voice to scare him off. It had the desired effect and he rushed away, pursued by the smoking man who no doubt thought him guilty of some crime he had not perpetrated and perhaps mistaking him for myself as he ran from the same direction. Afraid that the constables would be upon me I slipped undetected from the gateway mere moments before a horse and cart was driven into the yard and my latest victim discovered. I had not the time to finish my work of art and had to abandon it unfinished.

Furious at myself I headed East along the High Street then into Commercial Street. The anger that swirled around me was greater than any I had known, it even surpassed this morning's wrath.

My foot was sticky from the blood that had trickled inside my boot, but I cared little, it did not hinder my ability to walk. I had wondered from the main track and was unsure where precisely I was. I was cornered within an enclosed courtyard, warehouses stood tall and threatening over the square broken up by houses, some of which were derelict and silent, a shop that was closed for business hidden away in the south-west corner.

I collapsed onto a crate, tears stinging my eyes as I let my emotions rise to the surface and bubble out. I berated myself for losing control, but I couldn't stop the tears from rolling down my cheeks. A lifetime of shame and pity had come to a head with the latest in a long line of my failures.

Footsteps rang out as someone entered the square and for a moment I thought I had been tracked but a gentleman would not walk with such a light step. I barely gave a glance in their direction consumed in my own self-pity I cared none that I should be arrested as it would mean that my suffering would be lived for only a short time further.

The stranger that approached was neither a policeman nor any other that would do me harm but a pretty slight woman with brown hair and a dark frock. At first, she seemed to think better of her actions and retreated but found that she could not leave a woman in distress and returned to offer a kind word and arm of comfort. It was an action that would prove fatal for her pity, paying the ultimate price.

I launched myself upon her before she had time to even raise her arms to defend herself. The knife plunging first into her throat. It had proved on many occasions to be a fast and effective means of silencing and incapacitating the whores so that I could concentrate my efforts on destroying the body's that they had used to their advantage. Her hands flew to her throat as she fell to the ground, her eyes bulging in panic as realisation set in. She tried to scream but only gargled blood, I had failed to complete the incision in one movement resulting in her eyes burning her pain into my soul.

Mad that I was an abject failure I buried the knife repeatedly in her abdomen, ripping the fabric with each blow. By this point her hands had released their grip on her throat, falling at unnatural angles, her eyes lifelessly staring back at the moon. As was my trademark modus operandi I slit her throat further to ensure that it would be seen as the primary method of death, I cut so deep that the knife scrapped upon bone. The hole that had been torn through her clothes gave access to her belly without the need to pull up her dress, and there was no need to conceal my surprise for the blood-soaked dress was evidence enough.

I hacked at the exposed flesh with a renewed fury, caring nothing for precise and neat incisions, how I longed it to be *her* belly that I was slicing but I could not kill the child of my love, even if I was not the mother so this poor soul would have to satisfy my need. Her insides were a red jumble of meat, hardly discernible from each other such was the level of mutilation. I pulled a handful of her soft insides from her gut and placed them within a piece of fabric that had been cut away in the frenzy. Exhausted and sweating from the exertion I stood up to admire my work in the scant light that the moon provided as it shone mutely from above, an unaccountable witness.

As I looked upon her she felt unfinished and I remembered

the promise I had made to the news office, that I would remove a part of her. Bending over her face I carved two identical V shaped makes upon her cheeks but her accusing look gave me the shivers, so I tried to close her eyes, but they would not shut. In a temper, I sliced each eyelid then earlobe, lopping off a piece which I placed inside my boot with the knife once I had wiped it clean. I had seen the blackened blades that were caused when the oxygenated blood had stained them, and I wished for mine to remain attractive and shiny. Already shaken from my near capture and the rush of the kill dissipating I stuffed my blood-stained coat inside the bag and retrieved the hat from the crate where I had placed it, my racking sobs causing it to have fallen from my head, in turn luring the good Samaritan to her doom.

I headed back in the direction of the nights first kill to observe the activity that was rampant over her deceased remains and to embrace the fear that was almost tangible in the air. With the stolen body parts weighing heavy in my bag I tempted fate for only a few minutes, retreating to head home as fatigue began to play upon my eyes. A snarling pack of dogs fighting over the pitiful remains of something provided the perfect disposal of the parts which I tossed at them as if flicking away a cigarette end. The piece of fabric cut away from the dress I held onto, not wanting the police to find the two pieces of evidence beside each other. The approach to Petticoat Lane was becoming populated with the market traders gearing up for the busy Sunday trade so I mistakenly threw the bloodied rag at a doorway on the approach.

I had seen many men stopped and questioned in the early light of the day. Nobody was looking for a woman, so I passed unnoticed, just another casualty of the worlds cruel fate who could fall victim to the crazed killer should I continue to roam the streets during the hours of dusk till dawn, were I not the source.

The journey home was fraught with delays which only hastened my negative feelings. My mind was in too much turmoil to rest, the sleep I craved eluded me and served to fester my feelings of anger. After an unsuccessful attempt to take a nap I paced my front parlour hoping that exhaustion would overcome me, but the movement stimulated my mind into action. My hands were shaking, still furious at the outrage that Frank had impregnated his whore that my next letter was a scrawl compared to my first. The kills had done nothing to dampen my hatred of that bitch, she had my life, so I took that of another.

"I was not codding dear old Boss when I gave you the tip, you'll hear about Saucy Jacky's work tomorrow double event this time number one squealed. A bit couldn't finish straight off. Had not got time to get ears off for police. Thanks for keeping last letter back till I got to work again."

Again, I finished with my alias 'Jack the Ripper'. I had failed to realise that a blot of ink had fallen onto the table and transferred onto the postcard when I wrote the address on the reverse, the situation made worse as I tried to wipe it away, smudging the letter but I cared none, they could have it as it was. I had stamped and mailed the letter before the stroke of noon.

The following day I again put pen to paper after a rather heart crushing visit from Frank, he declared his love for me but was torn due to the immoral nature of our union. This time I wrote with an outpouring of emotion to my dear Frank, no teasing or deceiving, just unadulterated honesty. He was so downhearted this morning that I changed my usual style of requesting his presence, the tone pleading, begging him to stay, swearing that I won't ask too much of him. On rare occasions Frank would scrawl a reply on the envelope but his hand was not precise, he would always leave it on the mantelpiece in the bedroom.

The newspapers bore copies of the letters that I had written, stirring further panic amongst the community's in a futile attempt to lure the culprit out from the shadows, baiting them to confess and admit their crimes. I particularly enjoyed the illustrated paper for it cost just a penny and came with copulas drawings of the murders and the investigating officers. Lost amongst the pages was the report of another murder that had taken place on the streets of Whitechapel, a mysterious death that was little reported and was not at my hand. I could only wonder who was attempting to impersonate me and why.

The Metropolitan police replicated the letters in hopes the hand writing would be recognised but no knock ever came at my door. Frank should have recognised the first at the very least for he had gazed upon my hand many a time although he had no evidence as I had burnt all the letters that he had returned, and I am sure that he, along with the police and general population did not conceive the notion that the perpetrator could be a woman. Post bills were placed outside the stations and handed out to public, every effort being made to circulate them. The publication of the letters led to a spate of copycat scribblings, illiterate imbeciles bombarding the relevant parties with pathetic ramblings, cashing in on my crimes but lacking the eloquence I displayed nor the guts to actually follow through.

I discovered through the grapevine that a counterpart had even forwarded to one unlucky individual a piece of human kidney. I had never intended for the slayings to cause a media frenzy, to be a bandwagon for the insane, they are a release of my pain, an act of revenge of the unworthy, a public service.

The next six weeks were a pleasant mixture of regular visits from both Charles and Frank. I could do nothing about the pregnancy except will it away although the thoughts and scenarios of *her* disposal amused me I could not cause another to suffer my own demise, I just needed to bide my time for good things come to those that wait and I had patience. I could have it all should I play my hand well enough.

Nature became my salvation, seeking solace in the many parks that nestled in the midst of the housing and the factories. Everyday brought a new site to behold, I even returned to the art of sketching, producing novice landscapes that I pinned to the wall at home, a few I sold to add scant coffers to the allowance Charles afforded me. On a warm day I could not look in any direction without seeing people take a turn around the grounds, lovers arm in arm, men strutting like a peacock to attract a mate, young woman fawning over their efforts as they giggled, hiding innocent smiles behind gloved hands, their frocks tickling the stones. Nannies brought their charges for a dose of fresh air, aprons wrapped around their frocks to prevent them becoming dirtied. Every ounce of human nature was on display of you looked hard enough. There was no discrimination or persecution here, the poor could walk the grounds as freely as the rich, providing that they did not interfere with or presume to engage the elite in conversation.

I thought that I had managed to tame the beast within for I felt no urge to release my pent-up anger on any, even those posing as myself brought feelings of humour after the initial annoyance receded. I had drawn a line under one of the darkest chapters of my life, ready to make a stand for my love and place my past deeds behind me. Life however had other plans and my peace was as short lived as my temper, the morn bringing devastating news that would seal my fate, and that of another.

12

Frank was too cowardly to break the news himself, the grapevine doing his biding rendering me incapable to putting a stop to the proceeding. Instead I bore witness to the wedding party returning from the church. Frank as handsome as ever, his beard freshly trimmed, his suit shinning and pressed. On his arm was his plum bride, all lace and smiles followed by family members dressed in their Sunday best. All were happy with the exception of a sour faced woman who resembled the bride, her face pinched with gloom. I watched them as they made their giddy way to a local tavern, tears silently falling like rainfall from my eyes as my heart broke in two. As much as it pained me I could not tear myself away. I was consumed by the thoughts that it should have been me in that lace dress, me marrying the man of my dreams, me getting the happy ending. She had the life I so longed for, why did she deserve it over me.

It took all my strength to walk away and not run to the man I loved however it didn't take long for the pain to whittle down to anger and wash over me, the familiar red mist falling over my eyes as the white wedding veil had for the newly made Mrs Hogg that very morning.

I returned home but could not quiet the rage that ran through me. I knew that there was only one way that I could ease my suffering, one that had worked before. I was of mind enough to collect my bag of essential kit and find my way to the station, but I was lost in a trance, the image of Mr and Mrs Hogg in the forefront of my mind, goading me. I had not laid eyes on *her* until this day. I was no longer able to visualise a crone of a woman who had ensnared my man for the vision that I looked upon had petite features prettily arranged and a figure, although evidently with child, slim in nature, her posture good and her life full of vitality. Her image was burned into my eyes and I could not be rid of it no matter who and what else I thought of. I would have to fill my brain with grotesque images to erase the Goddess in white.

Whitechapel was in a state of panic, more so than the first three murders had incited. Those not born of the British faith were travelling in packs for fear of being hunted like animals, sticking to the motto that *"The Juwes are the men that will not be blamed for nothing"*, their property's boarded to prevent further violence. The women of the night continued to ply themselves, unabated by the threat to their lives whilst groups of men roamed the streets after dark, their vigilance a small source of comfort to those that resided in the doomed hamlet, bats swinging in time to their pace as they stalked the streets in search of the killer.

Police presence had tripled, the tit headed officers stationed periodically around the town held a cautious hand to their batons, their whistles poised to alert their comrades should they encounter the Whitechapel terror.

The night drew in quickly, the skies turning dark shortly after seven and the cold wind biting at my exposed cheeks, still damp from the endless flood of tears that kept on escaping. I sought warmth and ale in the White Swan, not concerned that this was the very establishment in which I had befriended the ill-fated Martha. I used both my charm and my current vulnerability to deprive several gentlemen of a quart of ale thus saving the limited funds I had for when the sympathy pool was at a low.

As one kindly fellow began to become over familiar I discreetly took my leave and meandered down Commercial Street walking on the edge of the kerb stone as I did when I was a child, pretending it to be a tightrope but the weight of the bag I carried unbalanced me and I slipped several times onto the cobbled road that ran into the distance. Commercial Street was lined with four story buildings that towered skyward, gas lamps illuminated the street with an eerie glow, the shadows giving way to late night traders and those up to mischief under the cover of darkness.

As I neared Spitalfields I considered looking in on Mr Davis, but I knew that sex was not the answer to the gnawing need I had. I would have to be careful this time as nerves were still frayed and half an eye remained peeled for trouble or anybody acting with even a hint of suspicion or disregard for human life. Usually a patient person the lack of a suitable candidate was only serving to further anger my already taut temper, keeping the relief I sought at bay.

Most of the women were huddled in groups for security, the threat of death a temporary cause for friendship, only separating when a punter was identified, each goodbye potentially the last but a risk these women were prepared to take. Few expected the killer to strike again in this precise locality as the murders had been spread out across Whitechapel and they had had their death, in the slaying of Annie Chapman, but the threat was ever present.

I sat upon a torn stool, my bag of evidence tucked between its legs and nursed a quart of ale as I watched the patrons come and go or drink themselves into a state of oblivion, blacking out the woes that had caused them to seek consolation at the bottom of a glass. I could not recall the name of the tavern that I sat in, the Three Bells, the Three Cooks. It mattered not for it looked just the same as any other in the locality, a wooden counter that curved in an arc behind which bottles, and glass stood awaiting use, the same old foul smelling and foul-mouthed men and women complaining about the same hardships. Though most were forgotten in the blink of an eye one woman kept catching my attention. I had caught hers for our eyes made contact on several occasions and each offered a weak smile of acknowledgement although we had not been formally introduced. That being the very nature of adult interaction unlike the carefree nature of children who would have made merry, taking it upon themselves to strike up a conversation on a mutual subject thus forming an immature acquaintance that was accepted without prejudice and class.

Every time she returned she looked a little sullener yet jangled ever more money which was gobbled up by the greedy landlord as the cycle played out in a never-ending circle.

On her final return the women that had been seated with her had all found gentleman to occupy their night leaving her quite alone and vulnerable. I had slipped into their place like a bullet from a gun providing the perfect opportunity for the two of us to become acquainted. The trap was laid, and the bait was about to be taken. As she looked around the room in search of her comrades a spark of fear could be seen in her eyes, a fear that she could fall foul of the Whitechapel slayer. To assist my plan, I offered a feeble smile in the hopes that it would compel her maternal instinct into action, it did and as she approached I indicated for her to sit. My eyes were still swollen and bloodshot from the tears that I had cried over my lost love giving me the look of a woman in dire straits, perhaps the key to unlocking the caring attributes that would seal her future. Whether she saw in me a companion, a confessor or an easy target I allowed her to think whatever she chose, believing that she held the upper hand her suspicions would not be alarmed, and I could carry out my deed under the guise of a kindred spirit.

She was in more of a need of a shoulder to cry on than myself and spilled her guts, figuratively speaking, at the drop of a hat in an accent that I couldn't place, perhaps of a Welsh decent but defiantly not a local lass. She was yet another Mary and found it amusing that I too was a Mary. I am sure if you throw a handful of stones into a crowd you would no doubt strike several Mary's, such was the common place of such a name.

I was quick to learn that she supported herself, though prostitution, to reside in a small ground floor one bedroomed flat just around the corner, at thirteen Millers Court, although she was behind on the rent and feared that the landlord would be calling to collect what was owed. Her love life was in tatters, much like my own, for the relationship that she had with a former fish porter from Billingsgate named Joseph had come to an abrupt end thus leaving her short on her weekly rent. She said it was down to having invited a new acquaintance, who turned her to the art of seducing the men to earn her keep, that her fishy lover Barnett had left her. I confessed that my dearest had married another and lied that I had stolen his best coat and hat to prevent him from looking unsurpassed. We bonded over abandonment, our crushed hearts beating as one on a united path of redemption.

Rather the worse for wear we were unceremoniously ejected from the pub by a tired landlord who sought his bed. As a rouse, I suggested we play a trick on her house mate, I would dress in the top hat and coat before revealing my identify as a woman, what fun would be had as we could deceive any that we passed on route. Self-christened sisters we stumbled in the direction of Dorset Street, I supported her with an arm around her shoulder as she found the coordination to place one foot in front of the other a challenge.

The narrow archway leading down to the court afforded just enough space to pass two abreast, the near empty bag slung over my shoulder like Dick Whittington on his journey to the city with streets paved in gold. When we got to her place there was no candle burning, just a thick darkness coming from the room. Unlocking the door, she beckoned me over the threshold before falling back onto the bed in fits of laughter. She threw me the key and instructed that I lock the door, she didn't want to wake to find she had been murdered in her own bed and an unlocked door only begged for an intrusion. Her whore friend would raise them when she returned.

It took a well-placed strike before the match lit, illuminating the miniscule dwelling in a glowing light that danced shadows across the walls. The tiny room contained little besides the bed, a table beside the bed that served as a bedside table, a chair and a small stand that housed a basin, but it was private in the terms that the door locked, and they would not be disturbed as residents walked a communal passageway or thundered up the stairs. Being a corner plot, I had the added advantage of only a neighbour to the one side and the windows faced the court offering me an additional advantage in seeing the roommate return, the filthy glass and dirty ripped nets providing enough secrecy to my deed.

Mary, already sprawled out on the bed, found that the combination of alcohol and the means in which to earn the penny's to pay for it made a perfect sleeping tonic for she was out for the count and snoring daintily within minutes of the door closing. No matter that she seemed to have neglected to consider my sleeping arrangements for I would be gone before the larks began to herald the sunrise.

My arsenal had doubled, the sticking knife accompanied by a surgeon's scalpel and a carving knife procured from the Camden markets. I lay each instrument out on the table, the orange glow of the candle flame bouncing of the surface of the blades. I had never on my own had the opportunity to take my time, to dissect a person as Malt had done all those years ago to old Mr Ford. The notion that I could be interrupted by the return of Mary's house guest was ever present in the back of my mind, spurring me on as I released the stored hatred, every cut a relief, a soothing balm on my inflamed soul.

I took a moment to watch the angel sleep, about my age in years she had the classic English rose beauty to her, a porcelain complexion framed with a platinum head of hair and crystal blue eyes that once sparkled like diamonds but would now never see or be seen again. I twisted the image to fit into my deluded mind, convince myself that it was Phoebe that I had at my mercy. I could exact the justice she deserved for stealing the heart of a man that belonged not to her.

The first incision was my signature move, slitting the throat to prevent any screams. Used to having to place an element of strength into the initial cut I almost severed her head from her body such was the force of the slice across her delicate neck. Blood splattered across the mahogany head board of the bed. I carefully unbuttoned her clothing, her bare body laying vulnerable and innocent. As I had done before I pulled the blade the length of her body, the handle of the knife clasped in my intertwined hands. She split open as easily as an overfilled bag of grain. As with Annie I pulled out the yards of intestines that wound around her insides and decorated her as if it were Christmas, a festive banner hung around the body.

Plunging my hands into her warm insides I removed the rest of her organs and placed them upon the table. I was so used to the noise of blood and flesh parting that it raised in me no feelings with the exception of a slight bit of repulsion at the sucking sound. The smell was easy to combat with a balm smeared under my nostrils. Most parted with ease, only a little tug required but a few needed a quick nip of the scalpel to free them. It reminded me of removing the gibbets from a bird before roasting it. The pile of flesh on the side hardly amounted to the hollow cavity, I felt strangely cheated. Her breasts lay naked, mottled mounds of skin straining against gravity, her nipples eyeing me accusingly. I would not have her mock me in death, nor find peace in the afterlife so set about ensuring her body could not be resurrected. Every ounce of pain and humiliation that *she* had unintentionally inflicted upon me by marrying my man I would repay upon the corpse that lay invitingly at my feet. I removed the breasts, slicing the ample cleavage like butter.

I cannot say what possessed me to use a handful of the organs as a makeshift pillow, but I also placed bloody objects under each foot. Standing back to admire my creation I felt it was still lacking panache, an unfinished painting. I took my blade to her arms, mutilating the flesh, blood dancing in trickles as it seeped slowly from the wounds. I carved chunks of flesh from her thighs and abdomen, the skin wobbling as I inched my blade through the thin pink sheet that covered what remained of her body. I wondered if it would crackle under flame as a pig's skin did. As a final insult, an ultimate act of defiance I took my blade and savagely hacked at her face, for no reason other than being unable to commit my crime against the one person I desired too, her heart would be shared with the community, feed to the mutts.

I hummed to myself, gratified in the sea of blood, "Oh, Murder" I delighted, perhaps a little loudly.

I sat perched on the edge of the bed as I caught by breath and composed myself to make my escape. With the blades wiped clean and my male persona zipped away inside the bag I fastened a bonnet that I found in a basket under her bed over my head and wrapped a maroon shawl over my shoulders and left, locking the door behind me. The horrific scene was locked away like a forgotten treasure, waiting to be uncovered and revealed to the world.

With my head down, I hurried back through the archway to freedom, hoping that if any witness saw me they would assume me to be the victim or an acquaintance of hers.

Thankful that at this time of year the mornings were overcast with dark skies and the cold kept anybody that had no need to be out inside, my journey away from the centre of death was a swift and invisible one. My appearance was noted by the station master who was deceived with the lie that I had been performing midwifery duties into the night and was simply returning home. The bag accounted for my uniform and birthing tools and the blood splatter on my face was explained away with a graphic description on the arrival of a new life. Males had no constitution for such knowledge and I was quickly waved on my way, a handkerchief offered to remove the blood so that I offended no other on the course of my homeward travels.

Exhaustion again claimed me, leaving me to an extended troubled sleep and a morning that would bring news of a fifth victim attributed to the vicious Ripper.

Frank and his new wife took no honeymoon although he stayed clear of Priory Street for a little over a week following the ceremony. Our reunion was bittersweet for I knew that she had a hold on him that I could not break with words and promises. Frank was conflicted in his actions and his lust, an internal struggle was waging war inside him and it was evident he was on the losing side, his conscious revealing in a moral victory that had altered his mind, if only temporarily. Sleep was not my bed fellow that evening, and I tossed and turned to no avail.

With his presence fresh in my mind I tried again to convey my feelings for Frank through the expression of written verse, I hoped that it would also ease the thoughts that were preventing me from my bed. I knew that Frank would be strong and battle through the darkness, but I urged him none the less to be brave, that his love for me could conquer the theory that taking his own life would be a solution, that I would love him and love those that loved him, that it would work should he be as strong as I and that I would do whatever he so wish to keep him in my world. No matter how much love I had there was still that little part of me that was filled with anger and would sabotage my happiness and indeed my life with brazen hints at my hidden identity such as the challenge that I thought no other would know my handwriting, in a letter by my own hand.

Life regained a sense of normality and the Ripper name was ignored as London prepared its streets, shops and homes for the coming of Yule and the arrival of a new year. One that I was determined would not reflect my former mistakes and would bring me the happiness that I strived for but had eluded me, staying for only brief moments in time before fleeing. Frank and I continued to meet, our get togethers carefully timed, permitting meeting up to four or five times in one week.

Charles had always spent the holidays with his family but this year I was graced with his presence for which I was grateful as Frank's absence would have been noted by his in-laws, not that he had attempted to make arrangements to the contrary. Charles was subdued in his manner, suffering a loss he chose not to share with me, but his company was appreciated. The room was decorated with paper ribbon and a diminutive tree stood in a pot in the centre of the table. A small turkey cooked in the stove alongside potatoes while vegetables steamed in a simmering pot above. I had not prepared a gift for Charles so offered myself for him to unwrap and use at his pleasure. He presented me with a bar of scented soap that smelt like flowers, wrapped in tissue paper with a silver ribbon.

Frank parted himself from his pregnant bride for the

evening of boxing day, probably with the excuse of sharing a festive drink with an old friend for he only stayed a handful of hours. He brought me no gift other than himself. I took a slow delight in unwrapping him, his hairy bulbous stomach heaving with pleasure as he grew harder under my touch. I begged him not to leave but he returned none the less to her.

My new year started on a positive note, a happy equilibrium balancing my two lovers on a reduced alcohol intake, I had even started sewing again, taking in small jobs from neighbours so that I could be more reliant upon myself and not the charity afforded to me by Charles. Lizzy Crowhurst who lived above me kept me in regular employ and Charlotte Piddington, who lived next door, was too idle, her husband worked for the railway, so she could afford for another too darn his stiff socks. The first three months of 1889 were unchallenged by means of normality. The Whitechapel murders had abated, the autumn of terror ended and life's preserved by the absence of the monster. I made regular visits back to the familiar streets of Whitechapel and Mile End, the area's unchanged through progression, the plight of humanity no more improved.

On my most recent visit back to my childhood home I was greeted with the news that my baby sister was to embark on the next journey of her life for she had reached womanhood herself and was courting a fine young gentleman whose occupation was that of a school teacher on a respectable salary that would see my sister well. In time, she would become a wife and mother and supersede the trappings of a life of poverty and have the existence that I had always craved though I bore her no ill will, she was my flesh and blood and would excel in this lifetime as I could not. Preparations were underway for the Easter celebrations, excited children chattering and clergy dressing their houses of worship.

I sat at my kitchen table reading a Dickens book by candlelight when the key turned in the lock and my door opened. It was one of two as only three people had a key and mine was in my pocket. To my hearts delight it was Mr Hogg but my pleasure was short lived for he brought news that would again crush the life from my soul. The child that Mrs Hogg was carrying inside her had made its entrance to the world, conceived illegitimately but born within wedlock the baby girl was to be named after her mother Phoebe Hanslope. I queried the parentage of the child and why she was not a Hogg but received no answer from Frank except a look that was both painful and conflicted. He took his leave to return to his new born child leaving me in turmoil.

I itched to retrieve the bag I kept hidden underneath my bed and head out to the streets I had turned red, but my resolve held fast, and I drowned my desire in excessive amounts of ale and any other liquid that would dull the pain. Frank continued to visit me and placate my mood, but I could feel the old darkness creeping into my mind, turning my thoughts black and crushing the desire I had to improve my prospects. Months passed in a blur, I cannot say how I survived them, but I came through them. My twenty third birthday passed by uncelebrated. I had hoped I would emerge a different person, but I was the same Mary as before, cursed to repeat the same mistakes and follow the same path, fated never to make it to the bluebell clearing in the wood of my dreams.

I sustained an injury to my right hand that almost saw me admitted to the infirmary for I developed a fever and shook severely for a day. I had been carelessly cutting a piece of cheese from the small yellow slab when the knife broke away from the handle and nicked the side of my palm. The cut was not deep, but it opened whenever I flexed my hand and required a bandage to stem the flow of blood. I retired to bed under self-imposed incarceration, mindful to keep my feet warm for a change of air was not a possibility, a recommended course of action should the doctor have been called.

The self-pity only served to fuel my melancholy mood thus on one dreary July day the old coat and hat came out and I headed to the streets that I knew had served me so well.

The smell and the smoke that rose from the clay pipe alerted me to the presence of another, one which I had expected to be a gentleman but turned out to be a lone woman entering a narrow street known as Castle Alley. Her swaying hips indicated that she was the worse for wear through intoxication. She passed me with barely a sideways glance and I acted upon instinct, abandoning the bag where I stood I had caught up to her within five or six paces and sunk the knife into her neck but from behind, with my strongest hand bandaged, I did not have the strength to entirely slit her throat. She fell to the ground clutching her neck, the shock stemming the scream that her open mouth was trying to release. I was on top of her like a spider on a fly trapped in its web. Her body convulsed as her life began to leave her body, so I had to hold her down whilst I ensured that she would not bear witness to her death. I lacked the lustre that I had on previous kills, the second incision in her neck no more dramatic than the first but it had served its purpose and silenced her. As I had done before I pulled up her dress, as a child does to examine the under garments or to discover if their dolly was anatomically correct.

This was my hardest kill for I lacked the control I needed to wield the blade effectively, my dominant right hand incapacitated through my own carelessness. I cut her from her breast to her stomach, but she did not split open as all the others had. Disheartened that I was failing to live up to the reputation that I had created for myself I played at her genital region, the blade scratching at the skin that had been stroked by so many men, the blade separating flesh between her thick wiry midnight curls. A light came on in a nearby window ending my tepid mutilation. I hurriedly pulled her dress back into position.

Angered at the interruption I childishly kicked her a number of times before scurrying back to the bag I had left on the street. I retraced my steps back to the station as the rain that the night sky had promised began to fall. I was on a train back to Camden before the body was even cold. I promised myself that I would stop, that she would be the last, that I had to take control of my destiny before I swung from the hangman's noose. I would be the master of my own fate and was the only one that could alter the course that I was careening down. I would make this a new chapter and it would be the best one yet.

13

The longing for the ale that I had quit was almost as fierce as the desire to be with Frank. His new family were putting strains upon him both financially and emotionally, the release he sought in me was mainly physical, but he did get a sentimental release as he could confide in me the thoughts he was unable to share with his wife. Mrs Hogg had not satisfied her husband since the babe was born claiming tiredness and frailty, so I received every thrust and kiss that should have been hers, his manhood finding comfort and gratification inside my well versed laycock.

I spent the best part of four happy months in this fashion, Charles filling in when Frank was absent. I only had a handful of wobbles that had me almost drinking the tavern dry but rose above myself, keeping my dark demons at the door.

My friendship with Charlotte next door had helped to fill in the gaps when I was feeling lonely or tempted to leave the path of redemption and surrender to my past. I found her whiny in character and feeble in her conviction, but she was close at hand and accepted me for the Mary I portrayed, we spent many hours in each other's company. She often called out to me over the back fence that divided our property's and would use her windows as a look out post if I had been on a trip to the market and was out when she called.

She was also in the habit of borrowing my possessions, but they were always returned in the same condition as they were loaned.

Sarah Butler and her husband Walter had moved into one of the rooms on the second floor and she became a frequent visitor alongside Charlotte, neither had children that needed their care and attention. She had been present many times when Frank had called and had assumed him to be my husband, the legendary Mr Pearcey, I had failed to correct her assumptions, rather pleased that I could pass him off as my own when in fact he belonged to another, for the time being.

I had befriended Elizabeth Rogers who lived a short distance away on Priory Place whilst visiting the zoo, somewhere I hadn't been since childhood.

The experience was less exciting for I could see the beasts imprisoned in their cages for the pitiful creatures that they were, their majestic nature crushed, their lives a hollow shell of what they should have been. Myself and Elizabeth had struck up conversation whilst idly looking at the mammoth tortoises as they sat almost motionless in their enclosure. Her husband William kept long hours as a bricklayer and she lacked the interaction that I frequently rejected but which had become common place in my life since my resolve to better my prospects. We visited each other once or twice a week from that moment on. Despite the friendships that I had built up my existence was still a lonely one.

Frank was still struggling with the adulterous affair but was as unable to leave me as I was him. I still wrote him letters to assure him of my allegiance to his love, that I would go mad if he removed it.

As hard as I tried to be a different person the Mary that I had always been lurked just under the surface threatening to overwhelm the new and improved version at any moment and drag her back into the pits of hell for a fiery eternity. The presence of Mrs Hogg with the man that my heart yearned for was a constant stone around my neck. I could not and would not give him up so had devised a wicked plan that would see me in her place within a year. I would make the joyous festive Yule the basis of my plot, dressed up in the guise of goodwill to all men.

At first Frank was reluctant to accept and deliver my invitation but saw in it the merits of sharing a Christmas without the lies that had to be told to be together. I was unsure if Phoebe would accept, it would depend on Franks delivery, and, as the man he could insist although he had proven to be feeble in matters of confrontation. Her acceptance brought a mixture of delight as well as trepidation, but my bait had been taken so now I had to reel in my catch. I borrowed an additional plate and cutlery from Charlotte and a beaten straw filled cushion from Sarah that would serve as my bed for the night. I would offer my own bed to Frank and his wife, laughing in the knowledge that he had taken me upon it on countless occasions, a silent insult that she would sleep upon the memories of her husband's sweating naked body.

Although I had seen Phoebe before we had yet to be officially acquainted. I was introduced as a spinster friend of Clara's and it was seen in Phoebe's eyes that the Hogg's were doing a good deed in spending the day with a less fortunate and solitary woman. The windows were steamed from the heat of the oven as a small feast cooked upon the stove and a fire crackled in the hearth. We each sat supping a glass of gin whilst the roast browned, Phoebe junior asleep in her perambulator. I found the food tasteless to my palette for I desired her blood, but my guests were gracious and offered kind thanks. After the food had been consumed we played endless rounds of cards into the night, the babe entertained with cuddles and a silver rattle. I slept listlessly in the knowledge that my dearest was under my roof but in the arms of another and would have done her harm but restrained myself for fear that it would be my love who would be implicated. The couch made for an uncomfortable bed fellow. I sat with the babe for some time as she gurgled to herself, a glass bottle standing by with her morning feed.

They stayed for the most part of Boxing day and it played out in a similar manner to the day previous but with a meal of left overs and bread. My heart felt as used and discarded as the paper that I had screwed up and thrown upon the fire last year as I had penned my letters. The darkening of the sky signalled the departure of the Hogs. I hoped that I had played my part well and felt that Phoebe had warmed to my disposition opening a door into Franks world that could be manipulated to my own end. I savoured the kiss that Frank planted upon my cheek by way of a thank you for being a gracious host, but it cut me like a knife that he walked away from me with his family at his side. Mrs Hogg left with a hug that repulsed me and an invitation to visit.

I took up Phoebe's invitation and made the short journey to one hundred and forty-one Prince of Wales Road before the year came to an end. I had already seen Frank early that morning and knew that he would be occupied with work for the remainder of the day so seized the opportunity to engage with his wife while he was not present to be privy to our discussions. I rushed home and hastily baked a small ginger cake. It required all the spare cash I had, and a small tab at the bakers, to purchase the ingredients. It would mean that I would have to go without nourishment for a few days, but it would worthwhile and I had done so on many occasions in the past and I did not need the strength to earn a living. I made sure that each cake was baked in individual dishes for I did not want to consume the cake with the additional supplement of a spoonful of crushed rat poison. I hoped that the ginger would mask any taste that came from the poison. Once the cakes had cooled I wrapped each in cloth and tied them in ribbons of a different colour so that I could identify which was safe.

Arriving in the royally named street I was impressed with the grandeur of the four storey houses for they looked clean and prosperous, there wasn't a ripped curtain or muddied step in site. The two upper floors were clad in brick while the ground floors were painted a heavenly white, one disappearing below ground level, behind a wrought iron fence. Nervously I climbed the six steps to the wooden door, painted a deep blue, the knocker polished and gleaming in the afternoon sun. I clasped the cold metal in my hand and knocked three times. Feeling slightly out of place in such an affluent street I shamefully wiped my fingerprints from the knocker as I waited for the door to open.

My plan was almost scuppered for Clara and her mother were having tea with Phoebe when I arrived. I chatted with Clara and made small talk with Mrs Hogg the senior, bidding my time. Thankfully Clara left to run an errand and the mother returned to her room on the floor below. I suggested we take a turn to get some air. I took my turn to push the perambulator, rocking little Phoebe to sleep. When I was sure she would not wake I suggested we sit upon a bench and take in the scenery.

Mrs Hogg was not one to overly exert herself so was keen to take a seat providing with the opportunity I had baked earlier that day. She noted that a delicious smell had been coming from my basket and queried why I had waited until now to reveal the goods. She had unwittingly provided me with the opportunity to explain that I felt guilty that I had not enough cake to share and I begged her forgiveness for my needy circumstances and prayed that she would not think bad of me. She took the parcel of ginger cake she was offered and proceeded to daintily nibble at it until she had eaten the whole morsel, not a crumb remained. She made no comment on the taste and showed no ill efforts. We walked back to the home she shared with Frank. I left her to attend to the baby who woke as we manoeuvred her carriage up the front steps. I returned home perplexed that my ruse had failed.

I encountered Frank the following day who informed me that his wife had suffered a mild sickness the evening previously yet had enjoyed the ginger cake so much she would be much obliged if, the next time I visited, I could bring her some more. Pride seeped from my pours for I was not akin to compliments and felt rather smug that my baking had been so desirable. The fact that I had been granted a further chance to achieve my goal was not lost upon me and added to the smile that was fixed upon my face.

I made sure to visit Clara and gage her movements so that I would not be interrupted or have unexpected company. The family kept no servants. I learned of the perfect opportunity when the house would be empty, with the exception of my intended victim. I paid the Phoebe's a visit, my basket smelling of freshly baked ginger cake, this time with enough poison to ensure that the young Mrs Hogg would feel the effects. I made my excuses shortly after the cake was eaten for I did not want to be present when the rat extermination powder took effect.

It was the best part of a week before I saw or heard anything from any of the Hoggs. Frank's face was ashen but not as crest fallen as I would have expected for one that had just lost his new bride. Ready to provide comfort and take my place beside him I was dumbfounded to hear that my plot had again failed. The woman was still alive. After two doses of poison she had not succumbed, the bloody cow must have the constitution of an ox. Frank was frantic that his wife had been seized by a mysterious illness and was at a loss as to what to do. The doctor could provide no remedy. I offered to nurse her and care for the infant as Phoebe was unable to attend to her domestic duties.

I was given a bed for the first few nights as her fever kept Frank from his own slumber which would have rendered him unemployable through fatigue, but I required him fit and able to satisfy my own needs and desires. Those days I spent with the Hogg's were a bittersweet reminder of what it was to be part of a family again, to have a house full of love and disagreement. I had not realised how much I had missed the company of kin for at the time I was too centred on escape to appreciate what I had.

I helped Phoebe with every aspect of her life from bathing and dressing to performing her motherly and domestic duties, I performed her wifely duties too but not to her knowledge. My bedside manner was without reproach and I even brought her luxurious gifts, a tiny bottle of scented balm, a posy of flowers and un-poisoned cake, for fear that it may be consumed by my love.

For the remainder of the twenty days or so that I played nurse I would travel to my own home for the evening and return with the dawn the following day. Frank would sometimes walk me home, other times he leaves it a short time before he would arrive at mine. He was becoming increasing short with his wife, but I saw him give no ill treatment or withhold her food, he just lacked the loving devotion that a new husband should shower upon the mother of his child. The babe was thankfully too young to miss her mother's affection for she received it from her father and her temporary nurse maid as well as her aunty and grandmother, she wanted for little.

Frank had been afflicted with a cold, serving to dampen his mood further and I found myself caring for a snuffling bag of self-loathing as well as his wards. He had complained that work was short, so he would not be missed, though the income would be. His mother ensured that none went hungry. As well as Clara and Mrs Hogg the Senior the room was often occupied with Franks niece, a slight young woman by the name of Elizabeth Styles who had taken it upon herself to represent Phoebes family and ensure that her aunt was receiving appropriate care. I could tell from her expression that she believed Frank treated them both with some difference, but she kept her tongue until the end of February.

It started as a hushed conversation but escalated into a full-blown shouting match with Elizabeth making accusations that Frank was holding her aunt under deplorable conditions and providing her with insufficient food to overcome her sickness. Frank did not stand to be spoken to in such a fashion and forcibly ejected Elizabeth from the property, forbidding her re-entering the house and dispatching her with a flea in her ear. From the look that she left me with I had no doubt that she suspected that Frank and myself were familiar although we had been careful to avoid physical contact whilst under the same roof we may not have been as discrete in body language as I had thought.

Phoebe had made no comment but much of her time she was confined to the bedroom. During a lucid period, Phoebe showed me a revolver that Frank kept in his drawer. I do not know why she showed it to me, but I asked if I could have it for I lived alone and desired the protection a firearm would offer. I had far more sinister designs for it, a back up to my method of choice.

I took the weapon before I left along with the cartridges for it would be of no use without the ammunition. Upon my return to Priory Street I placed it in the kitchen draw where it would stay, forgotten. Her illness had been developing for near on two months and no improvement had been made, nor had she deteriorated further for I had been prevented from tampering with her due to almost constant companionship.

I had a few errands to run the following day so was late in getting to Prince of Wales Road. I arrived to find that I had no patient to care for. On orders given by Phoebes mother on hearing the report of her treatment from her granddaughter the frail Phoebe was whisked away by the matronly Martha Styles to be cared for and revived to good health. They held her for ten days, in which time not even her baby daughter was permitted to visit. I continued to visit Clara at number 141 but never again did I climb the remaining stairs and set foot inside Franks home. Even upon Phoebe's return, and when I was in the room below I never ventured further than Clara's door. I would meet with both the Phoebes through chance in the street and share a kind word and coo over the growing child.

Not one of them ever approached me to question why I ceased contact with Phoebe after such an intense period of care and I never offered an explanation for my actions.

I was content to continue my existence as it was. The overwhelming urge to dispatch Phoebe with haste had dulled to a work in progress. Frank's visits persisted, and I had the ability to raise a smile in the hairless tot when I happened upon them, a pang of longing gripping my heart. I had to fight the temptation to run away with her and raise her as my own but that would mean losing her father, so my hands were rather tied. I kept away from the streets of Whitechapel, but my boots walked the familiar paths of Mile End once or twice a month, primarily to see Lottie but it also served to prevent me from calling upon Mrs Hogg and causing her mischief. I had also taken the hat and coat from its hiding place and pawned them using fictitious details, leaving them to be sold on when I failed to return to buy them back.

My neighbours called in regularly to partake in a chat and cup of tea, Charlotte darkening my doorway almost daily. I learnt that Elizabeth was struggling so offered her my laundry, I was never enamoured by the mangling, I found the process laborious and it made my arms ache. Carrying the buckets of water left my shoulders throbbing so I was glad to be done. The water pump was nearer to her own dwelling than mine, besides I cared little for the populated area. Miserable wives and mothers pumped endlessly at the large handle before staggering away under the weight of the water they had collected, triangular strips of fabric holding back their dirty hair.

I opened the door one day, expecting to find either Charlotte or Sarah on my doorstep but was greeted by the face of Mrs Hogg, the babe gurgling in the perambulator. I invited her in, curious as to the purpose of her visit. It turned out that she had missed my company and now that she was stronger she had sought me out. She had come to thank me for caring for her through her illness.

As she left Sarah came from her upstairs room, an empty basket over her arm. I introduced the two women and told Sarah I would catch her up at the market. I walked with Phoebe through the winding streets that separated my home and the one I longed to belong to. She lacked vitality and suffered from crippling pain but she still on the mortal plain. I left her at Victoria Road to complete her journey, the itch to make it her last was so strong that instead of meeting Sarah as I had promised I spent the money that I had for food on ale, in an attempt to drown the feeling to wield the blade, an act that Frank may never forgive me for.

I had means to call in on Charlotte to reclaim the stand that I had lent her for a purpose I cannot recall but I used it little so decided against knocking at her door, she would only bore me with uneventful details of her day and I was far too drunk to hold my tongue civilly.

The summer came, and the city filled with tourists, the attractions burst at the seams with flowered bonnets and children in silk suits. The open spaces that offered a place of quiet contemplation were now noisy avenues that even the birds avoided. The usually sullen merchants had renewed vigour and some even attempted pleasantry's, which was an alarming spectacle. The end of the summer season signalled a mass exodus from the city leaving the inhabitants with a stench of sewage due to the increased strain upon the inadequate systems and the best of the produce had been sold.

I had reigned in my drinking again, but I felt the darkness of my mind closing an icy grip around me as the night drew its icy fingers over those that slept under its mercy. I was able to keep my feelings in check for the most part, my friends seeing nothing other than the Mary that they knew but when I was alone I could not deny the crushing thoughts that rampaged throughout my mind. Every fibre of my being ached for Frank when we were apart and sung when we were together. I just needed to eliminate the obstacle that stood between my happiness and the destruction of my soul. Our last meeting had been so brief, I had requested his company for just half of an hour, but he refused, stating that he was expectantly due to do a little work that he had to finish post haste and could not spare the time but promised that he would try soon.

I had not seen John for many months, our paths no longer crossing through my determination. Thursday past he addressed me directly, rudely enquiring as to the state of my blinds for they were drawn during day light hours. I told him some fable about the death of my young brother, but no sympathy befell me despite the mourning I told him I was under.

The events that occurred on the twenty-fourth of October sealed my fate forever, I don't know if they would have played out any differently had I kept a lid on my temper. I would accomplish my goal but at the same time bring about an avalanche of woe that could only have one sure outcome. The day started as plain as any other, I initially had no murderous intent in mind but, as always, destiny had already laid the path that I would tread, willingly or not, I was a slave to myself.

After breakfast I retired to read a novelette that I had been given, sitting in front of the fire to keep warm for reading exerted no energy to warm me. I had much enjoyed the broody fatal union of Catherine and Heathcliff, but I was not as enamoured by the earlier writing of Miss Austen, she didn't quite enthral me as much as the young Bronte.

I thought that I had heard a rodent scratching from behind the dresser but could not find the filthy creature. A knock at the door signalled an uninvited guest. It was Sarah from the floor above, come to see if I wished to come for tea the following day. I did not but offered her pleasantry's that were a feigned as our friendship, I even offered her the romantic drivel I was reading, a pastime to distract my mind from unholy thoughts. She imposed further by suggesting that I make efforts to purchase a trap to rid the house of the vermin, for fear probably that they would invade her rooms. I dutifully went out to purchase the said trap, freeing me from the intrusion. It would be this venture that started an unstoppable ball that I had no wish to halt.

The encounter with John the previous day had ruffled my feathers and left me quite perturbed. That combined with Frank's dwindling affections caused something inside me to snap, to lose the proverbial plot, I would have been instantly admitted to Bedlam if anyone could see the thoughts that played out in my mind.

First, I would have to lure my prey away from the sanctity of her family and draw her to a place of isolation. She had made no secret of the fact that she felt intimidated by the Hogg clan and had confided that the illness of her father had shaken her to her core. I felt sure that if I requested her to visit she would oblige me. I hoped that she would leave the babe in the care of her Grandmother and aunt. I had every intention to deliver the request myself but the opportunity to distance myself presented itself in the form of a young lad who was on an errand for his mother. I had seen him frequently in the area of Prince W Road. The roughish lad was more than eager to earn a penny for the small task of delivering my message. I waited for him to return empty handed and asked for a description of the recipient before thanking him and paying him the deserved penny.

To delay the task further Charlotte called to request that I collect the stand I had lent her though why the lazy imbecile could not manage the task under her own steam was beyond my comprehension, I dispatched her with the request that perhaps Mr Piddington return the borrowed furniture as I was awaiting company and could not leave for fear they would call while I was out.

As I had requested Phoebe came to me, but she had brought the child which placed my well-planned scheme in jeopardy. Bloody woman. She insisted leaving the perambulator in the hallway outside my rooms declaring that there was insufficient space to manoeuvre it despite my protests.

A little after Phoebe arrived I heard the faint call of "Mrs Pearcey" a handful of times coming from the back of the premises, knowing the disembodied voice belonged to that of my neighbour Charlotte I assumed it was to assert my safety after undoubtedly hearing the crack of the glass as it splintered from the frame and fell in an iridescent waterfall onto the cobbles in the back yard. The broken panes in the kitchen window were as a result of myself dodging the paperweight missile that Phoebe launched at me as she learned that her husband was not the faithful man she had thought him to be.

A woman scorned Phoebe would not take her leave, instead

torturing us both with questions, disbelief and sorrow. A calm had befallen the room following the frayed tempers, the exchange of heated truths and the ultimate sacrifice of the innocent glass panel, smashed to preserve the sanctity of human life.

I had seen the stand laying abandoned on the floor as I stared through the drafty hole in my window, the start of a drizzling downpour bouncing off the dark wood. I retrieved the stand before it too suffered a destructive end, taking with me the curtains that had hung in the window, a smear of my own blood bright against the ivory material, the jagged glass cutting my hand as I attempted to clear away the shards that had fallen inwardly. I had hoped that Mrs Hogg would be gone when I came back in, but luck was not taking pity on me and she was ready with a fresh assault of words.

In my absence she had taken her fury out on my dark blue felt hat for it now lay misshapen under her foot.

My temper erupted like a volcano and I raised my voice in protest. My arms were moving wildly as if shaking an invisible milk churn. My body shook from the sheer madness that rampaged through me. I inadvertently knocked a bottle off the table which smashed to the floor into a million sharp pieces frightening the baby causing it to let out a piercing cry of alarm. Phoebe was so concerned with questioning me that she barely gave her own child a passing glance let alone make a move to comfort her, instead chastising me further for causing the babe to cry.

Pained at seeing Franks own daughter distressed I made a move past Mrs Hogg to reach the child but I was dragged to the floor as she pulled me back by my hair. Rage filled me as it had never done before, this bitch had my life, my love, the child I could never carry but she was squandering it all, caring for her own needs. I had tried but failed to take them from her so now I would take her from them. Phoebe made a fatal error in throwing me to the ground for I landed near the remains of the bottle that has smashed to the floor. Grabbing the jagged remains by the intact neck I lunged at Phoebe. She raised her right arm to protect herself and the glass left a large ragged cut down her forearm. She cried out, the shock of the pain registering in her eyes as they grew in size. With the argument being conducted in the kitchen it kept prying eyes and ears on the streets from overhearing the disagreement.

The wound left her defenceless for she attempted to hold the skin together with her left hand so could not fend off another attack. It took only a moment for her tongue to regain its focus. She bent down to comfort her baby when I silenced her with blow to the back of the head. I used the handle from the poker that stood beside the fireplace. The sound reminded me of the first time I stood upon the gravel that lined the pathways up at Kenwood House, a sickening crunch. The blood was captured within her hair, causing a matted mess upon her beautiful head. As I wiped it clean I felt a small crack in the handle which must have been caused as it impacted with her skull. I felt vindicated, she just kept taking from me.

Phoebe lay unmoving at the feet of her babe, blood flowing from the cut to her arm onto the novelette that had been an innocent victim, swept into the fray as Mrs Hogg fell to the floor. A welt began to form on her forehead. I placed the blooded glass in a bowl and reached for my weapon of choice. Wielding the sharp blade, I took a fistful of hair and lifted her head from the ground, exposing her porcelain neck. I made several incisions just for fun, to poke at the woman as her life ebbed away, then with one mastered stroke I slit her throat. The angle of the incision combined with the angle of her head meant that I nearly removed it.

When I was sure that the knife was no longer needed I wiped the blade and returned it to the family of knifes that lived within my dresser drawer.

I was faced with the task of having to dispose of the body. I was unsure of how to proceed for I could drag her out of the building but how far would I get before I was seen? Little Phoebe sat contentedly upon my bed, nestled in pillows she was placated with a bottle and a comforting hum for she had known my voice throughout her infancy. I happened upon the idea of using the perambulator to transport the remains so wheeled it into the kitchen. It was a struggle to manoeuvre it through the narrow passageway and negotiate the curve just before the kitchen door, but it was manageable. It was one of my most challenging physical feats to fold the body enough to fit it into the perambulator. It wasn't perfect, and I had to cut off her close-fitting cardigan, a duplicate of the one that John had gifted to me, to allow the flexibility needed but I had achieved it, aided by her inability or refusal to gain weight from her period of sickness. A stray button from her clothing must have come loose when I cut the fabric and ended up in the fire with the rest of the sweepings, an insignificant little item that would have Phoebe exact her revenge from beyond the grave.

It was almost impossible with the body loaded to wheel the perambulator back though my home, but I accomplished it at the expense of my walls which suffered was many knocks and scrapes as seemed to line my hands. The babe had fallen asleep as I worked so I swaddled her in a blanket, leaving just her face exposed. I pulled down the hood of the perambulator to reveal the space that I had created for her, behind the body of her mother she would be safe as my plan played out.

I was preparing to leave so that I could dispose of the remains when I encountered Mr Butler as he returned from work, the perambulator was holed up in hallway outside my rooms reducing the already narrow walkway, but it was now laden down with the weight of a human twenty years too old for it. I had not lit the oil lamp for the darkness drew no attention to the bundle that was crammed awkwardly into it.

I had only meant to be a minute, but the arrival of Mr Butler had delayed the operation as I offered to take Mr Butlers hand and steer him around the obstacle, he obliged thanking me in the process. I pushed, heaved and dragged the bassinette perambulator over the threshold and into the street with a bump, the contents weighing heavy, threatening to snap the metal that supported it on its duel sized wheels. I struggled to push the heavily loaded perambulator up the hill away from the scene of the crime, keeping to the centre of the road to avoid any pitfalls that may dislodge my secret in front of witnesses. I saw what resembled the figure of Elizabeth Rogers in the distance, but I pretended I had not seen her, instead bowing my head and ploughing on with my journey.

I was heading in the direction of Prince W Road before veering off in the direction of Belsize Square to find a quiet neighbourhood in which to dispose of the remains.

I thought about the picturesque setting of Primrose Hill, but she did not deserve a resting place of beauty, she would lay in the streets as the others had. Activity led me to the less populated Winchester Road and into construction of Crossfield Road which would serve my purpose. My arms and legs were burning from the effort that it took to wheel the over laden perambulator around the uneven and steep streets of Camden, the sky turning from a deep blue to black in the time it had taken me to reach a spot to deposit my newest piece. I was so close to having Frank to myself, I would return triumphantly having found the young babe abandoned in her perambulator, her mother nowhere to be seen and we would be the family that I so craved.

She was such an adorable little tyke and she had been as good as gold on the journey, not a peep had come from her. I pulled off the clothing that I had placed over Phoebe's body and heaved her corpse from the perambulator, the weight almost making the task impossible but the thought that I would be a wife and mother gave me the strength that I needed. The carriage rocked and threatened to spill its contents onto the street such was the struggle to extract the woman that the handle snapped. I left her where her body fell, the angle of her limbs unnatural in pose but I had not the energy nor inclination to pose her.

Her eyes seemed to follow me as I moved, even though they were as lifeless as her soul they seemed to burn into my conscience, so I threw the commercially manufactured brown cardigan jacket over her head and left her alone in the cold damp street amongst the bricks and debris.

Little Phoebe looked peaceful swaddled in a thick blanket, just her petite facial features on show, I smiled merrily to myself as I wheeled her away from her old life and into a new one. I must have been walking near on ten minutes before I realised that I was heading away from Camden and my love for I was nearly at the fields that spanned into the distance from

Finchley Road. It was then that I smoothed the fabric away from the beautiful child's face that I felt the coldness of her skin. I instinctively jumped back in repulsion.

With my heart in my mouth I lifted the child from her death carriage and looked upon her face. Under the dim light of the moon I saw that the eyes I had taken to being closed through sleep had in fact closed in death, her features slightly swollen, her mouth slightly open. I held her tight to me and I rocked the body, tears of loss streaming like a waterfall as I mourned the loss of the family I no longer had and for the death of a child I had hoped to raise as my own.

The confusion overwhelmed me, she had been alive when I had placed her in the perambulator, had her own mother crushed her? Any will that I had to live within this world flew away like a migrating bird, caught in a snowstorm of grief, never to return. I was sure that I had given her ample room, perhaps that body had moved as I hauled over the front step. She was beyond help, life had left her prematurely.

I carefully unwrapped her from the blanket that had protected her miniature clothing from the blood that stained the perambulator. I gently kissed each little fist and her forehead before placing her face downwards in a cradle of nettles, her resting place one of nature. I took from her one little sock and booty so that I would always remember her, remember the child I had ripped from inside me and remember the dream of the perfect family.

I pushed the perambulator a further handful of yards to Hamilton Terrace before carelessly leaving it though I removed the skin rug that lined it despite it being covered in blood that could not be detected in the feeble moonlight. My heart and head filled with death it took all my soul just to walk away from the babe in the bush. I know not how I got home but I did. I must have passed a hundred people, but I could tell nothing of them, not even if they had been wearing a top hat or a skirt, hell I could have walked into Joseph Merrick and not even battered an eyelid at the disfiguration.

When I returned that evening, I learned that Frank had been over to Chorley Wood for Phoebe's father was gravely ill and was not expected to last the week. He had called to trace the whereabouts of his wife but found neither of his lovers that night, a scribbled note the only evidence that he had been. He had not observed the disarray in the house for he showed no concern in the note he left.

I wiped away what blood caught my eye in the dim candlelight that flickered in the room. Every letter that had been retained I burnt on the fire, the flames crackled as the paper was blackened, the writing erased for an eternity. I had forgotten about a pile of letters that I had in a black box beneath my bed. I threw the burnt evidence of our relationship into the yard, to be left to rot, as the bodies of the Phoebe's would be in their wooden coffins beneath the hard, unforgiving ground.

I threw the bonnet that I had worn out onto the fire, not wanting to wear anything that would bring memories of this awful night.

I placed my blood-stained clothing in a copper in the little washhouse that stood at the end of the communal passageway, the blood-soaked novelette used as fuel. The bedding that I had used to scrub the blood from my carpet floated in zinc baths that I had overfilled, spilling pink water all over the floor. I vowed to return before the break of dawn and ring out the wet cloth, but the sandman had other plans, keeping me in a slumber.

I was raised the following day by an urgent hammering on my door, it must have been shortly after nine o'clock in the morning. I feared it was the police and that my deed had been traced back to me, but the knock held a more frantic than authoritative tone. On my doorstep stood a dishevelled looking Clara, her unkempt frantic hair barely contained within a bonnet, a wild expression in her eyes. She immediately pressed me with queries about the whereabouts of Phoebe, asking if I had seen her at all yesterday to which I lied that I had not.

To avoid any scandalous accusations, I invited Clara into my rooms in the hope that I could placate her, but she was like a dog with a bone and continued to press me with the same questions. I crumbled under the interrogation and confirmed that Phoebe had indeed paid me a visit at around five the previous evening in the hopes that I would mind the baby or lend her some coppers for a reason that she did not disclose.

Phoebe had caught me at a time when my purse was suffering for I had the total sum of only one shilling and three half pence to my name and would not part with even one of those half pennies. I failed to inform Clara that I knew of what had happened after this point, choosing to end the tale with a refusal of help. Clara beseeched me to help her now to find her missing sister-in-law. To appease Clara and divert any suspicion falling upon myself, as well as keeping in good favour with the family I wished to join, I agreed to accompany her on her search.

Again, Charlotte called at my door, this time to ask if I had retrieved my stand from the back yard and to beg my pardon if it had been damaged, I assured her it was all fine, but she could not stop as I was needed to accompany Clara on the search for her sister-in-law. She waited quietly but anxiously for me whilst I put on my hat and jacket. She wished to first visit the Kentish Town Railway Station to enquire if Phoebe had booked the pram onto a trip to her ailing father in Chorley Wood. We had to walk though Prince of Wales Road to access the station. I managed to convince Clara that her time would be best spent at home and that I would go alone to make the enquiries, happy that an alibi had presented itself.

After enough time had passed to warrant a return visit to the station I presented myself at the Hogg property.

I meet Frank leaving as I mounted the steps to the front door.

I fraudulently told him that the Perambulator had not been booked at the station. He was on his way to Phoebe's father for that was the only place on earth that she could be, having no other family and few friends. He would have a fruitless disappointing journey.

The harrowing look in his eyes will stay with me for all my days, an icicle in my heart that will find no release. Clara had gained control of her wits and was able to challenge me regarding the prominent scratches on my hand that I had not the foresight to conceal. I flippantly voiced the first thing that came to mind and told her that I had "been killing mice", that thousands of the little blighters had invaded my kitchen, that the smears on my dress were a result of the rodent cull. I was midway through a cup of tea when Clara came into the room brandishing a paper and talking of a death up on Hampstead, claiming that the description fit that of Phoebe.

I swayed her on the notion that it was indeed her beloved sister-in-law and that Frank would return with his wife and child on his arm having been to Rickmansworth on an errand to visit the sick. I dutifully went out several times to purchase different newspapers so that Clara could read aloud all the facts reported and used all my charms to keep her from running to investigate further.

The latch-key that she had handed me to regain entry sat comfortably in my pocket, the cold brass hard as it brushed against my fingers. The key remained safely in my pocket, the small chain that hung from it made a tuneful jingle as I walked. My charms were not as persuasive as I had hoped, with Clara as hard to contain as an excitable child I found myself offering to accompany her on her detective trail.

On reaching Hampstead police station my heart hammered a treacherous beat against my chest threatening to unveil my deepest secrets. The constable on duty introduced himself as Inspector Bannister, the fur lined collar of his knee length coat denoted an air of authority.

He was happy to humour the deranged ramblings of an insistent woman, eager to have a hand in solving the grisly murder. We were solemnly escorted by Bannister and a sergeant by the name of Nursery across the road to the building that officially housed the dead as they waited to be interned in a peaceful everlasting sleep.

The cold lifeless body that lay on a slab in front of us was as she had been found, dried blood and mud caked her face, disguising her features. Clara faltered, the dreadfully shocking sight affected her weak female constitution nearly ending the expedition, but she tamed her emotions, recognising the dress of the deceased.

I tried to convince her that the body was not that of Phoebe, that she was mistaken over the clothes. I felt a little pang of guilt at my attempt to sabotage Clara's justice for had Lottie suffered the same fate I would certainly hang if I learned who was responsible.

The Inspector pressed that we could surely form a reliable opinion if she were a relation. I was perhaps a little too quick to point out that I am no relation, only a friend. Viewing the body for a second time, the face having been freshly washed, showed her to be the missing wife of my lover. I tried to drag Clara away and implored her not to touch the body, but she brushed me away, grieving over the woman that lay extinct and grey on the table.

Upon the positive identification of the remains we were escorted to the Portland Town police station where we were shown the perambulator that had yesterday rocked the precious body of Franks little girl. It was the one that had stood for months as a fixture in her brother's rooms and been wheeled around the streets of Camden by all three women. Also, a non-descriptive rag covered in oil and the skin rug that Clara recognised and declared as belonging to her brother and his wife. We walked in silence back in the direction of Prince W Road to confirm the horrific news that Phoebe had meet her end and would no more grace the rooms of 141.

I found it alarming that no-one sought the fate of the child nor had her passing been noted by the officers. The shock of seeing the body of a loved one in the initial stages of death had rendered Clare quite senseless, her wits thoroughly tried. In the aftermath of Phoebe's murder, the Hogg's would be dealt a double blow, but I would have no more to do with them, this chapter in my life was in its final sentences. Frank was at home when we returned and in the company of the three officers tasked with investigating the murder. They had searched the home and person of my beloved where upon a key was found that fit no lock in Prince W Road, for it was the key to my own dwelling. We were all escorted back to view the body by the three solemn faced officers for the convenience of their inquiries.

As Inspector Bannister talked his moustache moved in response to his speech, he said that he desired to search my lodgings, should I have objection. I replied that I had not the slightest objection and offered him my keys. I knew that any objection would result in further suspicion, besides they had Franks key in their possession so could enter regardless of my permission.

Eager not to draw attention by acting as a guilty party I requested that I should like to go with the them as the locks could be temperamental. Bannister offered a predatory smile before agreeing. I noted the raised pitch of my voice as I tried desperately to still the rising panic that was threatening to consume me, but I hoped that the inspector had not, though the manner of his person would suggest that he had. I left the tearful Hogg's to mourn their loss, the sorrow in the air palpable.

Frank would not look at me.

I trudged a weary path back to my own door, the two officers tasked with my custody flanked behind me, the exhaustion of the day was catching up with me with every step I took. My body was ready to collapse but my mind worked at break neck speed to ensure the lies and half-truths I was about to tell would be convincing enough to pass as the truth. My ears were ringing and a bead of sweat nestled beneath my bonnet as I approached the street door of two Priory Street. I had to hold the keys firmly to stop them from jingling in my shaking hands.

As each door was unlocked the cold grip of dread buried itself deeper, pushing the limits of my control. The officers followed me through each door, eagerly looking around the room, surveying and mentally cataloguing the situation, a picture of normality until the final room was breached. The kitchen was in darkness, moving to the window the bumbling sergeant fumbled with the blinds before admitting defeat and pulling them aside exposing the broken panes of glass. He looked closer, straining in the poor light, his back stiffening as the realisation began to sink in. With a cool tone he asked how the window had sustained such damage to which I replied with a rehearsed line about catching mice. The smell of paraffin was burning my eyes, so we retired to the front parlour, my lamp must have been knocked over during the course of the frightening events that had played out within the walls of this nondescript terrace.

Sergeant Nursey was dressed in a fine suit and matching waist coat, his moustache a characteristic of the time, his head topped in a bowler hat. He began to interrogate me about my interactions with the deceased, questioning my answers, stirring the bubbling pot that was about to explode. I tried to keep my responses calm, but the agitation was betrayed in my voice and demeanour.

I persisted with the tale that Phoebe had come seeking money and for me to take care of her child, adding that Clara had asked for my silence so no disgrace would befall the family name. I knew that my trembling voice had given me away. Nursey left the room leaving just myself and Detective Parsons, who so far had not spoken other than to acknowledge orders. I sat in the arm chair as he stood, as straight as a rod, beside the open door. I again repeated my take in the hopes that I could persuade him of my innocence. I even played the frail woman card, stating that I did not enjoy good health and the presence of blood should be attributed to a violent nose bleed.

After what seemed an age Nursey returned with Inspector Bannister in tow. They proceeded to search my home paying particular attention to the kitchen. The bedroom that separated the two rooms made it hard to understand what was being said but I heard the clangs of metal as they riffled through the kitchen drawers. Bannister returned presently, an assortment of knifes and the poker in his hand.

My heart stopped, eyes fixed on the very items that would convict me. I felt like a human statue, frozen in time. A faint whistle filled the suspended atmosphere and it took a moment to realise that the sound was coming from me. My breath returned in shallow puffs as I continued to whistle to myself. Sensing he would get no joy Bannister, followed dutifully by Nursey, descended upon the other residents to shed some light upon his investigation. He was gone for some time leaving me in the company of the uniformed Parsons, the mute guard! I kept him entertained with my endless tuneless whistle.

Bannister swept into the room, a stern look plastered upon his face and announced that I was to be arrested on the charge that this last night I did wilfully murder Mrs Hogg and I was to be held on suspicion of the wilful murder of Mrs Hogg's female child.

The accusation that I had caused harm to that sweet child snapped me out of myself and I leaped from the chair. I shouted that they could arrest me if they liked, that they had made a great mistake. My efforts did not impress them, and they treated me with as little dignity as they could allow. Defeated I returned to them the key I had to Franks home knowing that I would never have cause to use it again.

I was taken in a cab to Kentish Town police station. On the journey, I tried to protest my innocence, make him believe that I could not do such a dreadful thing, that I had never hurt anyone. The womanly wiles that had entrapped so many seemed infantile against his righteous exterior.

I had never travelled in a cab before, the experience was rather exhilarating, if not somewhat uncomfortable. I imagined myself being whisked away to a ball instead of to my doom.

I was to be charged with the wilful murder of Mrs Phoebe Hogg and the death of the sweet child. I made no statement, keeping my own counsel.

Upon reaching the station Bannister removed his cowboy style hat and requested that I remove my gloves, exposing the healing cuts. As I was transported to the holding cell I passed a bench of inebriated whores, held in place by a length of rope that prevented them from slipping to the floor in their drunken slumber.

I was removed to a windowless room where a portly female searcher removed my clothes like I was a child and inspected my naked person, passing my clothing to an attending constable as evidence. My mind distracted, running through all possible scenarios and escape options I engaged the woman's query on my guilt by needlessly informing her that I had requested Phoebe's presence via letter and that "despite our pleasantry's over tea one-word lead to another", though fortuitously I had the sense of mind to stop before I disclosed any more, reigning in my tongue before it passed sentence upon me. I could not be sure if they would find any splatter upon my clothing, the dark stripped material of my dress would disguise some of the stains, but I had not the chance to scrub the clothing that remained in the washhouse at Priory Street. I was supplied with other clothes, an itchy grey fabric infested with lice.

After the search I was placed in a barred cell that was crowded with the foulest specimens and smelt worse than the streets, hardened eyes watched every move. I made myself as comfy as was possible on the cold hard floor and buried my head in my hands as the gravity of the situation hit me like a train. If I could not persuade them of my innocence I would lose my love as well as my life.

The night passed in a tormented sleep, haunted by the image of the baby, walking now in God's own kingdom and of the disappointment and hate that I imagined would now fill Frank's heart. My body and mind were numb having been woken regularly by the pained and drunken cries of my inmates and the nightmares that stalked my dreams.

A bowl of gruel was offered as substance although I think the workhouse slop would have a better taste.

The day turned out to be no better than the night, tempers

rose as the efforts of the previous evenings tipple wore off and demands for release were bellowed through the bars. I was neither interviewed nor did I make any admissions. Other than the delivery of food I was addressed only once and escorted back to the windowless room. I was introduced to an attractive gentleman with a frowning moustache below a bulbous nose by the name of Thomas Bond who was a fellow of the Royal College of Surgeons. I received an ample view of his commonly parted hair as he examined my hands, obsessively turning them over again and again, documenting every little scratch and abrasion on both hands. He worked in silence, asking questions as to how I came to have such injuries and he voiced no conclusions as to how they were caused.

I was held for a further four days before any further developments in the case. I had no visitors. I was housed amongst debtors, murderers and thieves of every colour and creed.

My home was searched over the course of two days with items of interest removed to present as evidence of my guilt.

I was taken from the cell and placed in restraints before being transported to my committal hearing at Marylebone. The same three officers were in attendance and the evidence was presented for me to challenge or confirm. I did neither.

I refused to acknowledge any of the material presented nor confirm where the blood had originated though it had been proven some belonged to a mammal which supported the presence of mice within my rooms.

They reported on every knife that I owned and found one of particular interest on the sideboard in the front parlour behind tea-trays, though they found no trace of blood, which they wouldn't as it had been used on fruit and never inserted inside a human or a mouse.

The Hogg's missing revolver was held as evidence though it was quickly dismissed as nothing more than a miscommunication or petty theft, which was insignificant to the outcome, as neither body had gunshot wounds and the pin-fire cartridges were located separately to the weapon. I had no claim for the shimmering band of gold that I now wore upon my finger, the first ring belonged wholeheartedly to myself but the other was the ring that Frank should have placed upon me.

A great deal of time was spent focusing on the letters found hidden under by bed that I had exchanged with Frank in the trial though no-one ever questioned the handwriting or even attempted to match it to the infamous Whitechapel letters. Perhaps if they had discovered the hat and coat then the connection would have been made but as it was they were now being paraded around London along with hundreds of matching black top hats and long coats. The most tragic blow since the death of the child I wanted as my own were the lies Frank told about the timescale and depth of our love, but I allowed it. It was the only thing I could do for him now, to permit him to protect his reputation and avoid being prosecuted for criminal intimacy. My actions had not only killed his wife and child, but they had slaughtered our love. I had ripped his heart out and would be forsaken for an eternity, the depth of my betrayal would see me out of this life and haunt me into my next.

There were no witnesses to either the murder nor the disposal of the corpses but there was undeniable evidence of a struggle within the walls of Priory Street and the presence of blood was as good as any to convict, some had been convicted on much less. I was fighting a battle that was stacked against me, I had no allies to defend me nor any artillery to fire back at the accusers. All I could rely upon were the fabrications that were as thin as the bloodied curtains.

I was presented for trial at the Old Bailey on the first day of December. Just a decade from now the world would be celebrating a new millennium. I had marvelled at the grand exterior, yet the interior of the court was a painted masterpiece, as gilded as any place of worship I had seen. It was hard to comprehend the beauty in a building that had been the end to so many. Hatless gentleman filled every inch of the hall, the occasional bonneted woman broke up the sea of masculinity.

The panelled walls and polished oak would have been at home in any of the fine rooms at Kenwood House, but the purpose of the room could not be denied for it bore the trademark sword and royal insignia and carried an echo of the tragedy and loss that had been heard since it's conception. On a raised podium on the opposite side of the room sat the gentleman that would determine my fate. All were over fed with rosy cheeks and donned lengths of fur and fine cloth. Gold chains hung around their portly necks and caught the lamp light. I entered a plea of not guilty.

The inspector presented the evidence, highlighting the blood stains on the cloth that he had retrieved from my person and from the zinc bath. He made a well voiced case against me which was swallowed hook, line and sinker by the educated gentleman, their facial hair as down turned as their faces. The counsel, comprised of Mr Arthur Hutton, that stood by my side was as assured of my guilt as the Inspector had been. The pity in his eyes reflected his experience in the sentence I would receive though he tried the feeble defence with the assertion that my build would hinder my ability to commit such an atrocity. He reminded me of Frank for his beard covered the lower half of his face, snowy coloured, his tightly fitted jacket buttoned to the collar.

He barely blinked an eyelid when the judge returned the verdict, resigned from the beginning to my fate. Frank, Clara and Mrs Hogg senior as well as my mother and Lottie sat in the gallery to hear the outcome of my trial. Tears flowed from the Wheeler eyes but the Hogg's remained resolute in their resolve to have their justice. Clara and their mother fixed me with a glare that would kill the dead, hurt and betrayal radiated from my former friend as steam rose from a kettle, but it was the look on Frank's face that I would take to my grave.

He looked haggard, like he had not slept in days, his usually groomed appearance was raggedy, his expression haunted. Where I should have seen hatred in his eyes I saw nothing but sorrow, hollow pools of nothing started out over the court room. His admission of our affair had enraged the general population, many of whom considered him as guilty as myself in his wife's slaying and treated him as a leper, a social prior to be degraded and insulted for his part in his unwholesome relationship.

The wigged judge called for silence which fell instantly upon the court room. The authoritative voice of Justice Denham brought the courtroom to order as effectively as a school master disciplining a truant. I had no say in how the final chapter to my story would unfold.

I had remained impassive throughout the proceeding providing a well-rehearsed script to preserve my life when permitted. Mr Fulton and Mr Gill had expertly presented the prosecution's case against me, delivering each statement with conviction. It was up to the men of London to dictate my future.

I was asked one final time if I had anything to say that would prevent the court from passing the lawful sentence of death should I be found guilty. I made the simple reply to say that I am innocent of the charge against me.

A verdict had been reached. The judge donned a black cap that hung from his head as limp as a wilting flower.

I was found guilty on both counts.

I was to be sentenced to death.

I would hang for my crime.

14

The few days that I was held in the communal cell was a blessing compared to the isolation that awaited my final duration on this earth. Some of the worldly black toothed inmates were the scourge of society, others juvenile in their crimes but they were at least company. Though the conversation rarely reached a level to touch on any intellect it was distraction enough from the limited future that was my own. Once moved to the larger prison the confinements became far harsher, silence was required, and manual labour was expected. My fingers bleed from a day picking oakum, separating the strands of the coarse rope that probably once suspended a like-minded soul.

I was held in a single occupancy cell. The isolation was manageable, but the smell was over powering. It was not any one odour but a mixture of scents that combined to produce a toxic aroma. I had never been inflicted with a phobia of confined spaces so the box like dimensions were no punishment.

The white washed walls were stained with the existence of past criminals and the sounds of the city rang throughout the night, amplified around the tiny cell via the bared hole that served as a window, mounted so high that I could see little but the pale winter sky.

There was to be no escape, the bared window would hardly take the width of an adult, who would be meet with a drop to their death and the heavy metal door was solid and fit perfectly into the frame that supported it.

Simple pipe work provided a small basin, a bucket acted as a lavatory. I think there were more rats than people. I enjoyed the hammock, sleeping suspended above the floor. I would have liked one for my rooms at Priory Street.

I think the solitude was to induce us to repent against our sins, to be consumed by the guilt of our own actions. It did not work on me for I repented for nothing. I did the world a favour, a few less diseased whores spreading their filth and an undeserving wife dispatched for one that had longed for the position.

I quickly came to terms with my own fate, in the depths of my heart I knew that my actions only had one reward, but I was not prepared to show the world my true colours so kept up the pretence of my innocence. After all was said and done it was the words that stung more keenly than any knife, words that had imprinted in my head and been branded into my heart, words that would sing a melody to my grave and taunt any peace that I should find there.

Though my defence saw through my pleas the solicitor that was attached to my case was less convinced of my guilt and went to great lengths to secure my release. Mr Freke Palmer was young and eager to listen to my version of events. A notebook in hand he took notes as I spoke, a spark of hope gleaming in his educated eyes. He left me with a feeling that all may not be lost, I tried to ignore the pang of expectancy as his infectious positivity chipped at my resigned surface. I fancy that if my predicament had not been so dire that I should have pursued him, his face was a handsome mask of manliness and his physique appeared strong under the fine suit that he wore.

During my incarceration mother came to visit on several occasions. The first was full of shame and disappointment yet the tiniest spark of hope for my innocence shone from her eyes as she talked of the day I would walk the streets of London again. More for her own peace than mine but it was good to lose myself in her fantasy for a few moments. She always wore her Sunday best with the addition of her black mourning veil and carried herself with an air of self-importance, her nose wrinkling in disgust at the conditions of the gaol. Our interactions had to be carried out through the bars that kept the prisoners from their freedom.

When I was transferred to Newgate Mother knew that all was lost for this particular prison housed those awaiting the gallows, I would not be transported nor fined, I would die.

My solicitor Freke was still working tirelessly on my defence, the young whippet was desperate to prove to his peers his worth, yet I felt he was fighting a losing battle and may well fall alongside me, vocal in his attempts to defend me. His ingenious angle was to take the insanity approach and prove that my actions were due to an unstable mind, that I suffered from diminished responsibility due to the illness of fitting that I had suffered since childhood. He alleged that someone in control of themselves, someone of sound mind would not attempt to commit the unholy act of suicide.

I knew that all his actions would achieve would be to draw out the timescale of my execution, but I was grateful for the additional time despite the fact that I had made peace with my fate, beside I had none to blame but myself and I would take joy in the secrets that I would take to my grave. None would know my true nature but myself and Malt. Every night I would dream of our life together, what was and what could have been. The festivities never reached the confines of our cell, the jailers were merry with the spirit of the season but for us it was just an endless routine of silence, work, gruel and sleep.

Despite the fact that I had been convicted and sentenced to hang for my crime Freke had been granted a medical enquiry under the criminal lunatic's act which meant that I would be formally assessed to determine the extent of my lucidity. Three well-spoken suited gentlemen joined me in my cramped cell to conduct the interview.

I had no desire to join the ranks in any asylum, no wish to spend my days with the rambling drooling insane so I answered all the probing questions with as much intelligence as I could muster. I could have acted the fool, played on my womanly charms but I was done with this life. After what seemed an age but was probably only about an hour the three learned gentlemen took their leave to consider the evidence they had gathered and deliver a verdict that would either support or quash the case that Freke had painstakingly put into place.

The final days of my life were guarded round the clock by female wardresses who oversaw the bath that all condemned souls were required to take, so that they entered the kingdom of God, should they repent their sins, clean. The water was tepid, but I was permitted to scrub myself retaining as much dignity as possible with a stranger watching my every move.

The look of defeat etched on Freke's face said all that I needed to hear, he had been unsuccessful. The doctors had found no evidence of legal insanity, my case was sealed with the words "the law must take its course". I had only one request, that Frank be granted permission to visit me. I had to lay this ghost to rest before I became one, Frank had to know that I meant no ill will towards his little girl, that it was a tragic accident for which I was truly sorry.

I waited in vain for him to come.

The date for my execution was set for Tuesday December twenty-third, just two days before Christmas.

I had become accustomed to being a spectacle, to be gazed upon like a freak. The Judas hole in my cell was opened and a familiar face filled the space. It was one that I had seen before but took a moment for me to place. It was the executioner, Mr James Berry, who made a living from ending the life of another, the only lawful manner to extinguish an existence. My mood was especially light, free from the worry that daily life brought. From my understanding, he was several days early.

The day before my execution was scheduled was the busiest I had had. I was inundated with visitors though the one I wanted left me with nothing more than the sad image that stood in the court as my trial unfolded but I hoped to the very end that he would find it in his heart to forgive me.

The jailers treated me with unprecedented kindness allowing Mother and Lottie unrestricted time so say their farewells, though they stood guard over the entire visit they did not intervene. No matter how I had vexed mother during the course of my life she still grieved for the daughter she was to lose. Of the few regrets I had I was soured that I would not see

Lottie become a wife and mother, that I would leave her with no sisters, only brothers that cared only for themselves.

Mother questioned me relentlessly, but I maintained my innocence throughout, making no admission of guilt. They both looked beautiful, their clothes pressed, mother's waist was pinched to a point, her dress gathered behind her in metres of fabric, a pathetic thin shawl draped over her arms. I complimented them as we exchanged pleasantry's though I did not question why Lottie wore a child's straw boater, dressed in attire far suited to someone of a younger generation.

I was pained to release Lottie from our embrace, I inhaled deeply so that I could commit her scent to memory, to savour her. I kissed her tenderly on her forehead. Holding mother, I was reminded of all the love that I felt as a child and my heart ached for her as she wept on my shoulder. I kept my composure as they walked away, never would I gaze upon them again.

Freke made a final visit, persistent that I submit to his questioning so that a reprieve may be applied for before the home secretary, but my fate was set, Freke would have to admit defeat. I would not confess. I had one last bequest, that, on my behalf, he place a personal advert in the main Madrid newspaper. The message was to my dearest Malt and was to read "MECP Last wish of MEW. Have not betrayed. MEW." Despite the intrigue that such a coded message brought I refused to elaborate on its meaning nor on the recipient. I just hoped that Freke would carry out this concluding act and that

Malt would see my message. I had no notion as to whether he was keeping abreast of English news or if he was even still in Madrid but that had been his last known location and I wanted him to know that I took to the grave what we had done.

All I had left was to wait. I sat in my cell nauseous with anticipation that Frank could arrive at any moment. He did not. It felt like a stone was weighing down my heart when I admitted to myself that Frank was not coming. I cried myself to sleep, inconsolable. A piece of me had already died so tomorrow would be a release from the torment of my existence. I would handle my upcoming death with remarkable fortitude. The last sleep from which I would wake, in the condemned cell, was surprisingly peaceful.

I was prepared for one last moment of fame, to be shown as the murderess I was, though I maintained my innocence. This was snatched from me by the Sheriff of London, Sir James Whitehead who deemed the presence of the press as vulgar, owing to me being a young woman so he excluded them from attending my private execution.

It had been almost thirty years since hangings were a public spectacle though the sentence being carried out would still be announced through the ringing of the bells at St. Sepulchre, a chime to serenade the departed souls on their journey to heaven or hell. Many a time I had seen the black flag flying above Newgate that denoted the death of an inmate at the hands of the country.

How many people would gather outside as I swung for my crimes? Ten, twenty, maybe a hundred or more, surely the greater the crowd the more I would be remembered.

My body would hang for the customary hour, dangling lifelessly at the end of a rope inside the brick lined pit through which I would fall as the trap door was opened via a lever by the hangman. I would then be placed in a coffin for inspection by the coroner's jury who will confirm that I am life extinct. My final journey will be a short distance away to my place of burial where I will lay eternally in an unmarked grave. To be walked over by future inhabitants of London who may or may not know my story.

I would never know the notoriety that my actions would bring. If they were deemed wicked enough I may even be immortalised by Madam Tussauds as one of her famous wax works. I could see it now, standing beside the bloody perambulator a knife raised high in my hands, ironically adjacent to the unchallenged Jack the Ripper. Notorious crimes highlighted in all their glory in the Chamber of Horrors.

I woke on my final morning refreshed yet I could not shake the feeling of trepidation I felt as my last minutes on earth ebbed away. The priest came in to listen to any confession I may have, to release my soul to God but I dispatched him having no need or want of his service. Mr Berry entered my cell early in the morning, the oil lights still lighting the passage as the dismal day kept it as dark as a cow's guts inside.

Mr Berry sported a moustache and a beard like no other I had seen for it seemed to shy away from his chin and cheeks and seek point like an accusing finger. He had boyish features that hid below a wide forehead, his hair as afraid of his head as his beard was of his face. My executioner was solemn in his duty, taking no pleasure in the task at hand. He greeted me with a "good morning Madam" and wearily shook my hand. The law dictated a standard set of procedures that had to be followed to the letter, but Mr Berry was kind in the application of his duty. He asked me if I was ready for him to place upon me the straps to which I replied that I was quite ready.

The well-used large leather belt was strapped around my waist. My body was squashed as the corset type device was tightened around my slender waist, my breath winded from me with every buckle strengthened. Mr Berry secured my wrists in front of me to the hooks in the belt. I protested that it was unnecessary for I had nowhere to run but it fell on deaf ears, my hands would remain in a downturned prayer. It was nothing against my character, just an adopted procedure that prevented those hanging from clawing at their own necks in an attempt to loosen the rope that would bind them to the afterlife.

I was given the opportunity to make a closing statement to which I replied, "my sentence is an unjust one and much of the evidence against me false", keeping true to my own defence but not to the events that took place. With the party ready to proceed to the gallows Mr Berry took the lead while two of the wardresses took their positions at my side. A requirement put in place by the home office though I pleaded to walk unaided they ignored my protest and escorted me from my cell.

I was secretly pleased that I had so many to accompany me on the short walk down the corridor and into the cold yard which lead to the shed that housed the gallows. I kissed each woman in turn then the procession to my doom commenced.

I was flanked by clergymen, male warders, prison officials, several police officers and of course Mr Berry who lead the way. Why I was such a spectacle I am unsure, many a woman had hung before me for murders that were more heinous. I do not think that it required eleven grown men to be present to witness my death or prevent my escape. Maybe they were privy to a great escape plan that would result in my freedom though I doubted it greatly.

As I emerged into the yard the bitter chill of the harsh weather bit at my cheeks and brought tears to my eyes. Mr Berry placed a white hood over my head, preventing me from seeing the instrument of my death. Whether this was for the benefit of those who watched or from a kindness that he felt inclined to apply to young woman I did not know.

I was determined to remain calm throughout.

Through the fabric I heard a remark that I was the calmest

person he had ever seen approach their death. I prided myself in my resolve. I presumed this to be Mr Berry for hundreds had passed from this life to the next at his hand. Most I assumed would have been man handled into the noose, fighting for every last breath.

I was manoeuvred blind and incapacitated towards the gallows. I had heard that the Newgate gallows was a large construction that could hang up to four individuals at any one time.

The lack of activity in the yard indicated that I would die alone, no companion would swing beside me. I visualised a single lonely noose hanging from the beam. I assumed that the end was near for a sudden silence had fallen. The only beat I could hear was that of my own heart humming a rhyme that quickened in pace as I was helped up the wooden steps that lead to the platform. I was pulled into place by the strap around my waist.

A deep voiced gentleman informed me that I would be held while my legs were pinioned, a practice that prevented the legs from jerking around as the body fought a desperate battle to survive. A rouge leg jamming the dropping motion would be both humiliating to the hangman and would cause unwarranted suffering and disgrace to the criminal.

As the noose was placed around my neck I heard a jangle of metal as the iron chain chaffed against the hook ready to brace against my weight. Despite the hood I felt the coldness of the metal eyelet dig against the soft flesh below my jaw and press upon my neck. The frantic drum of my pulse echoed against the restraint. The coarse rope was tightened around my neck, not to the point that it cut off the limited air that flowed in and out but enough to quicken my breath and encourage the rise of panic that had started to flood my body.

I heard footsteps vacate the platform leaving just myself and Mr Berry. His experienced hand hoovering above the lever that would open the trap doors through which I would descend to my end. I imagined the men watching sombrely, their hats held in their hands, waiting for the drop so that they could pay the dutiful respects and be in the pub before the rope had stilled.

With no proclamation I plunged to my death. The decent was swift, I could only guess how many feet I dropped. Instantaneously the thunderous sound of the trap doors opening penetrated the hood as my stomach lurched due to my body dropping through the air. I did not hear the sound of cracking bone as my neck snapped.

The world went black forever.

Jill

The End

N.Joy   Jill

N.Joy   Jill

Nickie is a cat-loving married mum of two who was born and bred in Bideford, a pretty little town in North Devon. With a love of books from a young age and a passion for writing stories Nickie's debut novel, Jill, is her self-published lifelong ambition on the literacy world. She's not stopping there so keep an eye out for other works by N.Joy.

She writes under her maiden name of Joy and hopes that you will 'enjoy' her work.

N.Joy   Jill

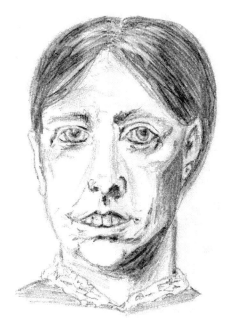

This is an image of Mary Pearcey, drawn by the author.

Sources:

www.london1868.com

www.casebook.org

www.capitalpunishmentuk.org

www.thehistoryblog.com

www.ancestry.co.uk

www.oldbaileyonline.org

www.google.co.uk

www.victorian web.org

Jack The Ripper The Casebook by Richard Jones

N.Joy   Jill

Printed in Great Britain
by Amazon